Pretty Boy
Problems

Also by Michele Grant

The Montgomery Series

Heard It All Before

Pretty Boy Problems

Any Man I Want

Sweet Little Lies

Heard It All Before

Crush (with Cydney Rax and Lutishia Lovely)

Published by Kensington Publishing Corp.

Pretty Boy Problems

MICHELE GRANT

Kensington Publishing Corp.
http://www.kensingtonbooks.com

DAFINA BOOKS are published by

Kensington Publishing Corp.
119 West 40th Street
New York, NY 10018

Copyright © 2012 by Michele Grant

All Kensington Titles, Imprints, and Distributed Lines are available at special quantity discounts for bulk purchases for sales promotions, premiums, fund-raising, and educational or institutional use. Special book excerpts or customized printings can also be created to fit specific needs. For details, write or phone the office of the Kensington special sales manager: Kensington Publishing Corp., 119 West 40th Street, New York, NY 10018, attn: Special Sales Department, Phone: 1-800-221-2647.

Dafina and the Dafina logo Reg. U.S. Pat. & TM Off.

ISBN-13: 978-0-7582-4224-2
ISBN-10: 0-7582-4224-7
First Kensington Trade Edition: August 2012
First Kensington Mass Market Edition: July 2014

eISBN-13: 978-1-61773-299-7
eISBN-10: 1-61773-299-0
Kensington Electronic Edition: July 2014

10 9 8 7 6 5 4 3 2 1

Printed in the United States of America

For the fellas: Frank Sr., Errington, Frank II, Mel, and Ted—classy guys who keep me grounded.
To the s/o's past, present (and future?). Men fascinate me. If nothing else, it's always a learning experience.
To all the pretty (and not so pretty) boys and all their struggles.

If you don't like something, change it. If you can't change it, change your attitude.

—Maya Angelou

ACKNOWLEDGMENTS

One of the fun things about writing is creating these vivid worlds for people to visit and stay a while. One of the challenging things about writing is creating accurate portrayals of actual places and professions. Granted, setting a plot in Dallas is not a challenge. I was born here, raised here, and came back here. But the world of fashion was foreign to me beyond watching a few episodes of *America's Top Model* and having an insatiable love for Michael Kors clothing. So I must take a moment and acknowledge a few groups that help lend some flavor.

A million kisses and thanks to the folks at Fashion Institute of Technology in New York for answering my endless stream of questions. Thanks to the good people who manage Fashion Week Dallas for indulging my rampant curiosity. Last, but not least, to the good folks at Jet Charters who allowed me to treat a private plane like my own for a few hours.

I'd also like to shout out Cheris Hodges, Farrah Rochon, D.L. Sparks, and Phyllis Bourne for the author solidarity this last year. You are appreciated!

Prologue

You're No Gentleman

Beau—Friday, March 25, 1:36 PM

I finished zipping up my pants and surreptitiously glanced at my watch. Dammit, I was late . . . again. I was going to catch hell, without a doubt. May I be perfectly honest? Linda (or was it Laura?) hadn't really been worth it. I couldn't even use the excuse that I had lost track of time. It was a lunch date that turned into a lil something else. Sure, she had four of the five *w*'s going (woman, wet, wanton, willing) but there was no wow. Without that wow, sex was just routine aerobic activity. Sad to say, somewhere between "Are you sure you want to do this?" and "Oh God, Beau, you're so good!" I found myself going through the motions. To me, that was unacceptable. Any woman worth doing is worth doing well.

Hoping none of these thoughts played across my face, I glanced over at her as she shimmied her perfectly toned body back into her clothes and sent a radiant smile in my direction. At least *her* world had been rocked. If I hadn't given it my normal effort (and I really hadn't), at least she wasn't disappointed. Then again, let's be honest: a half-hearted effort of mine still knocked it out of the park on a lukewarm day. I grinned back at Lisa, hoping she wouldn't press for a repeat performance.

"So . . ." she said tentatively, stepping into the sexy heels that had caught my attention in the first place. Sexy shoes on a slinky woman are my weakness. Well . . . one of them, anyway. I'd admit to having a few.

I knew what was coming next, and I wanted no part of it. I dialed up my most charming grin and walked around the desk. Tilting her chin up, I dropped a kiss on her lips, stroking my finger along her jaw. "*Chèrie*, I'm late. I'll call you later, yes?" Without waiting for an answer, I turned and headed toward the door for a smooth exit.

"You don't have my number, Beau."

"Oh, but I do. I have your work number, doll." I threw a smile over my shoulder, two steps away from a clean getaway.

"Beau," she snapped, "it's clear you're dying to escape. I'll make you a deal. You can walk out of here drama-free without a look back or a good-bye if you can tell me my name."

I closed my eyes with my hand on the door-knob. *Merde!* So close. I hazarded a guess, "Lovely Linda, why do you think I don't know your name?"

She slammed her hand onto her hip and scowled. "Maybe because it's Lydia? Son of a b—"

I cut her off there. No one disrespected Alanna Montgomery. "Actually, Leah, my mother is a per-fectly delightful woman."

She stomped her foot in obvious abject fury. "Tell me something—has there ever been a woman you couldn't charm out of her panties?"

I tried to think when (or if) that had ever hap-pened. I drew a blank. "Darling, a gentleman never kisses and tells."

"You're no gentleman, Beau. I hope to be around to see you get a taste of your own medi-cine: used and discarded for nothing more than a half hour's pleasure by someone who cares noth-ing for you and can't remember your name! I hope you get to taste the bitterness of wanting more from somebody who doesn't want you in the same way."

That wasn't likely to happen. But since I was genuinely sorry she felt used, I suppressed the smirk that was itching to appear on my face and decided not to share that thought. No need to be nasty. I'd had an okay time with her. "Laura, I thought you understood this was just *bon temps*—a little good time for both of us to enjoy. Did you not enjoy yourself?"

"Again, it's *Ly-di-a*, and you know I did. That's not the point."

I did know. I rarely, if ever, left a woman dissatisfied, and she had been quite vocal with her enjoyment. "Apologies, *ma douce*, did I make promises or give a hint of the possibility of anything more?"

Her face fell in defeat. "You know what? To hell with it; the mistake was on my side for thinking you were any different, any more than the shallow, sexy outside that I see. Just go, Beau. Just walk away. I have a feeling it's one of the things you know how to do best."

As I closed the door behind me, I heard what sounded like a shoe hitting the door. Should I try and make amends? I hated ending a nice if somewhat boring interlude on a sour note. I paused just long enough to glance back down at my watch. I was egregiously late, and there was no time for damage control. Silently, I made a mental note to make it up to Lisette later.

1

We're Done, Son

I was sorry that it had come down to this. Well no, I really wasn't. Enough was enough. I was only sorry that I hadn't put my foot down sooner. Looking into his handsome face, I could almost hear what he was thinking. He's thinking, *This kind of thing only happened to other people.* Not Avery Beauregard Montgomery.

Beau, natural-born charmer, all-around good-time guy, was not having a great week. He was fresh out of second chances and clearly hoping for a little mercy. I sincerely hoped he could tell from the look on my face, none was forthcoming.

"Beau, you have officially torn your last pair of silk boxers with me," I hissed while standing in the middle of my living room. Okay, maybe I did feel a little bad about arguing with the man who had become my brother-in-law less than two months ago. But facts were facts. Beau was delicious to look at, tough to live with.

He was six-foot four with the sculpted body of a man who worked hard to maintain that physique, close-cropped hair, and almost regal features encased in toasted-toffee-colored skin. His face was a study in symmetrical beauty: perfect spaced eyes, proud forehead, chiseled cheeks, and almost pouty lips. Beauregard Montgomery was an attractive, well-built man who knew exactly the effect his looks had on people and played it for all it was worth.

My husband, Roman, shared the squared jaw, the broad shoulders, and gold-toned eyes, but that's where the similarities ended. Where Roman came across ruggedly handsome, Beau was downright pretty. Roman tended to downplay his looks; Beau used his like a commodity.

Their personalities were also worlds apart. It was at times like this that I couldn't believe that Rome was related to Beau at all. Roman was responsible, straightforward, considerate, unswervingly monogamous. Beau? None of those things, as far as I could tell. I couldn't recall the last job or relationship he'd taken seriously. As far as I could tell, he loved women, his family, premium tequila, his wardrobe, and himself. Not necessarily in that order.

I motioned to the luggage and boxes stacked beside me. "As you can see, I have most of your stuff packed up already."

"Where is lil Chase?" He referred to his nephew, my stepson, LaChayse. Chase loved his Uncle Beau and would not have appreciated this scene one bit.

"He's with his mother this weekend. He can't save you. Would you seriously hide behind a child? C'mon now."

His tone turned cajoling. "Jewellen Rose Capwell-Montgomery! *Ma soeur,* can we at least talk about this?"

"I've only been your sister for a few months now. I don't consider you fam yet. Talk is cheap, Beauregard. Yours is downright bargain basement at this point. No more talking, brother. You're outta here."

"Ah *chérie* . . ." Beau tended to sprinkle a little Cajun-flavored patois into his speech when he was trying to be extra charming.

I wagged my head and my index finger in tandem. "Don't bring Bayou Beau to me, sir. That's not going to fly. Today it's not that kind of party. I have repeatedly asked you not to dally around with the women in my office."

Beau held his arms out in a "who me?" gesture. "Dally? I don't dally. I delight, I dazzle, I drink in, but I never dally."

My eyes narrowed. "You have a problem keeping your pants zipped, Beauregard. This is a well-known and well-documented fact. I would think you'd be exhausted trying to keep up with all the hot- and cold-running 'lady friends' you keep on tap, but hey, it's your life. Generally, I don't have a problem with your King of the Man-Ho act until it impacts me. Today, it impacts me. My account manager, Lydia, came back from lunch weeping

and wailing about doggish men. Guess which doggish man she was talking about?"

Beau grinned devilishly. "That Lynda, she was
surprisingly agile. You know she does Pilates?"

"It's Lydia, and that's TMI." I spoke through
clenched teeth. "That makes the fourth employee
traumatized by your triflingness. I've had it with
you." My company, the Capwell Agency, was a
small staffing agency with about twenty-five em-
ployees. That meant that Beau had broken one-
fifth of the hearts on my payroll.

"Jewellen Rose, that's not reason enough to put
me out; we're family! *Où est mon frère?*"

"Brother, I'm right here." Roman gave me a
quick kiss as he walked in, answering Beau's question. My husband was solidly built, wide of shoulder, lean of hip, long of leg. He was about one
inch shorter, ten pounds lighter, and three and a
half years younger than Beau. The expression on
his face said his patience with his older brother
had run out. Rome was wearing a lightweight silk
suit and a scowl. "The question is—where were *you*
on the James job this week?"

Beau's easy smile fell away. Technically, he was
employed as a site manager at Roman's landscape
design company. But standing out in the hot sun
overseeing people working in dirt and fertilizer
was not Beau's thing. Actually, hard work was not
Beau's thing. He was a gifted salesman, could sell
ice to Eskimos. But Beau didn't like to be both-
ered with the details . . . like pricing and budgets
and invoices. After his "creative accounting"
caused Roman to lose money on two projects in a

row, Beau was sent out to manage projects in the field.

I was quite sure of what had happened this week. The weather had been unseasonably hot and humid for springtime. No doubt Beau felt he was far better suited to the indoor pursuit of Lydia.

He shrugged sheepishly. "Bro, it was just this week. But everything is under control. It's just this heat, you know. I'll be back out there Monday."

Roman's jaw went granite hard and his rum-hued eyes turned flinty. He slowly took off his jacket, loosened his tie, and folded his arms across his chest. I had seen this stance before. It was his no-nonsense, "this is how it's gonna be" stance. My man was about to shoot straight, no chaser reality in his brother's direction. "No, Beau, you won't. You won't work in the field, you won't do office work, and you cost me over eighty grand in lost revenue last year. To put the cherry on top the sundae, you slept with my receptionist . . . at her engagement party. I don't need the drama. We're done, son."

Beau took a step back and glanced from Roman to me and back again. "Wait, you're firing me *and* putting me out? All in the same day? Seriously, *mon frère. C'est a froid.*"

I couldn't help it; I pursed my lips into a snarl. "We're cold?! You haven't contributed a penny to this household, you eat your way through most of our groceries, you cook and never clean up, you have me washing your nasty drawers, picking up after you, and taking irate messages from women all hours of the day and night. *That's* cold. Like your brother said, 'We're done, son.' " I'd had quite enough of his nonsense.

Roman walked over and clapped his brother on the back. "We do this with love. It's all with the L-O-V-E. It's time for you to get out there on your own and be about Beau's business, whatever that is going to be. It's time."

Beau gauged our seriousness one more time. Neither of us cracked a smile and most of his things were packed and stacked in the middle of the room. If nothing else, he was a realist. His free room and board, his money-for-nothing job . . . gone.

Beau stood silently for a beat, then nodded with a slight smile and shrug. "*Tout va bien.*" He snatched up the largest of the multiple suitcases, a garment bag, and his laptop case. He shook hands with Roman, came over and gave me a kiss on the cheek. "Time to be on to the next. Y'all been good to me. *Merci, ma famille.*" He slid his sunglasses on and headed out the front door. It closed behind him with a heavy clunk that resonated through the room.

I turned into Roman's embrace as he wrapped his arms around me from behind. "I know we had to do it, but I still feel kinda bad. Like we're letting him down."

"Beau's my brother. I love him but . . . Jewel, please. We have carried that man for over a year and that half-assed *merci* was the first thank-you we've heard. It was time. Trust and believe he will land on his feet; he always does."

"You're right. I know you're right." His hands traveled down my arms to rest at my waist.

"Babe, I'm always right." He gave a cocky grin.

I rolled my eyes. "Let's not get carried away. You moved him in here in the first place, cowboy."

"You have a point." He stroked his hands from my waist to my hips and pulled me a little closer.

"I usually do, Mr. Montgomery."

"But I wonder, Mrs. Montgomery; do you know what this *really* means?" His fingers started unraveling the knots holding my wrap dress together.

I liked where this discussion was heading. I started unbuttoning his shirt. Didn't matter how many times we did this, I was still thrilled by the easy heat between us.

"By most standard rules and customs, we're still in the honeymoon phase of this marriage, you know." My dress fluttered to the floor to crumple alongside his shirt.

"True." I tilted my head up and to the left a little as I leaned into him.

Roman inched me closer still. "*Umm hmm.* This means with him gone and Chase at his mother's . . . we can get buck naked and nasty in any room of our house again—anytime we like." He trailed kisses down the side of my neck.

I unbuckled his pants. "Naked *and* nasty? Why Roman LaChayse, what do you have in mind?"

"Come a little closer and let me show you."

His next action took any remaining worry or thought about Beau right out of my head.

2

Avery Beauregard Montgomery

Beau—6:23 PM the same day

"*Jesu Christo*, what a day!" I muttered under my breath as I slid behind the wheel of my black convertible Porsche. With a sigh, I tilted my head back and closed my eyes. Here we go again. This was getting old. By this, I meant having to start over from ground zero and rebuild.

I mean, *merde*! One of these days, I was going to do the right thing just because it's the right thing to do. Thirty-eight years old and not a lot of tangible achievement to show for it. No home, no job . . . no life to speak of.

This wasn't my plan when I started out years ago. As the first-born child of Avery and Alanna Montgomery, I planned to blaze a trail for my younger brother, Roman, and younger sister, Katrina, to follow. My childhood was golden; I had no recollection of Pops and Madere struggling to make ends meet. When we moved from Louisiana to Dallas, it was an easy transition for the whole family.

After years of civil servant jobs, Pops had opened a trucking company. Madere worked as his operations manager. They worked hard, and the company remained successful until the day they sold it a little over five years ago.

I grew up as an athlete, a scholar, and generally known as "that nice Montgomery boy" around the neighborhood. Sometime in junior high, I sprung up eight inches, all arms and legs. My ass was gangly. My head was too big, nose too prominent, lips too wide for my face.

Thankfully, by the time I reached high school, I had grown into both my features and six-foot-four frame. It seemed like overnight I went from being the smart, nice boy with quiet manners to "that dude" that guys envied and girls wanted. I liked the feeling; I liked it a lot.

I excelled in sports without very much effort and excelled in my classes with very little studying. Apparently, I looked good doing both. Vividly, I can recall the day that I realized the full advantage of attractiveness. I had stayed out with a friend enjoying a lil female companionship the night before a major project was due. For the first time, I skipped turning in a homework assignment.

When I got to class the next day, my teacher asked me why I hadn't turned in my assignment. I had no valid answer so I decided to wing it. On a whim, I walked up to Miss Whisler's desk and knelt beside her looking into her eyes. In a soft voice, I apologized, swearing it would never happen again. After a slight pause, she blushed. Then she told me it was okay, just this once.

My friend, who was just as nice, held the same grade point average, but wasn't quite as easy on the eyes, was given an incomplete and an afternoon in detention. It was a turning point for me. I got it. In an illuminating moment it was all clear to me. Beyond brains, beyond brawn, beyond brown skin, and whisky-gold eyes . . . I had "it"—that indefinable charisma that drew people.

You can call it charm, maybe it's second nature, I don't know. But I realized I had it, and I was going to make it work for me. Having "it" meant that, sure, I could work hard for extra credit, or I could spend that time in a more entertaining pursuit and charm my way to the grade I wanted anyway.

Yeah, yeah—I realize that the day I decided to use my looks, wit, and smile was the day I stopped trailblazing. It was the day I got comfortable. But I'm not sure that if I had to do it all again, I wouldn't do it exactly the same way.

I had a combination of academic and athletic scholarship offers. Baseball was the sport I loved. I played short stop; I could run, hit, throw, and jump with minimal contact. I chose Tulane because it was back home (still considered Louisiana home), and I knew I could be a big fish in a little pond there. Baseball paid for my first two years of college. Officially, I majored in marketing. Unofficially, I majored in women. I received high marks for both pursuits.

Right before my junior year, a talent scout from a modeling agency "discovered" me in Café du Monde late one summer night and sent me to New York. Modeling part-time paid for the last two years of college when I transferred to LSU. Once I graduated, I moved to New York and modeled full-time.

What they don't tell you about modeling? It's boring as hell. The majority of your time is spent waiting around or running to catch a flight. You are treated like a commodity and not a very smart one at that. But tell me what else I could do that paid me $5,000 plus expenses for two days' work?

I lasted for ten years; that's five times the average male model's career. I earned a decent nest egg that, contrary to popular belief, I have not blown through. I buy myself a new car every two years and pick up jobs here and there, as I see fit.

At thirty-eight years of age, I was a man still waiting for my purpose in life to reveal itself. I wished it would hurry the hell up. There had to be more than this. Forty was just around the corner. I had no intention of becoming "that guy"—the one who had all the potential and pissed it away. The one still chasing twenty-year-old tail in his forties. I couldn't be that guy. If I knew nothing else, I knew I was better than that.

But for right now, this instant? I needed a place to lay my head for a minute. Wiping my hand down my face, I started the engine and made a ten-minute drive south along Central Expressway.

That's how I found myself, fresh off a firing by my brother and an eviction by my sister-in-law, standing outside my sister's high-rise condo in downtown Dallas, hoping (praying) she was out of town.

Kat was a model as well and frequently jetted off for days at a time. I was pretty sure that she was doing a beach shoot on the other side of the planet and would be there for a week or so. At least I hoped so. If Kat was home, she would want explanations; she would want chatter and explanations, and I wasn't in the mood for any more soul searching.

With my laptop case slung over my left shoulder and a garment bag in my hand, I leaned on the doorbell. After a few minutes with no response, I dug into my pocket for the spare key I had made for emergency situations such as the one I found myself in now.

"Kat?" I called out as I stepped in the door. "Katrina? It's Beau."

Still no answer. With a relieved sigh, I set the bags down in the entryway and ventured deeper into the unit. I strolled past the open great room with kitchen and living area attached, ignored the guest rooms and bath for now, and headed for the master suite.

It wasn't until I was outside the master bath door that I heard the shower running and Maxwell crooning.

I sighed. *A brother cannot catch a break today*, I thought as I pushed open the door. Fog and the strong scents of ginger and peaches wafted heavy throughout the area. I stepped deeper into the

room. Kat's shower was a huge glass-and-tile enclosed box on the far side of the room. Without
pausing, I yanked open the shower door and dove
into my explanations. "Kit-Kat, it's Beau. I'm staying a few nights. No lectures, okay?"

A startled scream came from the wet woman
under the hot stream at the exact moment I realized it wasn't my sister, Katrina, in the shower. No
indeed, it was not. Instead, I allowed my eyes to
roam up and down the lovely frame of a tall sister
around five-foot ten, with short hair a la Halle
Berry, curves for days, high cheekbones, lush lips,
and widely set big brown eyes currently widened
with alarm.

"What in the entire hell is this?" The sudsy, angry,
and gloriously naked vision before me spoke.

Now you know I considered myself to be quite a
connoisseur of the female form; and this right
here was a mighty fine specimen. Taking my time,
I leaned against the tile wall and looked my fill in
blatant appreciation. "Well now . . . you're not Kit-
Kat."

Regaining her composure, the young woman
turned the water off and reached for her towel. "A
gentleman would have averted his eyes." She
spoke with a decidedly deep Southern drawl, all
warm and whiskey-laden. Something about her
struck me as familiar. I rarely forgot a face or a figure like hers.

"I've never claimed to be a gentleman," I answered honestly. I took a step back to allow her to
pass. She was a cool one, seemingly unfazed to
find herself near naked in my sister's bathroom
with a strange man.

She tucked the towel around her chest tightly and shot me a look. "You must be Beau."

I tilted my head in acknowledgment. "*Mais oui*, in the flesh and at your service."

"Well, Beau, I'm Belle. Your sister and I are designing a clothing line together. She invited me to stay here until I find a place of my own. She didn't mention anything about additional houseguests." Her tone, though pleasant, was stern. She wanted me gone. I needed to stay. So here we stood.

I gave a quick shrug. "She didn't know. I'm an unexpected drop-in. Just here for a day or two. Are you going to send me out into the hot Texas evening with no place to go, *chérie?*"

"How is it that you have an accent and she doesn't?" Belle inquired as she perched on the edge of the vanity chair and reached for some lotion.

"Some of us cling tighter to our roots than others." Truthfully, I liked to let a lil Louisiana roll off my tongue from time to time. The fact that ladies seemed to love it was all the more reason to sprinkle it in the mix. I flashed my most charming smile and headed for the door. "So what's it gonna be, Belle? Shall I start dinner or head for the elevator?"

Belle tilted her head to the side and assessed me with serious consideration. Long moments passed as she eyed me up and down. Finally she shrugged. "You have the weekend, and then I talk to Kat. I'm partial to fish on Fridays."

Score! My smile spread. There was never a deal Beau Montgomery couldn't close given forty-eight hours, a set agenda, and a beautiful woman. "Seafood it is." I slipped out the door and closed it behind me. I laughed softly when I heard the click of the lock. She might be a cool one, but she was no fool.

3

Delaney Mirabella Richards

Belle—7:42 PM the same night

Using a dry washcloth to wipe the condensation from the mirror, I shook my head and sucked my teeth. I took one look at the gleam in my eye and the flush on my cheeks, and I started talking to myself. "Baby girl, no. Matter of fact—hell to the no. That big piece of caramel temptation is the *last* thing I need right now. Brother Beau. Man like that? Sex on a platter, trouble on tap? No ma'am. We do not need the headache." Okay, I had officially started lecturing myself. Out loud. Not a good sign.

The well-earned reputation of Mr. Beauregard Montgomery preceded him. He was an angel to look at, heaven to sleep with, and hell to give your heart to. Hard to resist, hard to get over. I knew myself: inside the boardroom, I was hard as nails. Outside, I had a weakness for tall, pretty boys with killer smiles, tight bodies, and serious bedroom game. Beau was just my type of chocolate addiction. Addictions were nothing but time-sucking black holes. I had zero time for a beau or a Beau of any type or flavor right now.

This Southern girl had busted her ass way too long and too hard to get to this position in my life. I was not about to get sidetracked by anything or anybody. Coming up in the midsize town of Valdosta, Georgia, I dreamed of seeing the world and living a glamorous life. Or at the very least, a more glamorous life than my mother led. I swore to myself at a very young age that Delaney Mirabella Richards was an onward and upward girl—no looking back, no regrets. Success with no strings, no limitations, no excuses, and no complications.

For years I watched my mother, Delores, sacrifice her own dreams and needs. She was a brilliant artist who gave all that up when she married my father, Percy. Instead, she worked two administrative jobs and kept an immaculate house, all while raising five kids. There was me and my younger brothers, Dalton and Davis, along with two younger sisters, Loren and Tina. Five kids, two jobs, and a needy husband—that's how I summed up my mother's existence. In my mind, the most egregious crime was the way my mother catered to her husband, my father. I swear I never saw him load the dishwasher, iron a shirt, or make his own plate. Not once. Delores ran to do it each and every time.

It drove me crazy. My father worked long hours as a custodial supervisor at Valdosta State University. I appreciated the hours he put in to provide for the family, but did that mean he could not fetch his own iced tea at the dinner table? I never once saw him do a thing for her; it was always the other way around.

When my mother passed away at the ridiculously tragic young age of forty-seven, there was nothing that could convince me that my father wasn't partially to blame for my mother's heart giving out too soon. Would it have killed him to treat his wife like an equal and not like a servant?

At the time of my mother's death, I was a slightly rebellious seventeen-year-old who had been modeling for two years. During a spring break cheerleading trip to Miami my sophomore year of high school, a photographer asked if he could take my picture. Then he asked if he could send it in to an agency. My father hated the idea; my mother loved it. After a lot of back and forth discussion between my parents, I signed two weeks later at the tender age of fifteen.

I was a pencil-thin girl, five-foot ten and a half, with olive-tinged brown skin, long thick hair, and what I'd always considered to be just an "okay cute" face highlighted by doe-shaped chocolate eyes and a wide mouth. I was like nothing in the marketplace at that time. They tell me I was an immediate sensation in the modeling industry. All I knew was that I earned my own money, plus enough to send home for my siblings. The world outside of Georgia was mine to explore.

The agency that booked me called me poised,

told me I wore evening gowns and jeans with equal panache, and displayed the professionalism of someone twice my age. My parents made sure I balanced my schoolwork with my career. I had been accepted to FIT, UCLA, and Pratt Institute. My plan had been to head to California or New York right after graduation. But that very afternoon, two hours after my high school graduation, Delores Richards declared that she was tired and went to lie down on the sofa. My mother never woke up again. The doctors said she had a congenital heart defect that had been worsening for years.

From that day forward, I was determined to grab life and live it by my own rules. But at the same time, I was very aware of being forced into the role of matriarch in my family. I was the one the others called for advice and decision making and money. It made me extremely focused and driven.

I gave up pursuing a degree in fashion design and modeled full-time, until right around the time of my twenty-fourth birthday. Using the single name "Delaney," I was fortunate enough to grace covers of magazines and strut catwalks worldwide.

Sometime after the age of twenty-one, I started developing curves. Serious curves. The kind that apparently made me ideal for lingerie and bathing suit shoots. But even with bodacious curves, the industry was a tough taskmaster. After a memorable job where a photographer told me I needed to lose ten pounds—I was over six feet tall in heels and weighed 117—I decided enough was enough.

I had made enough money to put myself and

the rest of the family through whatever schools we chose. There was also the undeniable fact that I was a girl who liked chocolate and French fries. I wasn't meant to live on brown rice and tofu. I was a child of the South. I wanted my chicken fried and cozied up next to some mashed potatoes, not naked on top of brown rice. I missed gravy, dammit! So I semiretired from modeling, only picking up a gig here and there as needed. I moved to New York, enrolled belatedly at FIT, and lucked out when one of my swimwear designs was chosen at a "One to Watch" showcase during Fashion Week.

I launched BellaRich Designs with swimsuits and lingerie. My designs had a nod to old Hollywood and pin-up glamour but used flashy, sinuous fabrics and design elements to give them a modern update. My bestseller was and still is a turquoise halter top tankini with built-in bra and tummy support similar to a swimsuit Jane Russell wore in *Gentlemen Prefer Blondes*. Each of my creations has a signature pink rose stitched into the design somewhere. The fuchsia flower became the company logo.

A few years later, I launched the Trés Belle Women's Ready-to-Wear line with a splashy show in Times Square. That's how I met Kat. She was my headliner for the show. She made a completely inappropriate but hilarious joke about double-sided tape backstage. We've been good friends ever since.

After our last show together, Katrina approached me about partnering to launch a menswear line. Perfect timing. I had been thinking about expanding into menswear and was awed by Katrina's preliminary sketches. She couldn't draw worth a damn but I was able to ascertain her ideas from the rough work. We decided to give it a go.

To keep the new line a surprise, Kat suggested we set up a satellite office in Dallas. So here I was at the age of thirty-two, ready for a new challenge. That challenge did not include tangling with Katrina's older brother. No matter how smoking hot and tempting he was. And Brother Beau looked good.

In my experience, which I'm not ashamed to say is considerable, getting tangled up with men slowed you down, sapped your energy, and blurred your focus. Especially when a man clearly knew exactly how to tangle you up. I remember hearing about Beauregard Montgomery and his exploits among the modeling set. He quit modeling a year or two after I started, but he was legend.

Even without the stories, I knew men like Beau. I almost married a man like Beau. Lucas Turner. He was an aspiring model, aspiring business manager, and unfortunately, an aspiring adult. He failed to achieve any of those three titles. Luke was pretty, spoiled by countless women, and never worked hard a day in his adult life. Wonderful to look at, fun to roll around with until that one morning—the morning you realized you weren't building a relationship, you were supporting and raising a supposedly grown-ass man. No. Thank. You. Lesson learned.

Sure, having those caramel colored eyes scan up and down my body had reminded me of just how long it had been since I'd indulged in any type of naked aerobic activity with a man. And if even half of the rumors about his "talents" were true, he was worth falling off the wagon for an hour or two. The worst thing for a woman who needed a little loving was falling into the path of a man who loved women. And when he looked the way Brother Beau did? Dangerous.

I shook my head one more time as I finished moisturizing every inch of my body. Pulling on simple black cotton undies and matching bra from my latest microfiber line, I spoke sternly to my image in the mirror. "You should have kicked his fine ass out. You *so* don't need this."

"Dinner's almost done. Just simmering a bit. Ready whenever you are," Beau called through the door. He had a voice like maple syrup and somehow made a dinner announcement sound like an invitation to bed. Or was that just my needy imagination?

I sighed. I was making more out of this than was necessary. "Be out in a sec."

"Take your time; we're playing by your rules this weekend."

Damn straight. I stepped into tan yoga pants and a green tank top before looking at my reflection one more time. "Quit overthinking, Delaney."

"Did you say something?" he asked, clearly still standing by the door.

I swung the door open. "I'm starving, sugar. What's for dinner?"

He took a step back and appraised me lazily from head to toe.

I raised a brow. "Seriously?"

"A man can't look?" Beau queried with a careless shrug.

"Not in this direction. Don't even bother," I snapped, and instantly knew it was the wrong thing to say to a man like Beau.

"Is that a challenge?" Of course he saw it as such. Nothing piqued a hunter's interest as much as forbidden prey.

In lieu of an answer, I strode past him to the kitchen. The smells coming from the pans on the stove were amazing. Lifting the lid on one pot, I almost moaned. Shrimp, scallops, and veggies were nestled into a tomato-based sauce. I reached for a spoon.

He reached around and smacked my hand. "Get a plate, *chérie.*"

I rolled my eyes and pulled two plates out of the cabinet. "What is it? It smells heavenly."

"My version of a quick and dirty spin on étouffée—nothing fancy." He dished fluffy rice onto the plate before ladling the fragrant seafood and veggie mix over the top. He opened the oven and pulled out a tray of French bread. Breaking off a chunk, he added it to the plate before handing it to me.

My gaze ran from the delicious meal and then back to him. "You whipped this up in twenty minutes?"

He let a slow smile slide across his face. "You'd be amazed what I can do in twenty minutes, *ma petite chou.*"

I ignored the obvious double entendre and

headed for the dining table. "You can save all that, sugar."

Setting a wine glass beside me, he poured some Chardonnay for both of us and sat down in the seat directly across from me. "Save all what, *ma douce*?"

Clasping my hands together and bowing my head, I murmured a quick prayer over my food before digging in. Dear God, that was delicious. I closed my eyes and moaned appreciatively, "That's better than sex."

"You haven't been doing it right," Beau said in a husky murmur.

Blinking my eyes open, I set the fork down and took a long sip of wine before answering. "That. That's what I'm talking about right there."

"What?" He tried to give me an innocent look.

I wasn't buying it. "All the innuendo and the silky seductive tones—save that for someone else."

"You think my voice is silky and seductive?"

"Beau. I know you, okay?"

"Ms. Richards, we've never met. I would remember."

I slapped my hand down on the table. "I mean, I *know* you. You're the panty-getter, the best looking guy in the room, Mr. Charming. I've met you. I've been with guys just like you. I've seen you a thousand times over. I'm done with all that drama, sweetheart."

He looked at me over his wineglass as he swirled the liquid in a slow circle. I met his gaze unflinchingly. He dipped his head in acknowledgment. "Friends then?"

Finishing another bite, I grinned. "A man that can cook like this? You bet. We can definitely be friends."

He arched a brow. "With benefits?"

I threw back my head and laughed. He wouldn't be Beau if he didn't try. "You just couldn't help yourself, could you? I never say never. Let's just leave it at that for tonight."

4

Cotton Candy

Belle was lounging, stretched out with her feet up and twirling the ice in her glass when the realization hit me. She turned her head in the direction of the setting sun as we sat on Katrina's balcony enjoying our third and final dinner together of the weekend. No makeup, hair combed artlessly back from her face, and I couldn't remember seeing a more beautiful woman. She was flawless. And that was really saying something. I confess to having critiqued a good number of fine-looking women in my day. Okay, more than a good number. I love women; is it my bad they love me back?

People act like it's some sort of crime to appreciate the beauty and bounty of a woman . . . well, yes, women plural. I was always upfront. I never led anyone on. When you tell a woman, "Don't fall in love with me. I'm not sticking around. I'm not husband material," it doesn't get any clearer than that. Women seemed to find that a challenge. What's a man to do?

Yes, I've been in long-term relationships. My college girlfriend and I were together for about four years. And then there was Alexa. She was a model as well. We were actually engaged. I was never really sure why she broke off the engagement. I was doing a photo shoot in Milan, she flew in, gave me the ring back, wished me luck, and I haven't seen her since. I wasn't cheating. I mean, I wasn't around a lot, but I thought she and I would have made a beautiful couple. Had beautiful kids in a beautiful house.

So see? Not a complete dog. Or what did Jewellen call me the other day? A man-ho? That was so unfair. And patently untrue. A ho is indiscriminate; I consider myself very discerning.

What was I talking about before I got sidetracked? Oh. Belle. Yeah. If I was a man for serious relationships, I'd make a play. If she gave me half an indication of being interested in a fling, I'd make a play. I couldn't remember the last time I had spent an entire weekend in a beautiful woman's company when I hadn't made a serious move. More than forty-eight hours with no sex involved . . . and I enjoyed it.

If you had told me that I would enjoy running errands and grocery shopping, I would have doubted your sanity. But hanging with Belle while she picked through stacks of avocadoes and tomatoes in the quest for the perfect guacamole fixings was more fun than I'd had in ages.

After stocking up on supplies for the house, she invited me to go house hunting with her. Since she and Katrina were going to be working near the Fashion District in Dallas, she wanted a full-service place with relative low maintenance in the downtown area. Within a five to ten minute drive were the Dallas Market Hall and Trade Center, a mecca for those in the apparel business.

We drove around the area, and I played tour guide while getting a feel for what she was looking for in short-term housing. On a whim, I drove her to the W Residences near the arts district. She could have hotel amenities, concierge service, and a sleek loft-style condo only fifteen minutes from the Dallas Trade Center and less than five minutes from Katrina's condo. She loved it. As luck would have it, one of the units that was up for sale was also available for month-to-month rental.

I watched her bargain a lower price in exchange for paying six months' cash up front. She also got the owner to agree to leave a good portion of the furniture. She reminded me of Madere, my mother, the way she negotiated so politely the person thought it was their idea all along.

We celebrated her new housing over Mexican food and margaritas. We ended the evening with a fist bump in the hallway before she went to her bedroom and I retired to mine. That alone should have let me know that my mojo was missing in action.

We spent today chilling. Usually, I spent Sundays at Pops and Madere's house but I wasn't up to any more chatter from Rome and Jewel. Instead, I scanned the job boards to see if anything interested me (nothing did). I moved some money around, checked my stock portfolio, and caught up on my e-mail.

The whole day Belle remained hunched over her laptop and sketchbook. I finally suggested a movie. She agreed and had no issues when I chose the latest action blockbuster with car chases and explosions.

When we returned to the house, she offered to cook. We dined out on the balcony. It wasn't until right this minute that I realized what a cool weekend I was having. Drama-free. Breezy, full of laughter and light-hearted moments. The conversation never lagged, and the silence was never uncomfortable. It was just . . . easy.

Now that's pause-worthy. How often did a woman like that cross your path? A woman who looked like that, had her act together, and possessed that elusive cool factor thing, too? That's possibly all five *w*'s. That's a woman you had to give some serious consideration. That's not a woman to keep in the Friend Zone. Just as I thought about making a play, she tilted her head slightly, and it clicked where I'd seen her before. Oh shit! How had I missed that?

"You're Delaney!"

She turned fully toward me and beamed, flashing a trademark pearly-toothed countenance that had graced many a magazine cover. "Guilty as charged. Delany Mirabella Richards, to be exact. Why do you make it sound like an accusation?"

How did I not know this? I wondered. So I asked

out loud, "How did I not know this?" Me, who prided myself on possessing an encyclopedic memory of the hottest models of the last two decades; I should have recognized her at first glance. Especially since my first glance had been quite a glorious eyeful.

For a while there, Delaney was *the* supermodel of supermodels. Magazine covers, runway shows, and cosmetic campaigns—she rocked them all. She hit big just as I was getting out of the business, so our paths never crossed professionally but I definitely had her on my radar.

Looking at her now as she raised and dropped her shoulders in a *who knows?* gesture, I saw not much had changed. She'd cut her hair; it used to hang to her waist. She had added maybe ten pounds here and there, but it landed in all the right places. I took my time letting my eyes wander along her frame. Yes, sir. All. The. Right. Places. Good Lawd.

She raised a brow. "Beau, we had an agreement."

I leaned back casually. "What was that, *chérie?*"

"We agreed to keep things on a friendly basis."

"Am I not being friendly?" I loved a good banter. Lately, it seemed all I had to do was smile and crook a finger and women fell in my lap. It was hella-boring. Where was the challenge in that? But this right here? Maybe this was what I needed. An honest-to-goodness challenge worthy of my determined pursuit.

Belle sat back in her chair and wagged her head at me. "It's so funny. I can actually tell what you're thinking. Don't waste your time, darlin' man."

If she only knew, I had nothing but time to waste. I grinned wolfishly and lowered the tone of my voice. "Enlighten me. What do you think I'm thinking?"

"You're thinking I'm a challenge and you're a little bored."

Well damn. I had to laugh, "You got me, *chérie.*"

She smirked. "Normally, I'd be flattered, and I'd play the game with you."

"What if it's not a game?"

She gave me a look. "Isn't it all a game?"

I conceded the point. "Maybe. But? It sounded like you had a *but* coming behind that statement."

"I'm a busy woman, Beauregard."

"*Vraiment*—but, beautiful, I'll do all the work. All you have to do is say yes."

She raised her eyes to meet mine and let a slow smile spread across her face. Busy woman or not, she was enjoying the banter as much as I was. "You're good, sugar. I'll give you that."

I nodded seriously. "You don't know the half. You should try me and find out."

She flung her head back in a full-bodied laugh. "I've no doubt. Beau, we would be quite the fling, wouldn't we? But I have neither the time nor the energy for the kind of diversions you have in mind."

"All work and no play, Belle?"

She let out a deep sigh. "Beau, if you don't mind me asking . . . what do you *do*?"

"*Bonne question.*"

"You don't know what you do for a living?" She slanted me a confused glance.

"Ah well, there's a question. Let's just say, I'm between enterprises at the moment."

She rolled her eyes. "Let me break it down: ex-model, pretty boy, mid- to late-thirties, unless I miss my guess. No job, no home, no wife, no kids. Flashy car, elegant wardrobe, barely respectable bank account, off-the-chart charm, and ridiculous bedroom game. You are all play and no work. Mr. Montgomery, you are cotton candy."

She lost me on that one. She was close on most of it except my bank account. Happily, thanks to smart investing, I could probably buy and sell her company a few times over if I wished. That cotton candy thing, though? She needed to explain. "I beg your pardon?"

"You're a sweet treat. Tempting as hell. Good to look at and delicious to boot. But you're all good times and no substance. And, ultimately, too much of you probably makes people sick. It's not a knock. I'm not saying it to be mean. There's a place in the world for cotton-candy people."

Well, *le ouch*. Did she just reduce me to a sugar high at the state fair? Damned if I would let her know that stung. A lot. I sent her one of my patented smiles. "Don't you ever just crave something sticky and sweet, *chérie*?"

She got up and started clearing plates from the table. Turning toward the door, she looked over her shoulder at me. "You'll be the first to know if I do. Good night, Beau." She disappeared into the house and closed the door behind her.

I sat there looking over the Dallas skyline. What just happened? It wasn't that I'd never been turned down before. I had, most definitely. At some point.

But no one had ever dismissed me. She called me sugared fluff, for Christ's sake! Sitting here on my sister's patio without a plan of what to do when the sun rose in the morning, I had to acknowledge some truth to her words, and that smarted more than I cared to delve into.

I was back to my thought from Friday night. I was too old for this shit. I needed to pull it together. Looking down, I saw Belle's sketchbook. Pulling it toward me, I began to flip through the book. Her ideas for a menswear line along with some sketched designs filled the pages. It looked like she was blending old Hollywood glamour with modern fabrics and unique tailoring details.

Picking up a red pen from the set she'd left on the table, I jotted a note next to one of the designs. And then I added another and another. Before I knew it, ideas were pouring out of me onto her pages. I may be sugared fluff but I knew what clothing looked good on men. The least I could do was offer a male perspective to her and Katrina's designs. Apparently, that was all I was good for this evening.

5

More than Just a Pretty Face

Belle—11:52 PM the same day

Dammit. I couldn't sleep. I felt bad. I shouldn't have said that stuff to Beau. I just wanted to dissuade him from whatever pursuit he was about to mount. I knew it was coming. I'd enjoyed his company all weekend long. That surprised me. I really didn't think he was that three-dimensional. It turned out that Beau had a keen mind to go along with that sense of humor, wit, and charm. Disconcertingly, he had the same taste in movies, music, and loft space that I did. Beyond the crazy, sexy, pretty exterior beat the heart and personality of a likeable man.

But I knew there would come the moment when he did what guys like Beau do. They have to do it.

They turn on the charm, dial up the heat, and next thing you know—naked shenanigans. My current rule in that regard? Don't start none, won't be none. So I shut him down before he got started.

Not that what I said was wrong; it was just raw and coming from a mean-spirited place. And even though he tried to hide his reaction, I could tell I hit a soft spot. Then again, who wants to be told they are pastel, spun confectionary sugar? I should've known better. Especially from one former model to another. I knew what it was to want to rock a "I am more than just a pretty face" T-shirt 24/7, just to be taken seriously.

With that in mind, I rolled out of bed where I had been tossing and turning anyway and went in search of Beau. I peeked inside the second guest room that he was using but he wasn't there, and the bed hadn't been slept in.

I cut through the living room and only as I was heading toward the kitchen did I glance outside. He was sprawled across one of the deck chairs sleeping soundly. Stepping closer, I noticed he had my sketchbook in his hands. "What in the entire holy hell?!" I raced onto the deck and snatched the book out of his hands.

He blinked up at me sleepily. "Hey you."

Dammit, the man even woke up sexy. I wasn't having it. "What are you doing with my designs?" Flipping open one of the pages, I noticed notes scribbled in a different color pen and handwriting. "Did you *write* in here?"

Sitting up slowly, he shrugged. "Just a thought or two."

I started to deliver a scathing barrage of scorn

when I actually read the note next to the drawing of a man's dress shirt. *Add pale blue contrast stitching at wrist and collar. If produced in silk and linen, good for club and vacation wear.* My mouth fell open. I would have never thought of that, and the contrast thread would add a custom touch to make buyers feel as if they were buying a one-of-a-kind product. I tapped his legs so he would swing them out of the way and kept reading. All of his suggestions took my designs to the next level. That elite couture, recognizable on sight level. The man was a genius.

"You're a genius!" His random thoughts were going to elevate my designs from pretty good to all-world epic.

He wiped the sleep from his eyes and blinked at me. "Can't say I've ever been accused of that before."

I nudged him. "No, seriously, these ideas are brilliant."

He looked embarrassed and shrugged again. "Glad you like them."

"No, you don't understand. I need you."

"I've been telling you that, *chérie*," he said with a raised brow and a slow smile.

I smacked his arm. "Beau. Not now darlin', I'm being serious. Come work with me."

He sat silently looking at me as if waiting for a punch line.

"Beau Montgomery . . . stunned into silence? Now this I don't believe. What is it? You have to know that you have an eye for this."

"I know what looks good. That's all."

"That's a talent, Beau. You have the ability to look at a garment and figure out how to make it better. It took me six weeks to design these clothes; you upgraded them in an hour and a half." I tilted the book toward him.

"Are you serious about me working for you?"

"Would you have a problem working for me?"

"What's your policy on interoffice relationships?"

Laughing, I patted his thigh. "They are strictly forbidden, sugar. I don't do drama."

"You really want me to come work for you?"

"Why are you so surprised? Been a while since someone saw you as more than just a pretty face?" I meant it as a joke but he shifted as if uncomfortable with the topic, and I hurried to reassure him. "Beau, I'm serious. You have a designer's eye, a model's experience, a quality-control mindset, and a little something extra. I don't know what to call it."

"*Lagniappe*." He nodded, taking the design book out of my hand and setting it on the table. I suddenly was very aware of the fact that I was in a short nightgown practically sitting in the lap of a really fine specimen of man. Ah jeez.

"*Lagniappe?*" I asked as he leaned in closer and braced his hands on the table, bracketing me in.

"*Mais oui*. It means *a lil sumthin' extra*, down on the bayou." He nuzzled the side of my neck as he explained. "It's an indefinable sumthin' sumthin' that adds just the right touch of spice." He stroked a hand down my back and I couldn't help but shiver a little.

"Beau?" I tilted my neck to give him better access. Dammit! I didn't mean to do that. I tried to lean back but there was really nowhere to go.

"*Umm hmm?*" His tongue came out and traced along the curve of my earlobe. Something started to melt inside me. Good Lord, the man should come with a warning label.

Concentrate, Mirabella, I scolded myself. "What are you doing?"

His lips paused as he trailed his way from my ear to my cheek. "If I have to explain it, either I'm not doing it right or you are way out of practice, *fille.*"

I *was* way out of practice, but he didn't need to know that. "I guess what I'm really asking is why are you doing this?"

"You said you have a strict no-fraternization policy in the office, right?" His lips grazed mine, and I literally forgot to breathe for a second.

"Right."

"Since I'm coming to work for you in the morning, I thought I'd get my fraternizing in tonight."

I raised my eyes to meet his gaze. We stared at each other trying to get a read on what the other was thinking. Just a quick taste wouldn't hurt anything, would it? I could tell the moment he saw my decision. He leaned in and I closed the distance between us. His lips pressed against mine and my breath hitched in my throat. He sucked my bottom lip into his sinfully warm mouth before releasing it. Then he placed light, soft kisses around the perimeter of my lips.

I leaned closer and angled my head to taste

more of him. I felt his lips curl into a smile before he took my face in his hands. I opened my mouth to take a deep breath and he slid his tongue inside. In slow and deliberate movements, he entangled his tongue with mine. It was a sensuous dance. He led and I followed. His mouth learning mine in delicious determination. He circled once, gauged my reaction, and delved in to try a different tempo. It was the most blatantly sexual kiss I'd ever received. I'd never quite been kissed like this before. As if the kiss was the whole thing and not a prelude to something else. His lips lingered and tantalized for long, heated moments. It was . . . divine. He literally took my breath away. Slowly I pulled back, shook my head, and eased backwards on the chaise. "No. We're not doing this."

"We're not?" His voice was a silky rasp against my already inflamed senses.

My hormones were screaming the same question. *We're not?* "We're not."

He dropped his hands to his lap and nodded slowly. "Why not?"

"You're better than this. I'm smarter than this. I'm not going to seal an employment offer by having wild, raunchy sex with you out on your sister's balcony."

"Wait . . . was it going to be wild *and* raunchy?" he asked teasingly.

Hot and steamy, too. "Focus," I said to him and my wayward thoughts. "I'm not doing it as some sort of power play between us."

"Why not do it because you want to?"

"Too easy."

"Does it have to be difficult?"

"Sex is your fallback position, I get that. But I like you, Beau."

He frowned. "I'm confused. You like me. You want me. But you won't sleep with me."

"Not tonight and not tomorrow." I eased away from him and stood up. Plucking the book off the table, I headed back toward the sliding glass door. "If you like, we can ride into work together; I'd like to start at eight. We'll discuss salary and job description on the way. Good night, Beauregard." He would never know how much I longed to throw caution and decorum to the wind. To just say "to hell with it" and pounce back on that lounger taking everything he had to offer.

The knowing glimmer in those eyes indicated that maybe he did know after all. "*Bon nuit*, Mirabella." His voice was a deep bass gilded with undertones.

His every word was a temptation at this point. I gave myself silent kudos that I walked away without looking back once. Congratulations to me.

6

What Have We Here?

I was abruptly awakened by the sound of my baby sister's not-so-dulcet tones shrieking at me. "Avery Beauregard Montgomery, why are you in my guest room?!"

"Audelia Katrina Montgomery, what time is it, and what are you doing back from Bora Bora?" I stretched and opened one eye.

"It was Bali, idiot. It's just after six." Katrina was half an inch shorter than six feet. We called her the Golden Child because she was the youngest, the only girl, and literally looked like she'd been dipped in gold. Her hair was long, wavy, and sandy-colored. Her eyes were gold. Her skin has been described as honey-coated bronze. To me, she was just my baby sister. Snarky, smart-mouthed, and always in someone's business. She was border-line brilliant and did have a heart of gold, though. You'd never meet a more genuine or loyal person. Her timing, however? That was inconvenient as hell.

"Bali, Bora Bora, Bahamas. I knew it was some white, sandy, beach-type destination that started with a *B*. Whatever. I thought you were on location until next week at least." I opened the other eye, looked over at the clock to confirm the time, and wondered if I was going to get that extra half hour of sleep.

"You mean you *hoped* I was on location until next week, *mon frère*. I wrapped early. Did you miss me?" She yanked the covers off the bed and took a flying leap to land on top of me. Dammit, I would not be getting those extra *z*'s after all.

"Oomph! Kit-Kat, watch the jewels!" I shifted as her knee came dangerously close to a sensitive area. Wrapping her up in a hug, I kissed her fore-head. "Hey, brat."

"Hey, handsome." She kissed me back before digging an elbow into my side. "What are you doing here?"

"Hanging out," I evaded.

She heaved a sigh. "Beau, what did you do to get kicked out of Roman's?"

"You mean *who* did I do?" I said with a sigh of my own. It really had been one of my stupider moves. And I'd had plenty over the years.

"Jesus, Beau . . ." Katrina muttered.

"I think her name was Linda. She was the proverbial straw."

"Straw?"

"Yes, the one that broke the camel's back. If in this metaphor Rome and Jewel's tolerance is the camel's back, Linda was the straw."

Katrina frowned. "Lydia? From Jewel's office? Cute, chesty, a Pilates nut?"

"That's the one."

"Was she worth it?" Katrina wondered.

"She totally wasn't."

"Will you ever learn to think with the big head?"

"Must we discuss this now?" Like I mentioned, Katrina tended to lecture.

"Fine." Katrina changed the subject. "Did you meet Belle?"

"I did." And I liked her. A lot. I liked a lot about her. Did that make sense?

Her eyes narrowed. "Don't even think about it."

"Already thought it." Still thinking about it this morning, if I was being honest with myself.

Kat winced and smacked my arm. "Please, please, please tell me you did not sleep with her."

"He did not sleep with me," Belle said from the doorway. She was dressed and ready for the day in a short dress that was bright, silky, and showed off her curves and long, toned legs. Nice.

I couldn't help but grin at her and a slow answering smile spread across her face. I'd like to think that we came to an agreement of sorts over the weekend. She was definitely one of a handful of women who saw me as more than a diversion. A woman that talked to me like she really wanted to know me, the real me. Not just the me I showed to keep things light and easy. She wasn't a frivolous woman and saw me as more than a frivolous man.

I know, I know. Boo effin' hoo, Beau—right? These are what my friend Carter calls "pretty boy problems." Complaining that women only want to sleep with you or have you on their arm, complaining that people don't expect much out of you: pretty boy problems. I got that. But with the exception of that tart "cotton candy" jab, Belle hadn't treated me that way at all. So if my morning smile was part appreciation and part predatory, could you blame me?

Katrina looked from Belle to me and back again. "What have we here?"

Belle rolled her eyes. "I hired your brother last night."

"You did what? As what?!"

My eyes narrowed. "Professional gigolo and good-time guy, isn't that all I'm good for, *'tite chat?*"

Katrina jabbed me in the ribs. "Don't bring it here, AB. I know you can do whatever you put your mind to, and your talents lie beyond the bedroom and the bar. When are *you* going to figure that out?"

I shifted uneasily, trying to act casual.

"Well, I figured that out last night," Belle shared from the doorway. "Your brother single-handedly repaired the spring line in an hour or two." She walked forward and handed Katrina the sketchbook before looking at me. "You gonna be ready to go in an hour?"

"Yes, ma'am." I watched as she swiveled on one tall, skinny high-heeled shoe and exited the room. Once a model, always a model. She knew how to leave an impression on a room. Katrina jabbed me in the ribs again. "Girl, what is your problem now?"

She was flipping through the pages. "Why didn't you tell me you knew how to design clothing? We could have launched a line years ago. These are really good, Beau."

I shifted her off me and eased out of bed. I wasn't entirely comfortable with all the fuss the two of them were making over some scribbled suggestions next to some drawings. I had an eye for what looked good on people. That was all. I didn't consider that a marketable talent, but if they did, so be it. Heading toward the bathroom I called over my shoulder, "It's just a few ideas, Katrina. Hardly a design."

"Stop selling yourself short; these add a completely different depth to the designs. This is going to be awesome."

I paused from brushing my teeth. "So I can stay?"

"Can you promise not to sleep with Belle?"

"I can promise not to do anything she doesn't want."

"Not the same thing, Beauregard." Katrina stood up and started pacing with the sketchbook in her hand.

"That's all I can promise. You want me to lie?"

"She's a friend of mine, Beau. And she's good people. Plus we're in business together. I don't want any broken hearts."

"What if she breaks mine?" I stepped into the shower and set the temperature to just under scalding.

"Is that even possible?"

"Are you calling me heartless?" I raised my voice to be heard over the water as I soaped up a washcloth.

"I'm calling you . . . aloof."

Rinsing my face and head, I disagreed with her. "I'm the warmest guy in the world."

"I'm talking about your heart, not your libido."

"I took anatomy, *ma soeur.*"

"*Mais oui*, wasn't it your major?" My snarky baby sister came to stand in the doorway, hand on hip.

I turned off the water and stepped out of the stall. "Funny girl." I wrapped a towel around my waist.

"Just saying. Maybe Belle is one you can just skip."

"Skip?" I started the electric razor and glided it over my jaw.

"Not play with?"

"Who says I'm playing?"

She swallowed and let her mouth fall open. "What happened this weekend between you two?"

I kept my expression stoic. "We just hung out."

"You . . . just hung out?"

"Indeed. So can I stay?"

"At least promise me you won't pull a patented Beau hit and quit, please?"

"I beg your pardon?" I dared her to elaborate on that.

She heaved her second deep dramatic sigh of the morning. "Never mind. You can stay."

"Appreciated."

"But why do you want to? You have enough

money in the bank to buy homes all over the globe. Why don't you pick a place and settle down?"

I turned off the shaver and started to dress. "With a wife, a dog, two kids, and a pool?"

"Most people say picket fence."

"Are we most people? Anyway, *chérie*, it's way too early in the morning for one of your 'it's time for you to grow up and settle down' speeches. Believe me, I'm thinking about it. I know I'm not getting any younger."

"I only say these things in love, Beau."

Roman said a similar thing when he booted me out of his house three days ago. Pulling out cufflinks, I walked past her toward the closet. "Love me less, *mignon chat*; I'll be all right."

7

Interesting Times

Belle—6:32 AM the same day

Tiptoeing away from the guest suite where Katrina and Beau were talking, I couldn't help but be more intrigued by Beauregard Montgomery than I cared to be. If pressed, I would've thought Beau had spent every last dime he ever made and was a happy-go-lucky guy. The man I overheard? He had some depth to him.

I shook my head; I had no time to be concerned over whatever Beau was or wasn't. I had a business to run. Glancing at my watch I called out, "Who's coming into the office with me?"

"One second and I'll be ready," Beau called back.

Katrina appeared in the hallway with the sketchbook. Waving it at me, she smiled. "Who knew?"

"I did, the minute I saw the notes. I made him a job offer on the spot. Even though I'm comfortable designing clothes for women and was pretty sure I could pull off the mens' line, I have to admit I wondered . . ."

Katrina nodded. "Me, too."

"What?! The menswear line was your idea, ma'am."

She shrugged. "I know. But I have to admit that I thought about it with dressing my brothers in mind. There is Roman, who will throw on cotton shorts and a tee, as opposed to Beau, who looks runway-ready every time he leaves the house. All I had was big picture ideas; I was going to lean heavily on their input."

"Well, now we have it."

"Like I said—who knew?"

"Your brother is a genius," I told her.

"Dear God, don't let him hear you say that. The last thing he needs is more reason to swell his considerable ego."

Beau stepped out into the hallway wearing a perfectly tailored light summer silk suit in a pale gray, paired with a mint-green shirt and butter-yellow tie. It was an outfit only the truly confident could pull off. Like Katrina said . . . runway-ready.

"Mornin', Belle. You two know I can hear you, right?" He brushed past me, casually running his hand across my shoulder and down my arm. He strode on the way to the kitchen and started pulling things from the refrigerator.

I deliberately ignored the tingling that started the moment he touched me. When he pulled a skillet out and set it on the stovetop, Katrina and I exchanged glances and sat down at the breakfast bar. Nothing sexier than a man who cooked well and often. I reached for the coffeepot and two mugs. I poured a cup for Katrina and handed it over.

He looked over his shoulder as he cracked eggs into a bowl. "What's wrong with this picture, ladies?"

Adding cream and sugar to the cup, I raised a brow. "Not a damn thing that I can tell—you, Kat?"

"Nope. All good here."

He diced and chopped ham and onion and tossed it into the pan. "I'm a man who likes to be catered to. Why am I doing the catering?"

I snorted. "I just gave you a six-figure job, sugar."

Katrina nodded. "I'm letting you live here rent-free."

"*Ça suffit!* Fine." He shook his head and muttered under his breath about *les femmes gâtées*.

I set my coffee cup down and looked at Kat. "What did he call us?"

"Spoiled women."

"Why does he sound more French than you and Roman?"

"He remembers our Cajun life more than we do, and he thinks it's sexy."

It kinda was. But I was not going to admit it. I was saved from making a response by the insistent ringing of my BlackBerry. Glancing at the screen, I rolled my eyes. "Yazlyn, what's up, girl?"

Yazlyn was my best friend and managing director; she was overseeing the office in New York while I was launching Dallas. We met on a beach shoot back in my swimsuit model days. She pranced out to the set stark-naked, all six feet of gleaming ebony skin and another full six inches of majestic curly Afro, and announced, "I want the suit that she has on, or I'm going home."

Just as I was about to jump up to break off a piece of my mind, she winked at me. The photographer/director was a known grab-ass, and she wanted to make him suffer a little. Nothing like a fit of divatude to throw a shoot off schedule. And everyone in the business knew that time was money. We were close in age, and she was also from the South. We bonded immediately. When I launched my first line of clothing, she agreed to do all the initial shots free of charge. When she retired, I thanked her by giving her a place in the company.

But by nature, Yazlyn was not a morning person, and even on the East Coast, it was early. "So, what's wrong?"

"It's Arizona." Arizona Marks was a former classmate of mine from FIT. We'd been friends and collaborators. She and I were both in the running for "One to Watch," but when I won the prestigious design award and she didn't, things turned ugly. I would call us rivals, but really, she made it her life mission to copy my work (poorly) and pass it off as her own.

I sucked my teeth. "What is it this time?"

"I just got a sneak peek at her fall line."

"And?"

"It looks eerily familiar."

I resisted the urge to stomp my foot. "Scan it

and send it. I'll be in the office in an hour. Wow, that girl can hold a grudge, can't she?"

"Like no other. How's it going there?"

Beau slid a fluffy omelet alongside some fruit on a plate and dropped it in front of me. "*Bon appétit.*"

I smirked into the phone. "Better than I would've imagined. I hired a creative director."

"Really? Who?"

"His name is Beauregard Montgomery."

She drew in a breath and let out a whistle. "Sweet Jesus, are you talking about the former model Beauregard Montgomery?"

I frowned. "Yes, why?"

"He's the hotness. Just hot sex on a platter. *Oooh wee*, the stories on him! Is he still fine?"

I flicked a glance in his direction. "He looks all right."

"Oh. We must not be talking about the same man. Oozes the sexy, killer body, smile that says 'you know you want some of this'—that guy."

I bit back a sigh. "Same guy."

"*Ummm*," she moaned. "He was looking right the last time I saw him. You gonna get on that?"

Something about her tone gave me pause. "You haven't slept with him, have you?"

"Define *sleep*." Her tone was silky.

"Yazlyn!"

"Ha, no—I never slept with him or entered into sexual congress with him. I did work with him once. Nice guy. He was engaged at the time. But, by God, I would do him on a bed of quesadillas at high noon in the middle of Times Square, given half a chance."

I blinked twice and looked down at the phone before putting it back to my ear. "I don't even know what that means."

She clucked her tongue. "Oh, sweetie, are you still living in Abstinence Land? Chillin' on Celibate Lane?"

"I'm hanging up now before you start talking about Dickless Drive." I hung up and looked up to find both sets of Montgomery eyes pinned on me. His whiskey-colored and full of humor, hers more golden and full of curiosity.

"Dickless Drive?" he asked, one brow raised.

"Who did Beau sleep with?" Katrina inquired.

"No one." I dug into my omelet. It was delicious. Where did he find fresh crab?

"Well, we all know that's not true," Katrina said in a dry tone.

"Watch it, Sis." Beau took a sip of coffee.

"No." I shook my head. "I meant . . . Lord. You know Yazlyn. I told her I hired Beau, and she knows him."

Beau nodded. "Yazlyn, yeah—ebony goddess with an Arkansas twang. We did a shoot for a winery. She said I slept with her?"

"No. She said she *would* sleep with you on a hot bed of quesadillas in the middle of the day in Times Square."

Katrina choked on her omelet. "Bad visual. Bad visual!"

Beau smiled. "*Que caliente*! Mexican. That's new. With or without guacamole, do you imagine?"

"Can we change the subject?" I pleaded, trying not to laugh.

"Salsa?" he asked.

"Stop. It." Katrina put her hand up.

But by that time, I couldn't hold it in. I snickered. "You know, salsa might sting and avocado is hell to get out of clothing. Sour cream would be better, don't you think?"

Katrina snatched up her plate and coffee mug. "That's it! I rebuke this entire conversation. You two pervs carry on. I'll come by the office after I've had some sleep and can get the thought of Beau's naked ass covered in avocado out of my head. I hate y'all!" She ran down the hallway and slammed her bedroom door shut. "*Hate. You. Both*!"

Beau and I chuckled in between bites of food.

"Are you going to explain Dickless Drive?" he asked.

"No indeed, sir. I am not." I shook my head. Share with virile Brother Beau that I was abstaining? A man with whom women (like Yazlyn) who hadn't laid eyes on him in ten years still longed to get freaky with on a stack of appetizers? No. Wasn't. Going. To. Happen.

He nodded. "All right. Then, tell me the breakdown of the company and what I'm walking into this morning."

Now that I could do.

"We're a more casual design house. I prefer to bring in smart people and let them multitask. Yazlyn is my second-in-command and acts as managing director. She'll take point driving the oversight of the women's line as I get this men's line underway. The women's line is broken into couture, ready-to-wear, swimwear, and intimates. Even though I'm the head designer, I can't do it all. So I have assistant designers as well as fashion and design specialists. We have a visual director who handles the showroom in New York and will split time in Dallas. We have finance, logistics, graphic designers, brand managers. We have garment construction specialists and a media/interactive director. On the sales side, we have account executives. We had a talent manager who recently resigned, but with you and Katrina on board, I'll probably shift those responsibilities to get your input."

"So how many people are we talking about in all?"

"Around fifty. I don't want to grow too far too fast. Right now we have the revenue on the orders from the women's line to support the expansion into men's."

"Do you want to go bigger eventually? Accessories, shoes, handbags, household items?"

This was the thing about Beau that snuck up on you. Just when you thought he was all rock-hard abs, killer ass, and quesadilla sex, he dropped something insightful on you. "Great question. I'd like to inch that way but I'm not in any hurry. The most important thing is to provide a unique quality product that people think they can't get anywhere else. With your help, I'm hoping that's what the menswear line will be."

He nodded. "Let's go get 'em."

8

Family Dinner

Beau—Sunday, May 1, 4:28 PM

With Katrina on one side and Belle on the other, it didn't look like I was going to get out of this one. It had been a while since I'd been to Madere and Pops's house for Sunday dinner. Not so coincidentally, it had been just as long since I had seen or spoken to Roman or Jewel.

To say I wasn't looking forward to it? A massive understatement. The past few weeks I had valid excuses for staying away. The first Sunday after I started working at BellaRich, I helped Belle move into her new condo and finish setting up the new offices. Belle's office was an open warehouse loft concept near Mockingbird Lane. It covered two floors with the top story dedicated to design and merchandising. The bottom floor was all sales and display. The next five weekends, we had worked straight through. We wanted to host a designer's showcase party for Dallas Fashion Week, and the deadline to have the designs perfected, sewn, and ready for orders was looming faster than any of us expected.

Working with Belle, Kat, and the team was exhilarating, exhausting, and fulfilling all at the same time. I was in my element: creative, collaborating, and contributing. Belle, as CEO and designer, had the talent to turn ideas into garments. Kat was a big-picture idea person, technically called a design director. She would say, "We need Casual Friday wear and weekend wear and resort wear for men. And we need to call it all something specific, so men know. Men want to be told 'wear this for this' and be done with it."

Then Belle would sit down and sketch out four items. Then they would pass it to me, and I'd say, "What about a drawstring waist, a fabric that doesn't need ironing or can be wash and wear and not too matchy matchy with the shirt." Plus, I wanted the entire line of clothing to have a similar feel. I went through and made sure everything looked like a coordinating set of styled garments. They all played off each other; that's what pulled together a collection. I don't know if that's what creative directors did at other fashion houses, but it was what I was doing now. I loved it.

The process behind the design, creation, and manufacture of clothing was new and intriguing to me. An idea became a sketch. Sketches were tweaked, ripped up, restarted, and argued about, redesigned, and finalized. The graphic designers fed them into a computer program and created the technical sketches. And then we'd debate the hell out of those. We'd call in the garment construction team (just a fancy name for the tailoring experts) and begin debate on cut, fabric, thread count, buttons, zippers, stitching, the works. One time we spent three hours reviewing the proper vent on a man's three-button blazer. Who knew all of this went into it?

From there, a spec sheet was created. The spec sheet was what went to the manufacturer so that samples could be created. We had e-mailed forty-two spec sheets to the manufacturer last night. The design part was over except for minor tweaks here and there. Marketing and sales would start next. Today was a celebration. But before we went out and raised a glass, I'd been shanghaied into attending Sunday family dinner.

Another thing I'd learned these past weeks: Belle was a woman I liked and respected. Only through a deliberate decision had I not made a single move on her. She and I, we had a vibe and energy between us that went beyond the sexual. I liked that. I appreciated the novel of the unexpected and different.

A quick and dirty hit and quit during lunch break was not what I wanted from her. I wanted more. I didn't know how much more, but until I figured it out, I was biding my time. She knew it, and I could sense in the way I caught her assessing me and watching when she thought I couldn't see her that she might be feeling the exact same way. There definitely was something going on behind those beautiful chocolate eyes. There was a palpable static between us, and we both made a conscious effort not to touch.

That was new for me, looking without touching. Running my eyes along Belle's fine form, I relaxed a little. "You look nice tonight." She had on a simple, green wrap dress and wedge heels. But she made them look magnificent.

"Thanks, bro, that means a lot," Katrina teased, at ease in jeans and a dressy top.

"You're all right, but I was complimenting the boss lady."

Belle smiled at me. "I'd be more flattered if you weren't so obviously stalling going inside."

"Dig deep, AB. Back straight, head up, smile on," Katrina said, slapping me on the ass and ringing the doorbell. I rolled my eyes and put my party face on.

Belle looked from her to me and back again. "That works? We can just bark orders and Beau follows them?"

I slanted her a wicked side-eye and a grin. "Depends on the order, *chérie.*"

"Don't even start, Beauregard; we are standing outside your parents' house."

"That never stopped him before, *jolie fille.*" My father laughed as he suddenly opened the door. A tall man with honey-brown skin and salt-and-pepper hair, Avery Montgomery was an imposing but friendly character. Ignoring me and Kat for the moment, he reached in between us and grabbed up Belle, enveloping her in a warm hug.

"Don't crush her, Pops. She signs my paychecks."

"Paycheck? You have a paycheck?" Alanna, fondly

known as Madere, peeked out from behind her husband. She was a tiny woman, with flawless mahogany skin, sparkling coffee-colored eyes, and doll-like features. Her long, dark brown, wavy hair was shot through with silver strands and pulled back into her customary neat ponytail.

I stepped across the threshold and kissed her cheek in greeting. "*Salut, ma mère.*" I picked her up and swung her around before kissing her again. "Miss me?"

"Rascal," she said with a huge smile on her face before turning to her husband. "Put the child down, Avery. Katrina, you come in and eat, *bébé*. Like to disappear when you turn sideways."

Kat and I exchanged glances as we stepped toward the kitchen. Madere was in one of her sassy moods this evening—anything could fly out of her mouth. Jewel and Roman were on the sofa in the living room. Jewel's brother, Ross, was in an easy chair. Various cousins, aunts, and uncles clustered around playing cards, setting out food, or watching a basketball game on the television. Typical Sunday at Pops and Madere's.

"Unca Beau, Unca Beau!" My nephew LaChayse came flying out of nowhere and launched himself at me. I caught him and gave him a hug before hauling him up in my arms.

"What's up, lil man?" Chase looked and acted like a Montgomery man even at the age of eight. Long-limbed, long lashes, eyes that looked like rum when serious or like copper when not. He had a slightly silly sense of humor and tended to be direct to the point of outspoken. He reminded me of, well, . . . me.

He frowned at me. "Where have you *been*? Why don't you live with Daddy anymore? You left without saying good-bye. I missed you! When can we play?"

The room fell silent while I contemplated my answer. I decided to go the diplomatic route. "I had to go stay with your Aunt Kat. She didn't want to be alone. I'm sorry I didn't say good-bye. What if I come by next week and we'll play?"

"Sports on the Wii?"

I agreed. "Sports on the Wii."

He thought about it for a minute and then looked over at his aunt. "You really need him, Auntie Kitty?"

Katrina nodded seriously. "I really do. Don't know how I lived without him." To her credit, she said it with a straight face.

"All right then. You can put me down." Chase was done with the matter and ready to move on. I set him down, and he ran to his grandfather.

"Who's the lovely lady?" Ross asked, getting up from the chair and smiling widely.

I sent him the universal "don't even think about going there" look and stepped forward. "This is Belle Richards, designer extraordinaire."

Madere clapped her hands in excitement. "Oooo, I have the dress. The Trés Belle wraparound silk in red flowers. *J'adore, j'adore!*" She came forward and gave Belle a kiss on each cheek.

Belle smiled back at her. "If you loved it, then I'll have to send you some of the new line. Bright colors, splashy patterns, slinky tailoring. Very sexy."

I blinked. "*Merde!* Did you just call my mother sexy?" No son wanted to hear about that.

Pops clapped a hand on my shoulder. "She is, boy; accept it."

Roman stood up from the sofa. "Is the food ready yet?"

Katrina shuddered. "Yes, please change the subject."

Madere waved her small hands at all of us. "*Pah*, what do you know. How you think you got here, no?" She wound her arm through Belle's. "Is that Georgia I hear in your voice?"

"Yes, ma'am," Belle answered.

"Tell me, *tite chou*, what do you pay my son to do?"

"Your son happens to be a genius when it comes to figuring out the extra touch that takes clothes from looking okay to looking spectacular. He's the creative director for the men's line of ready-to-wear clothing that Katrina and I have been working on."

I looked around to see members of my family nodding their heads and murmuring in agreement.

"The boy does look good."

"Always a snappy dresser, that one."

"He's always had the eye."

"That makes so much sense. I always thought he should have stayed in fashion."

"Finally somewhere to put all the talent."

These were things I never heard my family say about me. I thought they all assumed I was some form of lazy, freeloading gigolo. Maybe for a minute or two there, I kinda was. *Hmm.* Learn something new every damned day.

Roman came over to me, laughing. "Leave it to you to find a way to get paid for *lagniappe*! Only you." He put his hand out. "No hard feelings?"

I grasped it and pulled him to me in a quick hug. "Between Montgomerys? *Jamais, mon frère.*" Never.

Jewel sauntered forward. "Are you ready to admit that us tossing you out was the best thing to happen to you?"

I narrowed my eyes at her, still not 100 percent over that "man-ho" line, when Chase dashed over with his hands on his hips. "Mama Bijou, you tossed my unca out like the garbage?"

The Montgomerys had taken to calling Jewel *Bijou*, her name in French. Chase had picked up on it over the years. Saving her bacon, I jumped in. "Over. They tossed me over to Kat's house."

"Oh. Okay then. Can we eat now?"

Madere, with her arm still wrapped through Belle's, nodded and propelled them both forward. "*Allons manger.*" It was time to eat. Belle looked over her shoulder at me and smiled. I expelled a breath I didn't even know I was holding.

9

I Didn't Have Time for Complicated

Belle—9:43 PM the same night

I should have known the night was taking a turn when, upon entering this jazz lounge, half of the crowd screamed, "Beau!" like he was Norm from *Cheers.* Less than a minute after we walked in, Katrina yanked a random man off a barstool and disappeared onto the dance floor, head bopping and hips swinging rhythmically from left to right. My next clue should have been the dancing giant who came over to greet us, who had the unlikely name of Big Sexy. Only Beau would have a best friend nicknamed Big Sexy. And it wasn't as if only one or two people called him this. It was almost

(*almost*) as if his mama had named him Big Sexy. But I had to assume that she hadn't.

Carter Parks was a retired Superbowl-winning linebacker who had been at LSU with Beau before turning pro. He was a mountain of a man with a huge smile, a soft voice, and a wicked sense of humor. The two of them together were something to see. Both of them stood in six foot three or six foot four range. Beau was lean and dressed in a black tee tucked into black jeans. Carter was thickly solid and dressed in tan pants and a navy polo. Beau was pretty; Carter was handsome. They both had smiles that caught your attention and held it tight.

I liked Carter immediately, even after I heard that the two of them were given the nickname "The Pontchartrain Poonhounds" on campus. I can only imagine the trail of broken hearts left in their wake. Pretty much confirmed what I already suspected: Beauregard was a hound of epic proportions back in the day. And maybe was still. I wasn't sure. I hadn't really seen him doing any chasing or hounding lately. Curious.

Anyway, the club was named The Jade Spot, for no apparent reason I could ascertain. It was a combination restaurant/lounge/club that catered to the over-thirty, upwardly mobile set. This evening the band was playing a Stevie Wonder tribute, and the menu featured a sparkling wine tasting. If that wasn't a slippery slope for a woman fighting an attraction to a man, I didn't know what else to call it. Anytime your champagne glass magically refills without your knowledge . . . that's a recipe for foolishness and mayhem.

Working closely with Beau for the past five weeks had been more than I ever expected. He was all quick wit, agile communication, and sizzly chemistry. I had never felt anything quite like it. It was almost a force field that buzzed when we were in the same room. It went nuclear when we touched. So we tried not to touch.

So I wasn't sure how, after spinning around on the floor listening to Carter tell hilarious stories about Beau, I found myself wrapped tightly against Monsieur Montgomery while he sang "Knocks Me Off My Feet" in my ear. My head was swirling, and I really didn't know if it was from the bubbly wine or the company. But it all felt really good. How unfair was it that the man was not only finer than should be legal but could also sing and move like he was born to it? *Is there anything you can't do?!*

Beau tilted his head to the side and looked down at me. "Did you mean to say that out loud, *chérie?*"

I most certainly had not. "Never mind. Keep dancing."

"*Tout à fait.*"

"Which means?"

"As you like, or of course, or certainly."

Apparently, I needed to learn more French. The few phrases I knew from my Paris runway days were not enough to keep up with Beau's affectations. Although I was starting to think it was just a part of who he was. Beau might be a little fancy, but he certainly wasn't fake.

"I can hear you thinking, Belle. What is it?"

"Just trying to figure you out, Montgomery."

"Let me know what you come up with; I could use some insight myself."

The song ended and we took slow steps as we separated, trying to gauge each other's thoughts. There was definitely something going on here. He seemed a man at ease with himself. He was comfortable in the moment. I, on the other hand, was uneasy as hell. Standing there I felt the struggle between my intellect and my feelings. I liked Beau. I genuinely did. God knew I was attracted to him. A part of me wanted to just go with that. But then the intellect stepped in. He worked for me. The man's college nickname was Poonhound, for Christ's sake. Plus I was friends with his sister. Messy. I liked things clean.

He quirked a brow at me. "Come to any decisions yet?"

"Let me marinate with it for a second."

"Fair enough." He held my hand as we walked back to the table. I saw Katrina's and Carter's eyes drop to our clasped hands, and I pulled away. This could get complicated very quickly. And I didn't have time for complicated.

As I slid into the booth, he glided in beside me and asked the table, "Another round?"

"Almost always," Carter said.

"Maybe just one more," Katrina added.

All eyes at the table fell on me. "I probably shouldn't."

Beau's eyelids dropped low. "All the more reason you should, then." He lifted a finger toward the waiter. "Once more for the table, please."

As the waiter scurried off, I heard Katrina sucking her teeth beside me.

"What is it?"

"Trouble. In stilettos. Headed our direction."

I looked over to see a lovely dark-skinned sister with a shoulder-length bob and a smile that screamed "up to no damned good," dressed to the nines and approaching our table with a determined gait. From her flawlessly made-up face, past the revealing but expensive clothes, down to her perfectly pedicured feet wrapped in five-inch silver sandals . . . everything about her announced, *Look at me and appreciate what you see.*

Apparently I was the only one at the table who didn't know her. Carter had an appreciative smirk on his face; Katrina had an irritated scowl. And Beau? Beau's face was remarkably blank. Only the tightness around his jaw indicated that he knew anything about this woman.

When she was only a few steps from the table, he rose and gave her a hug. When he pulled back, she squeezed tighter and let her hand glide down his back and across his ass. My brow shot up. *It was like that? Hmmm,* interesting.

"Renee, *ma belle fleur,* how have you been? You look exquisite, as always," Beau said in a voice that spoke of . . . familiarity. He took a step back but she kept a hand on his arm. I decided right then and there that I didn't like her. I hate women who cling.

"You know me, Beauregard. I'm always good. You're still looking like the best damned dessert on the menu." She dragged a bright red lacquered nail down his arm.

"*Merci,* I do what I can to hold the old physique together."

"I remember," she purred and sent a stunning smile toward the table. "Big Sexy! Still in the wolf pack, huh?"

He stood up and gave her a hug. "Whither Beau goes . . . you know."

"Katrina! I haven't seen you since Jewel's wedding. You look fab."

Katrina nodded once. "Renee." Her tone was tart and her expression did not veil her disgust. I'd never known Katrina to be unfriendly to anyone.

"Well, damn girl, who peed in your pear brandy?"

"Renee, you tried to break up my brother's wedding to Jewel. You hit on my date to the wedding, and you've slept with Beau. I got nothing good to say to your trampy pseudo-bougie ass."

Whoa! This was just . . . whoa. I absorbed all of the best that I could and settled in to see what would happen next.

She and Katrina locked eyes for a heated moment before Renee shrugged a gleaming bare shoulder. "So be it. Who's the silent diva?"

I blinked twice. "Are you talking to me?"

"You're the only one I don't know, sweetie."

I hated when southern women called each other *sweetie* without having the familiarity to do so. It smacked of pretention and rudeness. Everyone knew it was a put-down and meant that person didn't really care what your name might be. Yeah, I really didn't like this chick.

Beau took one look at my face and stepped forward. "Renee Nightengale, may I present Belle Richards?"

Renee's whole attitude changed at hearing my

name. "The designer? Former model?" She dropped down into the booth next to me uninvited. "I've been dying to meet you!"

I inched closer to Katrina and gave a tight smile. "And now here you are, sugar."

"It's providence! I'm in public relations, and my client, Royal Mahogany, is interested in doing a spread featuring your clothing. I was going to reach out to your people next week."

"How providential," Katrina muttered and motioned for the waiter to hurry bringing the next round over.

Royal Mahogany would be a nice get, for the promotional power they brought to the table. Working with this chick? Not so sure about that. None of those thoughts showed on my face when I answered her. "Well, let's do that. Call over next week, and we'll set something up."

"Wonderful." She smiled broadly before looking from Beau to me and back again. "Are you two together? Like *together*?"

I looked at Beau; he arched a brow to await my answer. "No," I said vehemently. "Not at all." Oops. That might have been a little forceful. The easy smile slid off his face, and the look he shot my way was not pleasant. "We work together. That's all."

"That's all?" Renee asked, sliding her glance back and forth again.

"*C'est tout*—the lady says 'that's all,' then that's all. Why do you ask?" Beau answered with more bite in his voice than I'd ever heard.

Renee slid out of the booth and wrapped her arm around his. "In that case, come sit with me for a minute, won't you?"

He glanced at me as if expecting me to say something to stop him. I met his gaze and shrugged. His life after work was his own. I had no claim to stake. *Do whatcha wanna do,* my look told him. He nodded slowly. *Message received, loud and clear.* He smiled down at Renee. "*Pourquoi pas?*" He reached into his pocket, drew out some cash, and tossed it toward the table. "Kit-Kat?"

"What?" she snarled at me, at Renee, at the money on the table, and finally at her eldest brother.

"Don't wait up." With that, he turned and walked away with that trifling-ass chick on his arm. My stomach twisted a little at the sight of him walking away, and I wasn't sure how to feel about that.

Said chick looked over her shoulder with a smug smile. "Nice seeing everybody!"

The waiter finally rolled up with the drinks, and we all gave a *Really, dude?* look that had him announce in a rush, "These are on the house. Sorry for the delay." He set the check down and disappeared again.

"So . . . who is Renee, and why don't I like her?" I asked Carter and Katrina while I reached for another flute of sparkling wine.

Carter laughed. "Do you really want to hear this story?"

I nodded. "I think I do."

Katrina caught a waitress passing by. "Miss, we're going to need snacks and shots." The waitress nodded and rushed away.

My eyes went wide. "Oh, damn. Really?"

"Really," Carter agreed with a head bop.

Katrina started in. "Renee was Jewellen's best friend."

"Was?" I prompted.

"Don't jump ahead, missy." Katrina downed her wine and smacked my hand.

"My bad. Do continue." I took another deep sip.

She continued. "Jewel and Rome met because Renee's former fiancé, Gregory, played basketball in a weekend league that Roman belonged to."

"Former fiancé?" This story was already off the chains.

Carter laughed. "Wait for it."

"Renee dragged Jewel to Greg's game. Jewel met Rome, and romance happened."

Remembering how happy they looked together earlier, I would say that's a vast understatement. "Clearly."

"Clearly." Katrina smirked.

Carter chimed in, "But Renee is one of those women."

"What kind of woman is that?" I thought I knew but I was curious to hear a man's perspective on it.

"Girlie, you want to hear the story or not?" Carter chided.

I put my hands up. "Sorry, sorry. How do you know all this?"

"I've been to enough Montgomery functions to have heard this story backward and forward. Plus, I was around for some of it."

"Okay. Carry on." I was dying to hear the rest of this tale.

"Thank you. Now, Renee is the kind of woman who is never—"

Katrina broke in. "Ever, ever, ever—"

Carter picked it back up. "—satisfied with

what she has. She always thinks there's something bigger and better just around the corner for her. So there she was deep into a romance with Greg, who by the way is generally good people. Then one day at a pool party at Jewel's house, her eye falls on Beau."

"Were you at that party?" Katrina asked him curiously.

"Yes; I came in late. Right around the time you started running folks off at the spades table."

"Ah, good times."

I knew I didn't like that woman. I pursed my lips. "So, in spite of being with 'good man Greg' Renee has her eye on Beau and . . ." I made a rolling motion with my hands to indicate that either one of them could continue the story.

Carter continued. "To be fair, Beau had his eye on Renee as well. He's been known to appreciatively scan a fine female form from time to time."

"Understatement," Katrina said under her breath.

"Nothing wrong with appreciating a good-looking woman. I'm sitting over here in heaven right about now. Every guy in here wants to know what the hell kind of magic I have to keep the two most beautiful women in the room riveted on my every word. And here I am telling a story about some other brother who abandoned the table. My life!" His face spread into the largest grin ever, and we couldn't help but laugh. The waitress slid an appetizer sampler platter in front of us with a round of rum shots. Katrina reached for a crabcake.

"Okay, Renee and Beau fall in mutual admiration of each other's form . . ." I prompted and grabbed some sort of a deep-fried eggroll.

Katrina started in. "Well, that's how it began between them. A few words and a shared dessert at a pool party. Next thing you know Renee was showing up places she knew Beau was going to be. Beau started receiving invitations to events and when he arrived—guess who would already be there?"

"Ah." I was beginning to see the writing on the wall with this story. It wasn't pretty.

Carter picked it back up. "Fast forward to this huge party. Some froufrou society ball for a cosmetic company or something."

Katrina cut her eyes at Carter and interrupted. "That froufrou ball was to launch me as the spokesmodel for Royal Mahogany, sir."

Carter loaded his plate and continued. "Oh. Well done, then. But the thing was at some point, we look around and Renee—"

"Who worked for Royal Mahogany at that time and was managing the campaign," Katrina supplied.

"Had disappeared, and so had Beau."

"Uh oh," I muttered.

Carter inclined his head. "Damn skippy, *uh-oh*. Later we find out that Greg and Veronica, another friend of Jewel's, go looking for dear fiancée and find both her and Beau doing the do in one of the hospitality suites."

Worse than I imagined. "Not caught in the act?"

"In. The. Act. Beau, with a face full of Renee all out in the open without the door locked."

"The visual. Carter—please! I don't need that in my head," Katrina moaned.

I could've lived without that as well. Slanting a glance toward the two of them, I could picture it all too well. "So that was it with good guy Greg."

"Oh yeah. Good guy Greg is now engaged to Veronica," Carter supplied.

"Wait, the other friend?"

"It's a cluster," Katrina snickered.

"That's the story of Beau and Renee's romance?" Seemed like more than a one-nighter between them.

Carter shifted uncomfortably. "Well that, plus the six months he lived with her after Greg moved out."

My mouth fell open. "That's just . . . ratchet. Completely tacky. That's just . . ."

Katrina offered, "Beau. That's just Beau."

I shook my head. "He's not like that."

"He's not like that *around you.*"

"Until tonight. When you sent him that *I could give less than a damn* look," Carter murmured.

Katrina snapped, "And shoved him back toward that trifling barracuda who was so pissed off that Jewel was getting married and she wasn't that she made herself a royal pain in the ass right until the wedding day, when we threatened to beat her ass if she didn't play nice."

Wow. "I didn't give him any such look!" Had I?

"You even added a *carry your ass on* shrug!" Carter supplied with a side-eye.

"Well, we're not together. I don't think we're going to be together. It's just a bad idea to pursue it all the way around. And now that he's—" I gestured toward the dance floor where he and Renee were simulating sex acts to the beat of "Hotter Than July."

Katrina sighed. "I have to admit that I didn't like the thought of you and Beau together. It felt a little too incestuous at first. You're like a sister to me. He's like a brother to me."

"He *is* your brother, girlie." Carter took the champagne flute out of her hand and pushed the last of the parmesan potato skins toward her.

"Whatev. I'm just saying that, now that I've seen you and Beau working together and hanging out, I think you'd be really good for each other. You balance each other out. You keep him focused, and he keeps you from getting too tightly wound. I think you're soul mates."

Did she just say *soul mates*? Seriously? I dropped the carrot stick I'd been nibbling on and stared at her. "How many glasses of champagne have you had, exactly?"

"Doesn't matter. I'm still speaking *la vérité de Dieu*!" Katrina slapped her hand down on the table and half stood in the booth. "Beau! Get off that skank and come sit with your soul mate."

"Ah, Jesus." I closed my eyes in silent prayer.

"Time to go. Shots up, people." Carter downed his shot, waited for me to follow suit, and grabbed Katrina's hand to keep her from taking another sip of anything. Beau looked over from the dance floor, and Carter warned him off with the universal *Don't come over here unless you want trouble* head shake. Beau turned back toward Renee.

I dug out my wallet and was pulling out some cash when Carter threw a large bill on the table. "That plus what Beau left covers us quite nicely. Let's say we all call it a night, shall we?"

"Is she leaving her soul mate to that floozy?!" Katrina's voice really carried. I grabbed Katrina's other arm to help steer.

"Definitely. That's a wrap." We all but ran to the exit, propelling a still-protesting Katrina out in front of us. Glancing to my left at Beau and Renee, I had to admit to feeling a tinge of jealousy.

Maybe more than a tinge. But he wasn't my man and at this point, I wasn't sure I wanted him to be. Beau was a grown man who made his own choices. I'd just have to get over my dislike of this one.

10

A Bad Idea . . . Dammit, Beau

Beau—Monday, May 2, 2:08 AM *(technically the same night)*

Renee had not changed. Not one freakin' bit. No pun intended. She was still an equally adventurous and avaricious bed partner. Not that we'd made it to the bed the first time. Renee was a girl who liked sex. And I was a man who liked women who liked sex. We'd never had a single problem in that arena.

The problem was . . . me. I shouldn't have gone home with her; I shouldn't have made love with her. Three times. You know what? I couldn't even call that making love. We had sex. Energetic, emotionless sex. We both had an itch, and we scratched the hell out of it until we'd had our fill.

The entire time I had the most uncomfortable

feeling that I was cheating on Belle. Rationally, I knew I wasn't, but that didn't make the feeling go away. I didn't want Renee. Physically for the moment yes, but all I really did here was (as Roman and Katrina say) "pull a Beau": jack up a situation that had no reason to be jacked simply because I didn't take a second to think things through.

I could see the truth in that. I made a bad decision off a knee-jerk reaction. That moment when Belle looked at me with zero feeling in her eyes and shrugged, that was a bad moment. I thought we were at least acknowledging the possibility of *une chose*—a thing—between us. But she said no. Quite vehemently. I wasn't one to wait around for a firm *no* to magically turn to *yes*. Not me. I wasn't that guy.

Still though . . . I couldn't shake the feeling that this had been a bad idea. *Dammit, Beau!* A very bad idea. I rolled out of Renee's bed and made my way to the bathroom. She hadn't changed too much in here, either. I availed myself of a few toiletries and climbed into the shower. Setting the temperature almost to scalding, I rinsed the night away.

Using the spare toothbrush and paste I'd found under the sink, I started brushing my teeth. Speaking of bad ideas, what in the hell had gotten into Katrina? Besides too many ounces of bubbly? One minute she was chilling, the next she was screaming about skanks and soul mates. I almost hated having to go back there tonight. Times like this, a man contemplated needing his own space. I rinsed, tapped the toothbrush against the ledge, and set it on the tile shelf. Turning off the shower,

I dried off and rapidly dressed. I knew where I had to go.

Stepping into the bedroom, I pressed a kiss on Renee's forehead. "*Merci*, Renee. *Bon nuit.*"

She fluttered her lashes open and smiled. "No, thank *you*, Beau. You used to stay the night. I know how you like to be awakened in the morning."

I trailed a finger across her mouth. "Such a naughty mouth on a pretty girl. Perhaps another time?"

"Rain check is always on the table between you and me."

I wasn't sure if I found that comforting, frightening, or depressing. So I just gave a short nod. "Good to know. Take care of yourself."

She burrowed back under the covers. "You know I always do. Turn on the alarm on your way out. Code's the same."

With that, I headed for the door. Locking up behind me, I was in my car and heading south toward downtown in no time. It was 2:30 in the damn morning, and still there was traffic on Central Expressway! They had been "fixing" this road the entire time I lived here, which was over twenty-five years now.

Shaking off the irritation, I exited to the service road and headed up the back way toward Victory Plaza. By 2:45 I was striding through the lobby of the W Residences, knowing that in a very few minutes Belle would really regret giving me spare entrance cards to her building and loft. "In case of emergency only," she had said. She surely didn't think I would be the one with the emergency.

But here I was. I had to see her. Tomorrow

morning (this morning, technically) in the office
surrounded by staff just wouldn't do. Letting myself in the front door, I slipped off my shoes and
padded quietly through the condo. Her condo
was a wide, open space with a great room that in-
cluded kitchen, dining, and living areas. She had
kept the previous owner's beige contemporary
furniture and spiced it up with rich pops of color.
The master suite took up the back end of the loft
and was the only enclosed space. I walked quickly
to the master bedroom. Turning the doorknob
silently, I swung open the door.

"What in the holy hell are you doing here?" she
shrieked. She was awake, sitting up in bed with a
remote control in one hand.

"Happy to see me?" I said. What else could I
say?

"Are you out of your tiny lil mind?!" she
shrieked with full Georgia in her voice.

"So that's a no, *chérie*?" I figured as long as I
kept her talking, I could eventually get a word in.

"You came stepping your ass up in my house,
my bedroom, after leaving *hers*? You must be crazier than a June bug in the middle of December."
I wondered if she knew that her Southern accent
snuck back in when she was riled up. Next thing I
knew, the remote control came flying at me. Then
the phone, followed by a bedroom slipper and a
book. I dodged them all and got to the bed before
she could throw the iPad, which I knew she'd regret.

I stopped her the only way I could think. I
climbed over her, pressed her back into a prone
position, and gave her a second to tell me to

move. With no protest, I took her wrists in my hands and kissed her.

She bucked up against me in protest once, twice, a third time before she started kissing me back. Slanting my head to the right, I teased her with just the tip of my tongue. I didn't want to overwhelm, just pique her interest a lil bit. She moaned softly and then stiffened. I knew what was coming. I jumped up and off the bed before her knee could hit its intended target.

She jumped out of bed, took two quick steps forward, and slapped me . . . hard. "You raggedy mother—"

"Language, Belle, language! You met my mother; that's just insulting." I couldn't fault her for the slap. I had it coming. My eyes ran down the length of her. She was wearing a sheer pink wisp of a nightgown with nothing underneath, and I knew that I had settled for a pale facsimile of who I had really wanted tonight. I lifted my eyes slowly back to her face.

Her eyes narrowed. I could see her struggling to get her temper under control. She was breathing heavily. From the kiss or the temper or the slap? She took a total of ten deep breaths. I counted. Who knew she had a serious temper? Finally, when she had made the gratifying decision to neither slap me again nor throw me out, she reached for a robe.

"You don't have to cover up on my account," I said in a low voice, hoping to soothe. It didn't work.

She slid the robe on and angrily yanked it shut, tying the belt once and then twice and then knotting it. "You are an indiscriminate asshole. To come from her bed and jump on me in mine . . . What the hell are you thinking?"

"I wanted to apologize for tonight. It . . . didn't turn out the way I'd planned."

"The way you'd *planned*?"

"The way I'd hoped and wished and dreamed about."

"Don't try and sweet-talk me, Beau. You are fresh outta another woman's bed!"

I crossed my arms, leaned against the wall, and narrowed my eyes at her. "You said you didn't care."

"I never said that."

"My bad. You said we were 'nothing,' and then you shrugged at me."

"We hadn't made any promises to each other. In fact, we'd agreed to be just friends."

She was trying my patience. "Are you deliberately being dumb or is this coy?"

"This is truth, sugar. We never *said* anything!"

"So you're splitting hairs. This is semantics. Fine. So if you don't care, why are you mad about Renee?"

"I didn't say I don't care, and I'm not mad!" She was screaming.

I watched her chest rise up and down in obvious agitation and observed as she clenched and unclenched her fist. I raised a brow in mockery. "Sweetheart, you're visibly seething."

"Kiss my ass, Beau."

Hmm. One of my better dreams. "Just say when. I would love to kiss every inch of you, but we're just friends right?"

"Aren't you the one who doesn't do relation-ships?"

"I never said that."

She seriously looked like she wanted to take a swing at me again. She instead took a step back and asked, "Why are you here, Beau?"

"I wanted to apologize. Renee was . . . is . . . was . . . a bad idea. A mistake."

"She seems to be a recurring one in your life."

That left me speechless for a minute. Someone had loose lips. "Who told you?"

"What does it matter? I know about the two of you. Maybe that's who you're supposed to be with. You two keep finding each other."

I wanted to make her understand. "God forbid I ever entertain more than a fleeting thought about Renee. She's not it for me. She's a barracuda who takes what she wants from men and moves on to the next. Trust me; she's no more in love with me than I am with her. We have an understanding, her and me. It's just sex, *chérie*. Something to *passer le temps* on our way to other people."

She looked at me like I had lost my mind. "Are you kidding me? Am I 'other people' that you're on your way to? Am I supposed to be flattered that you broke in here to apologize for sleeping with another woman? Sorry, what did you call it? Pass-ing the time?"

Now I was getting frustrated. If she would listen for just a second. "No. I'm not stupid, Belle. But will you just hear me out? Without the attitude? For *un instant, s'il vous plaît?*"

"Beau, if this situation was flipped—would you

listen to what I had to say? For one second, without an attitude?"

"If I wanted to hear what you had to say badly enough, yes."

"Fine." She walked over to a chaise lounge she had placed by the wraparound balcony door and plunked down. She pointed at the chair across from her and fastened a scorching glare in my direction. "Pray, enlighten me."

So she was going to hold on to the attitude. Fair enough. I sat down and leaned forward, placing my hands on my knees. "I think we both know there's something here. Between you and me. Or there was, before I tripped over my dick tonight. But I truly believe if you can get past it and give me a chance, it will be worth it. I swear I'll be a better person for you. Just give me the chance to make it right." I had never begged a woman for anything. It chafed. Was I even doing it right?

She wouldn't look me in the eyes. "To what end? You aren't a one-woman man."

"I could be for the right woman." At least I thought I could be, especially if she was willing to be that woman.

"I don't know, Beau. You seem to have a systemically failing history when it comes to women."

Couldn't deny that, even if I wanted to. "Not with the ones I'm serious about."

Belle looked supremely skeptical. "And how many of those have there been?"

"Including you?"

"Are you saying you're serious about me?"

"Deadly."

"Why?" She looked genuinely befuddled.

"Why not?"

She went from confused to exasperated in the blink of an eye. "Not an answer, but fine. Then yes, including me."

"Two."

"Thirty-eight years old and you've only been serious about two women? And you just met me two months ago? How am I supposed to believe you? How am I supposed to take that?"

I shrugged and put my arms out. "You just should take it on faith and be flattered."

"These are just words, Beau. You're very good with words."

"They're all I have right now. Let me back them up. Let me build something with you."

"I'm not sure you're worth the trouble."

"But you're tempted."

"That means nothin' in the big scheme of things, darlin'."

"It means you're tempted."

She shook her head. "Answer me one thing: Why did you sleep with her?"

I could've made up a smooth answer but I decided to just tell the unvarnished truth. "You didn't want me; she was there."

"That is *weak*!" She was outraged.

I shrugged again. "I'm a man who needs to be needed. Now you know my weakness."

"At least one of them, anyway."

I inclined my head. "I never claimed to be perfect. You have to take the good with the bad. Either you think the sum of the good outweighs the bad, *chérie*, or you don't. So what do you say? Will you take a chance on me?"

"I don't know, Beau. I just don't know."

I closed my eyes for a minute and took a deep breath. There was nothing else to do or say. It was all on her. I couldn't make her listen to what she didn't want to hear. As I got up to leave, the phone rang. I looked at my watch: 3:56 AM. Nothing good came of predawn phone calls.

She ran over to the door and began looking for where she had flung the house phone. Seeing it under a dresser, I snatched it and handed it to her. She glanced at the caller ID and answered. "Dalton, what's wrong?"

I leaned in to listen. "It's Dad, Mirabella. They think it's his heart."

She stumbled back, and I put my hands on her shoulders to steady her. "What do you mean? How bad is it?"

"We're not sure. We were in Atlanta, staying at Loren's house, so they've taken him to Emory. Can you come? He was asking for you."

"I'm on the first plane out. Give everyone my love. I'm on my way. Hang in there. I'm coming." She hung up the phone and went to the closet to grab a suitcase. She pulled out an orange and tan rolling bag and tossed it on the bed. Haphazardly, she started throwing things in.

"Belle."

"I can't deal with you right now, Beau. My dad, my family." Her voice wavered.

"I know. How are you getting there?"

"Next flight, I guess."

"What if it's booked?"

"Why? What are you saying?" She shot me an irritated look over her shoulder

I walked over and put my hand on hers. "Take a breath, *chérie*. Process. Carter has partial ownership in an Execujet—it's a private plane. I'll make a call. You need to call Katrina and tell her to handle the Dallas office, and call Yazlyn to keep New York in the loop."

She stared at me, unmoving.

"What? I'm a dick, but I'm great in a crisis. Let's move. Make the calls, throw two outfits and a cosmetic kit in a bag, and head to the airport. I keep a bag in the trunk so I'm set. Move, woman!"

She went to retrieve her BlackBerry from the charger. "Wait, you're coming with me? Why?"

"Because I want to, and I said so. Now put it in gear." Ignoring her stunned stare, I turned my back on her and dialed Carter. "Dude, we have a situation. I need the jet."

"Renee killed you with a Kama-sutra move and you need an emergency medical treatment? Belle tar and feather you? You need to make a break for the border?"

I cut him off. "No time for jokes. Belle's dad is sick. We have to get to Atlanta ASAP."

"Let me dial up the schedule right quick." Carter's tone turned serious.

While I waited for Carter to reply, I looked over my shoulder. Belle was in the living room talking on the phone. Her suitcase sat open on the bed, half stuffed with random clothing that didn't go together. Walking over to the closet, I selected three outfits plus jeans, and started packing them in her bag. I opened up the top dresser drawer to discover an explosion of lingerie. My mouth watered for a second, and I had to remind myself to focus. I pulled out three bras with matching panties and placed those in the bag as well.

Carter came back on the line. "You're in luck; the plane is sitting in a hangar at Addison Airport. The other owners just cancelled a trip, so it's yours. The pilot can meet you there in an hour."

"You're a prince among men," I told him as I walked into the bathroom to look for the travel cosmetic and toiletry bag I was sure she had prepared somewhere. Once a model, always a model, ready to go at a moment's notice.

"Don't ever forget it. But you owe me, bruh." Carter laughed.

"Name it." I rummaged through the drawers and under the left sink.

"Set me up with your sister?"

That gave me pause. "Anything but that." Katrina and Carter? I suppressed a shudder. Perish the thought. Like gasoline and a flamethrower, those two. I decided to pretend he was joking.

"No, huh? One day, tell me the whole story of what went down tonight?"

"That I can do. Soon as I finish living it." Under the right sink I found the travel kit. I tossed the smaller bag into the suitcase and began to select shoes. Pumps, flats, and sneakers; into the suitcase they went. I pulled out a matching carryon and put her iPad and cellphone chargers inside.

"Safe travels, my friend," Carter said solemnly.

"I'll do my best." I hung up the phone just as Belle walked back in the room. She glanced at the suitcase and shot me a look. Rummaging through it, she nodded and made a *hmm* sound under her breath. Then she looked in the carryon.

"You're a man of hidden talents."

"No comment. You need something to sleep in and whatever other electronics you want to bring. We meet the pilot in an hour for takeoff."

"How did you . . ." She sighed. "Never mind. You're damn handy to have around."

"Woman, I keep trying to tell you! Now put some clothes on, unless you really want to make an impression on the pilot."

She came around the side of the bed and gave me a hug. "I don't know what to think about you, but thank you for this."

"*Pas de probléme, mademoiselle.* Now shake that fine tail-feather of yours."

"Yes, sir."

11

Do You Want Me to Go?

Belle—6:52 AM that same morning

It was with no little bit of surprise that I found myself buckled into a luxurious lounge chair covered with a blanket at thirty thousand feet. Wordlessly, Beau handed me a bottle of chilled cranberry juice and two Advils. It was uncanny how he seemed to just know what needed to be done without being told. It was jarring. Really. Not to mention unexpected. I didn't know how to feel about him, us, my father, anything.

The past forty-eight hours had been a veritable rollercoaster of highs and lows for me.

We finished the technical specs for the spring menswear line. I met Beau's family. I met Beau's best friend. I met his ex-girlfriend. He slept with her and then broke into my house. He said things I wasn't sure I was ready to hear. And my daddy was lying in a hospital bed in Atlanta. It was all a little much to digest on no sleep and a slight champagne hangover.

Yet here we were. I tried twisting open the top of the cranberry juice bottle and failed. I tapped it against the armrest and tried again. Nothing. Beau reached over and took the bottle, smacked the bottom, and turned the top once before handing it back to me. I took a long sip and swallowed down the Advil before leaning my head back and closing my eyes.

"Everything starting to catch up with you?" Beau asked.

"You could say that." He was the king of shrinking down huge thoughts into one succinct sentence.

The pilot's voice came on over the speaker. "We've got clear skies all the way there; flight time is less than two hours. Sit back and enjoy the ride. Please let me or Samantha know if you need anything."

I didn't even have the energy to open my eyes. "How is that possible? Isn't it a two and a half hour flight?"

"We're flying from Addison Airport to Fulton County Brown Field so we don't have to wait to taxi in or out. Plus these small planes have some speed on them."

I nodded. "How far to the hospital from Brown Field?"

"It's fifteen miles. We'll be there before you know it."

"Did you call—" Before I could formulate the question, he stopped me.

"Be easy, *chérie*. We called everybody we could. They'll handle it. All you have to do is sit back and take your rest."

"But—" I felt his lips graze my forehead; my skin heated where he touched.

"*Faire un petit sommeil*, Belle. Go to sleep. When you open your eyes, we'll be there."

I closed my eyes for just a second . . .

"Welcome to Atlanta, Mr. Montgomery. We've arranged transport as you asked."

I blinked my eyes open as Beau responded to the pilot. "Thank you, I appreciate you coming on such short notice this morning."

"Not a problem at all. You have the number if you need a ride back."

I sat up, still half asleep, and trying to get my bearings. Plane. Beau. Atlanta. Daddy. I tossed the blanket to the side and unbuckled the belt. I hopped up and looked around for my carryon and my purse. Beau put a hand on my shoulder.

"Take a minute; splash some water on your face. I've got everything ready."

"But my father—"

"Is in surgery. He's doing well. I'll tell you more when you get back."

I blinked at him. *Okay, Delaney Mirabella, pull it together.* I nodded. "Thanks, I'll be right back." I snatched up my purse and dashed into the bathroom. I used the facilities and turned on the faucet. I glanced up and gasped. Oh my, damn. Well, that wasn't attractive, was it? This is what four glasses of champagne, two hours of airplane sleep, and not enough water would do for you. I placed a washcloth under steaming hot water, let it cool just enough to pick it up, and then pressed and held it to my face for a few moments. Then I repeated the process with ice-cold water. That was better.

In a crisis, I knew that my family would take their cues from me. If I came running into the hospital looking stressed and worried, that would set the tone. And that would never do. I opened up my purse and got to work. In less than five minutes I'd put on a light face of makeup, brushed my teeth, and fluffed my short hair into some semblance of style. A few strategic spritzes of body spray and I was ready to go.

When I stepped out, Beau was standing there. Even in dark jeans and an untucked white dress shirt, he managed to look runway ready. He had a leather laptop bag slung over one shoulder and my bright orange carryon over the other. My BlackBerry was clutched in one of his hands; the other one was held out to me. "Let's move, woman; we only have a few minutes."

"For what? Did someone call? Is the surgery not going well?" I was alarmed and grasped his hand to head out of the plane.

We flew down the few steps and followed a man carrying our luggage across the tarmac. "So far so good. We're catching a helicopter over to Emory University Hospital."

I stopped dead and stared at him. "Who is paying for that? That seems excessive!"

He propelled me forward. "I know a guy who

knows a guy. Or would you rather sit in Atlanta traffic while your dad's in surgery?"

He had a point. I picked up the pace and ran alongside him. "What's the surgery for? Did they say?"

"It's bypass surgery. You father had a blockage in one of his arteries. That's what caused the heart attack."

"Heart attack? Bypass surgery? Oh my God." I knew Dalton had said it was serious. I just didn't allow myself to think about what that really meant.

"They say they think they caught it early. Your sister Loren gave him an aspirin, and he remained conscious the whole time. They say it sounds good."

"Who is *they*, and when did you talk to them?"

"The doctors. Eisenberg and Jeffers. I spoke to them while you were sleeping."

I wanted to ask him who gave him the right. I wanted to say he was being presumptuous, but I knew he was just being helpful. And he was operating on even less sleep than I'd had. I was scared and tired and more than a little bit frazzled. This day just kept getting crazier, and it was still morning. As we rounded a corner, I saw the helicopter and could only shake my head. The pilot was a stocky black man in his late thirties wearing aviator glasses and dressed all in khaki. When he saw Beau, he broke into a huge smile. "Bayou Beau, how you been, son?"

Beau dropped my hand to clap his friend on the shoulder. "You know me, Batiste."

He nodded. "I see you still arrive with the prettiest woman on your arm. Ms. Richards, I'm Batiste Landry. Let's get you set up and on your way to see your *pére*."

"Thank you." I flashed a dazed smile and paid attention while he showed me how to buckle in and put on the head set. Beau stowed all the bags and climbed in beside me. He strapped in and we were airborne, just like that. "This is crazy." As I spoke I realized that the headsets were mic'd and both Beau and Batiste had heard me.

Beau smiled. "*Chérie*, you've been in a helicopter before, no?"

"For a shoot in the French Alps a million years ago, not to run across town."

Batiste said, "My boy Beau likes to go big or go home."

"I see that. How do you two know each other?" I wondered.

They exchanged glances and smiles. "We ran around a little bit as boys back in our Breaux Bridge days," Beau answered. I was positive he was leaving out legions of storied details.

"Breaux Bridge, that's near Baton Rouge? In Southern Louisiana?"

"About an hour away, yeah. In the Atchafalaya Basin. Saint Martin parish," Batiste explained.

I don't know why I asked. All I knew of Louisiana was New Orleans, really. But I nodded as if that gave me a greater understanding.

"What about you, Mirabella? What part of Georgia did you grow up in?"

"Southern. Almost as south as you can go without hitting Florida. Valdosta."

"Do you ever get back?" Batiste asked.

I shook my head. "Not very often. My two brothers and two sisters live here in Atlanta and we've been trying to get my dad to give up the house and move here, too, now that he's retired. He spends most of his time up here with them anyway." My voice faded when I realized I didn't know if my father would be around, if he was even alive right now at this moment. I grew still. Granted, I rarely saw eye-to-eye with the man, but he was my father and I wasn't ready for him to be gone.

Beau slipped his hand around mine. "It will be fine, *bébé*. Breathe."

Batiste said quietly, "*Cette fille est différente. Elle est spéciale. Vous l'aimez, n'est pas?*"

Beau took a deep breath. "*À ce qu'il paraît, mon ami.*" He looked at me with a completely unreadable look in his eyes.

I raised a brow. "What?"

"He said you seem special and he can tell I like you."

"And you said?"

"So it would seem."

"*Hmm.*" I was ill-equipped to dive into that hornets' nest of emotion right now, but I wasn't letting go of his hand.

"We're touching down. Wait for the signal, and then it's safe to get out."

It had been less than five minutes. I looked down and saw the huge block letter "H" on the rooftop. We landed smoothly, squarely in the middle. When the rotor blades had slowed a bit, Batiste gave a signal. Beau disentangled himself from the seat and headset and swung the door open. Then he reached in for me. I lifted off the set, unbuckled, and crawled out behind him. Batiste unloaded our things and gave me a hug. "Meet you again on a better day, *jolie*."

I nodded and hugged him back. By the time I turned around, Beau had everything gathered up. He handed me my purse and put out a fist toward Batiste. "*Merci beaucoup, frère*."

They bumped fists. "No thanks needed. Anytime. If you have a second while you're here give a call. Kim and kids would love to see you."

"Will do." With a final wave, Beau turned toward a door where a woman stood in light green scrubs. We headed in that direction.

"Mr. and Mrs. Montgomery? My name is Misty. I'm a charge nurse in the Cardiac Care unit. Your father is still in surgery, but he's doing well. Your family is in the east lounge on the third floor waiting for you. One of the doctors will be out shortly to talk to you. Right this way, please."

As we followed in her wake, I gave Beau a sideways glance. "Mr. and Mrs. Montgomery?"

He smiled. "Sorry about that. I had to tell them we were married so they would give me the information on your dad."

Suddenly I hit the wall. I was scared and frustrated. I felt out of control and out of the loop. "You know, sugar, you're kinda taking over things here. I didn't ask you to do any of this. I'm perfectly capable of handling my family, my father, and these doctors myself. I don't need you here to handle things or hold my hand. I'm a grown woman!"

He stopped in his tracks and gave me such a

look that I instantly felt bad for even bringing it up. "I know that."

"Then back off," I snapped, more than a little bit on edge.

"Do you want me to go?" he questioned quietly.

"I didn't say that," I muttered under my breath, already feeling chagrined for snapping at him.

"*Belle.* Do you *want* me to go?" he asked again, his normal light eyes dark and turbulent. He looked like he was ready to chuck my luggage at me and head back up to the roof. I had no doubt that if I told him to go he would be gone like the wind, no questions asked. I also knew that I couldn't have gotten here this quickly and drama-free without his help. I felt petty and mean.

"No. I'm sorry. I'm being bitchy." We started walking again. The nurse was giving us all sorts of curious glances over her shoulder.

"You're feeling scared. Maybe I overstepped, but I'll fall back from here on out, okay?" Beau's tone was conciliatory and light.

I nodded as we climbed into the elevator. "Beau?"

"Yep?" he replied casually.

I leaned up and gave him a kiss on the cheek. "Thank you."

He nodded once. "*C'est rien.*"

"It's not 'nothing'—it's a lot. Even if I don't act like it, it means something. So dammit, just give me the patented Beauregard smile and say, 'You're welcome.'"

He cocked a brow and flashed the classic grin that was his trademark. "You're welcome."

The nurse cleared her throat as the elevator opened. "Here we are. The lounge is at the end of the hall to the left. Someone will be in to update you shortly. Ring extension 427 on the house phone if you need something in the meantime." She fled in the opposite direction.

I almost laughed at the speed with which the nurse disappeared. "I think we scared Misty."

"Then she scares too easy. Do you want me to wait with you or leave you alone with your family for a while?"

I knew that walking into the lounge with Beau and having him stay with me was a step. A step I really didn't think I was ready for. But on the other hand, I really wanted him there. And I didn't have time to analyze that want.

"Your decision," he offered in that same easy tone.

"Where would you go?"

"I had a car delivered here. I have a room at the Ritz-Carlton in Buckhead. So I'm set. It's up to you." He waited patiently for my answer.

"I swear, for someone who pretends to be a lazy playboy, you're one hell of a detail guy."

He rolled his eyes. "Mirabella, you're stalling."

I was stalling. The fact that he recognized it told me he was getting to know me a little too well. I took a deep breath and offered a response. "Stay."

12

We Like Him; He Can Stay

Beau—10:03 AM, later that morning

We walked toward the lounge doors, and there was a literal wall of sound coming from inside. I slid a look toward Belle, and she was taking several deep breaths back to back. It was her way of evening out her turbulent emotions.

She glanced over at me as if gauging my readiness for what lay ahead. "You ready for this, playboy? This is not for the faint of heart."

"You've met my family—seen any faint-of-heart tendencies?" The Family Montgomery was easygoing but wildly protective of their own. Not a single one of us was shy or retiring.

"Duly noted. Seriously, you ready?"

"Stop prepping me. Inside already."

We walked through the swinging doors; all eyes turned toward us and the room fell silent for a heartbeat. Then everyone began talking at once and rushing forward for hugs and kisses. I shifted to the side and set down the luggage, prepared to take it all in.

"Auntie Bella!"

"Thank God, you're here, Mirabella."

"Who's the eye candy?"

"Did you hear about Daddy?"

"You must be Beau."

"How'd you get here so fast?"

Belle put her hands up. "Everybody calm down and back up two steps. Let's take it from the top. I caught a private flight. The surgery's going well; the doctor will be in shortly to update us on status. This is Beau Montgomery. He works with me and is a—"

My brow went up while I watched her search for the word to define an as yet undefined relationship. She slid me a look to see if I wanted to jump in with a helpful word. I just grinned silently.

She huffed, "A friend of mine. Now line it up and I'll get the introductions out of the way."

From the way the people in the room fell into a formation, I could tell this was a drill they had done before.

A tall, broad-shouldered, caramel-hued brother stepped up and gave me an assessing glance from top to bottom before sticking out his hand. "Dalton. We spoke on the phone."

"Yes. Pleased to meet you. Belle speaks highly of you." She actually hadn't told me a thing about her siblings, but it seemed the thing to say.

"I'm Davis." A younger male with a less serious air about him walked over and shook my hand. "This is my wife, Anna, and our four-year-old twins, Deidre and Diana."

I greeted his wife with a smile and knelt down in front of the twin girls. "Now who is the oldest?" They were cute as hell. Big, bright, brown eyes, hair parted in the middle into braids with ribbons on the end. They both looked at me like they weren't sure what to think.

The one dressed in pink stepped forward and smiled a smile with two front teeth missing. "Me. I'm Deidre, and I'm older than her."

The one dressed in blue stepped in front of her. "By a whole six minutes. Are you my Auntie Bella's new man?"

"Diana!" Her mother called out to her.

She looked over her shoulder guiltily. "What, Mama, don't you wanna know?"

I laughed. "It's okay, she can ask."

"So are you?"

"Not yet."

Then they took turns asking questions. "Are you trying to be?"

"I really am."

"Are you nice?"

"Most of the time."

"Are you rich?"

Kids are fearless. "I'm . . . comfortable."

"You're pretty."

I smiled. "So are both of you."

"Our grandpop is sick."

"So I heard. I'm sorry, *mes douceurs*."

"What language is that?"

"French."

"What did it mean?"

"*My sweets.*"

They both turned to their aunt. "We like him, Auntie Bella. He can stay."

"Thank you, ladies." I stood up and turned to meet the others.

Belle just sent me a look. "Next up are my sisters, Loren and Tina."

Pretty girls in their early twenties, they shared Belle's smile and skin tone, but both of them wore their hair long. They were dressed in similar sweatsuits. "Twins?"

"No," they said at the exact same time.

"Apologies."

One walked over and gave me a hug. "I'm Loren." She stepped back, placed her hands on her hips and took her time looking me up and down.

"Loren. Really?" Belle murmured.

The other sister was far more reserved and just nodded at me from where she stood. "Tina."

I nodded at them both.

"This is my Aunt Nita, Uncle Lon, and we'll get into all the cousins another time." Belle waited for all the greetings to quiet down and then asked, "Dalton, tell me what happened with Daddy."

He shook his head. "Made no sense. He'd been having a great day. We were just sitting around talking when he slumped forward. Loren put an aspirin under his tongue and we called 911."

"How long has his heart been acting up?" Belle asked.

"Far as we knew, never," Loren said. "It's only because of these medical prep classes I'm in that I recognized the signs."

"What medical prep classes?"

"Did she ever tell you, she's decided to go to medical school?" Davis asked.

Belle put her hand on her hip. "No. And we talk every week."

Loren said, "We decided not to tell you yet."

Her mouth fell open and a deep frown appeared on that pretty face. "Wait a minute. What? You all decided not to tell me? Why? What's going on?"

Tina stepped forward. "Mirabella, you've taken care of all of us for long enough. You have a business that is taking off. A new venture that you're excited about. It's time."

"Time for what?" Belle looked genuinely confused.

"For *you*, Sis," Dalton said, coming over to put an arm around her. "Daddy told us where all the money for the schools and the house down payments and the cars and the little extras come from. It's been you. You've helped us through all of the crises; with all our major decisions, you've been our rock. All these years, taking care of us since Mom passed. If we told you Loren was prepping for the MCAT, you would have started researching schools and put money aside for her tuition. We love you, Big Sis, but it's time to cut the apron strings. Live your life and don't worry about whether we'll make it. We will. You saw to that. You done good by us, Belle. Now let us return the favor."

I could see from the play of emotions across her face that she had not been expecting this and wasn't sure what to make of it. Before she could formulate any of those thoughts, the door opened and a short man in navy scrubs walked in.

"Richards family?"

Belle stepped forward. "Yes."

"I'm Dr. Eisenberg, the cardiologist assigned to Mr. Richards' case. Dr. Jeffers, the cardiac surgeon, did a great job. Your father came through very well. They performed a triple bypass today."

I asked, "Why did you do a bypass instead of angioplasty?" Everyone in the room turned to look at me. I wasn't about to admit that I used to date a woman who played a heart surgeon on a daytime soap opera. I recalled rehearsing a scene with her that talked about different ways to open blockages in coronary arteries. An angioplasty was a less rigorous procedure for a sixty-four-year-old man like Belle's father.

Dr. Eisenberg nodded. "Great question. There was too much blockage in the left main, so they opted for the bypasses. Looks like they got all the blockage and, barring any complications, the prognosis looks good."

The Richards family took a collective deep breath and sigh of relief. They were thanking the doctor when Belle asked, "So what's next?"

"He's in recovery now. The breathing tube will come out this evening. If all goes well for the next twenty-four hours, he'll be moved off the ICU floor tomorrow. Your father's health is good overall, so unless there are setbacks, he'll be back at home by week's end."

"What's the long-term care plan, Doctor?" I asked. Belle came and stood beside me.

"Lifestyle change, medications, and follow-up office visits. He'll be placed on an aspirin regimen and beta-blockers. He'll need to cut back on the fatty, salty foods. He'll need to exercise and keep an eye on his blood pressure. He'll need to see me in four weeks."

"Will he need to be monitored in those four weeks?" Dalton asked.

"No, he'll need to stay away from anything strenuous; but once he's released, he should be okay. Now, he will tire more easily while his circulation gets back to normal. He may have some pain from the incisions. But overall, we're optimistic for a full recovery." He handed his card to me. "Feel free to call me if you have any additional questions. Misty will let you know when he wakes up and is moved to the ICU. It will be a little while, if anyone wants to run home, grab a shower, or get something to eat." With a nod and a few handshakes, he left.

I handed the card to Belle. "Brunch, nap, shower—or stay here?"

Belle said, "First things first: Beauregard, when did you date the heart specialist?"

She knew me too well. "Oh *chérie*, you wound me. Maybe I read it in a magazine?"

"Could've happened, but I like my theory better." She crossed her arms and waited.

"Fine. She wasn't a doctor . . . but she played one on TV."

She chuckled. "I knew it. Well, for once, your

shady history with women came in handy. Thank you for asking the extra questions."

"*De rien.* So what's it to be?"

"A shower and then some food and then back here. I guess I'll stay with you, Dalton?"

Dalton looked questioningly from me to Belle and back again. "Sure, Sis. If you want. But that full-size bed is gonna be a little short for Stretch, dontcha think?"

"Stretch?" she said and then looked at me. "Oh. *Uh-hmmm.*"

Clearly, she hadn't given sleeping accommodations or arrangements a thought. I had. I always did. "I have a room at the Ritz-Carlton in Buckhead, Belle. You do what you need to do, don't worry about me."

"Wait a minute," Tina piped up. "Dela-Bella? You're going to let this yummy caramel treat sleep alone at the Ritz-Carlton while you opt for Dalton's lumpy-assed guest bed? What's really going on?"

Prudently, I stayed close-mouthed. Belle could try and explain that we weren't "there yet" in the relationship that she wasn't calling a relationship, or she could come with me.

"Not like you're saving it for marriage," Loren added with a twinkle in her eye.

Belle gasped and threw up her hands. "Oh my God, y'all are so trifling and wrong! Beau, I'll go with you."

"If you like," I responded lightly, holding myself back from letting a smug smile stretch across my face.

Dalton came over and leaned in to say under

his breath, "You might want to at least try and dim the twinkle in your eye there, bruh."

"What can I say? Your sister's an amazing woman."

"That she is. And you've been all right in the few hours that I've known you. Know this: you hurt her, and I'll hunt your pretty ass down and make you regret it the rest of this life and the next. *Tu comprends?*"

I understood. "*Ça se comprend.*" We shook hands and I turned to see Belle watching us with an irritated look on her face. My little control freak hated not knowing every single thing that was going on around her. "You ready?"

Belle nodded. "I'll be back in a few hours. My cell phone is on. Call me if anything changes. Does anyone need anything?"

Davis walked over and gave her a hug. Then Dalton joined in, then Loren and Tina. They rocked together in a tight circle, and I was delighted for her. It was good to see that she had this strong base of family behind her.

"Dad's gonna be fine, Belle. We're fine. We've all eaten. We've slept. We're good. Go," Davis said. They patted each other on the back and broke apart.

Belle stepped back and beamed in a way I hadn't seen before. It was dazzling, like everything in her world in that moment was where she wanted it to be. The sight of that smile shifted something in my chest. I knew in that instant I wanted to see that smile again. I wanted to be the one who put it there and kept it there. *I what?* All this emotion, family, lack of sleep, no food, deep thought shit had me tripping. *Just keep it simple, Beau.*

I wanted Belle, I wanted a bed, and I wanted a burger. In whatever order they came to me. I held my hand out to her as she neared, clasping her hand in mine. Not sure when that became natural. We headed for the door with all eyes on us again.

She called out over her shoulder, "We'll be back!"

13

Yes, There Is That

Belle—11:36 AM that morning

I was so wiped out, I really couldn't do more than raise a brow when Beau flashed his grin and gave his credit card to the front desk clerk and announced that one room would be fine. It wasn't fine. But I was tired and hungry and in need of coffee, so I let it slide. I'd deal with him when we got upstairs.

He requested two room keys and asked that two burgers be sent up. One well-done with cheddar and fries and the other cooked medium-well with Swiss cheese, bacon, avocado, and a side salad. He asked for a large pot of coffee and some bottled water.

We strolled in silence to the elevator. We rode up eight floors and exited. Turning left we walked to the end of the corridor where he opened the door to the corner room. It was a suite. I dropped my purse and tote bag on the coffee table and walked into the bedroom. There were two queen beds. When I walked back in the living room, he stood there looking at me.

"You think you know me so well, don't you?"

"What makes you say that?" He crossed his arms across his chest and fixed me a look. He was clearly wondering what my problem was now.

"The burger order, the two beds, the pot of coffee?"

"I'm observant, and I'm polite. Would you prefer that I wasn't?"

"I don't know what I'd prefer right now. I'm going to take a shower." I snatched up my suitcase and headed back toward the bedroom.

"Fine." He threw up his hands in surrender.

"I know it's fine. I wasn't asking your permission, Beau!"

He said nothing, just stood with his hands on his hips and watched me with those eyes that saw entirely too much. It irritated me. He irritated me today. But I didn't say anything because I recognized that my mood was all over the place. Too much going on to process and I hadn't even checked in with the offices yet.

I felt off-kilter. Thrown off my routine and tossed about by circumstances beyond my control. Shutting the door behind me, I unzipped the bag and pulled out some dark wash skinny jeans, a flowered orange and pink peasant shirt, and a pair of silver and pink peep-toe flats. And then I got irritated all over again. Jeans, shirt, shoes that *he* had picked out for me. He was taking over every area of my life, and I didn't like it.

I stomped into the bathroom with the travel kit and hopped into the shower. The heated water hitting my skin calmed me down for a moment, and I stopped to just enjoy the feeling. One of the great things about cutting my hair so short was that I could just wash it, throw a little product in it, and wear it wavy, or I could slick it back or blow it straight all in less than fifteen minutes. I massaged some conditioner into my scalp and used some scrub on my face. I reached for the razor and then paused.

What was I shaving my legs for? *Oh Belle, stop overthinking every damn thing. The man is here trying to be helpful, and you're being a total bitch.* It was like I had a devil on one shoulder and an angel on the other, and they were arguing heatedly.

C'mon, he's here for the sex.

He's had sex. Recently, remember? You're the one going without. You think he flew you to Atlanta and met your family because he wants to get laid? Really?

I guess not. Why's he being so nice?

Why don't you quit being so mean and ask him?

Maybe I will.

Shave your legs already; you're a designer, a former model. You can't be running around looking like Chewbacca. And get out of the shower; we have stuff to do!

We?

Me, myself, and I. Let's go!

Am I really standing in the shower arguing with myself?

You really are. Shake it off. We're hungry and sleepy, too.

I shaved quickly and rinsed everything off, laughing at myself. Climbing out of the shower, I decided that I was either more tired than I thought or losing it altogether. I smoothed rose-scented almond oil into my damp skin as a knock sounded at the door. It was déjà vu to the night we met in Katrina's apartment.

"What?" I snarled ungraciously.

"Food's here."

I decided to get one thing straight. "I'm not sleeping with you tonight."

"I don't recall asking." He had the nerve to sound amused.

I wrapped the towel around myself and swung the door open. "Are you deliberately being dumb or is this coy?" I threw his words from last (this!) morning back at him.

"I didn't say I didn't want to sleep with you. You know I do. I've made that obvious from Day One. But I'm not without some principles, Belle. You've had less than two hours of sleep, your father is just out of heart surgery, and—"

"And you slept with someone else less than twelve hours ago . . ." I couldn't resist tacking on that little unavoidable fact. Let's not forget that.

He tightened his lips and a hurt look passed across his face so quickly that if I hadn't been paying attention, I would have missed it. He blinked twice. "Yes, well, there is that. Food's ready when you are." He turned sharply and went back into the living room.

Ah damn. I hated when he showed flashes of

vulnerability just when I was feeling snarky. With a sigh, I closed the door and started pulling on clothes. I put my watch on and glanced at the time. It was almost noon already. I still needed to check in with the office, eat, and grab a half-hour nap before going back to the hospital. Glancing into the full-length mirror, I could only shake my head. Damn if he hadn't picked out a cute outfit, too.

I strolled out to the living room to find him on the phone. "Have her e-mail it to Belle. I would go with the lighter thread color, but it's her line. We're going to grab a bite, and then she'll call you right back. Okay, thanks."

I frowned. "What was that?"

"Katrina called. The thread we picked for the contrast stitching on the French cuff doesn't look right, according to the head seamstress."

"What does that mean?"

He leaned his phone toward me and pulled up the picture. I took a look and understood the issue immediately. "Oh, I see. It kinda—"

"—blends in too much," he finished.

I nodded. "Why didn't you tell them to go ahead and make the change?"

Both of his brows shot up. "And risk over-stepping? No, thank you. I'm Backseat Beau from now on." He set the phone down and started salting his French fries.

I plunked down in the chair next to him and took the top off the platter. The hamburger looked delicious. Perfect and made to my exact preferences. I reached for the ketchup and began putting the burger together.

"I'm sorry," I blurted out as I layered my bacon and avocado just so on top of the cheese.

He paused with his burger in midair. "I beg your pardon?"

"You heard me," I scolded.

"I must not have."

So we weren't going to do this the easy way. "I said I'm sorry."

He delved deeper. "For what exactly?"

"I know I'm flashing hot and cold with you." I cut my burger in half and reached for the salad dressing.

He snorted. "More like frigid and lukewarm."

"Whatever. The truth is—"

"Do tell."

"So this is snark?"

"Apologies. Pray, continue."

"The truth is that I appreciate everything you've done for me. Not just today but with the company and everything. You've been nothing short of amazing. But, Beau—"

He gave a wry smile. "There's always a *but, Beau.*"

"But, Beau, you and I would be a mess, relationshipwise."

"You think?" He took a large bite of his burger.

"I know, sugar. You're too spoiled, too smooth, too sexy, and too used to getting your own way." It was a rough combination.

"And you're smart and smoking-hot but totally anal and way too used to being in charge of everything and everybody around you."

I speared some of the mixed green salad on my

fork and lifted it toward my mouth. "So why even bother?"

Beau set down the burger and looked at me, willing me to meet his eyes. He'd never looked at me like that before. His eyes were the color of antiqued bronze and they were locked on mine. There was no teasing, no humor, no professional distance; it was just unvarnished interest layered with heat and hunger. I shivered under the intensity of that gaze. That searing glance was like a tactile caress. I felt it all the way to my soul. It took my breath away.

When Beau broke the charged silence, his voice was low, smoky, and urgent. "I haven't really even touched you yet, and you already know how it would be between us. It's not just sex. We have *quelque chose* between us. A certain something. A connection. You don't want to define it—that's fine, but let's stop acting like it isn't there, okay?"

I swallowed and let out a shaky breath. "Okay."

"You want to ignore it? You want to be business associates?"

I appreciated that he gave me the out. But I had to be honest with him and myself. "Even I don't think that's truly possible."

He picked up his burger and went back to eating as if he hadn't just incinerated my nerve endings.

I picked mine up. "Let's just see where it goes."

"Sounds like a plan," he acquiesced.

"Still not sleeping with you tonight," I felt compelled to add.

"Still haven't asked," he countered matter-of-factly.

"Are you the kind of man who asks?"

"What do you think?"

"I think you can be very persuasive and generally don't have to ask."

"*Hmm.*" That was his noncommittal answer.

"So I'm asking you not to persuade me tonight."

"I'm a gentleman. No means no."

"Because I can't be your second choice in twenty-four hours."

"You were my first choice, but I get what you're saying." His eyes flashed; he did not want to talk about Renee anymore.

Neither did I, so I changed the topic to something safe. "Is your burger as good as mine?"

"*C'est formidable.*"

"That means amazing, right?"

He grinned at me. "I'm sorry. I don't even realize when I switch. Does it bother you?"

"It's kind of sexy, actually."

"Only kind of?"

"You know it's hot." We fell into companionable silence as we ate. I made it through half the hamburger and all of the salad before I gave up. "Beau?"

"Belle?"

"Remember when you said you were going to be Backseat Beau?"

"Ten minutes ago—yes I vaguely recall."

"Smartass."

"Apologies. Please continue."

"I don't want you in the backseat."

"No?"

"No. I need you in the front with me. I'm used

to running things. Being in charge, making sure everything happens."

"I get that."

"But I'm tired. Literally and figuratively."

He nodded.

"So if you're offering to let me lean a little . . ."

"I am."

"Then I'm going to lean. But it's new for me, so you'll have to be patient."

"I'm Mr. Patience—what do you need?"

"Can you call Katrina back and handle whatever, so I can grab a nap?"

"Not a problem."

"I feel bad. You haven't gotten any sleep at all."

"I'll catch up later. You rest until we hear from the hospital."

I was so grateful; I leaned across and kissed him on the lips. And liked it so much I kissed him again. A thousand nerve endings sprang to life inside me. Swaying toward him, I put my hand behind his neck and pulled his head in close. His lips parted, and I dipped my tongue in for a taste. It was a sweet kiss, fraught with tenderness and emotions bubbling to the surface. His arms came around me. I snuggled in and nibbled his bottom lip. I felt it turn up in a smile.

I leaned back. "Whoops."

He ran his hands up and down my back. His voice was low and silky. "Don't stop on my account."

Tempting, but not right now. "I'm going to lie down. Wake me up if something's urgent at the office or if the hospital calls."

"Will do." He was still doing that massaging thing on my back. It felt amazing. My eyes drifted shut as he worked out a kink near my shoulder.

"Are you going to try and get some sleep, too?"

"Don't worry about it. I don't need a lot of sleep generally."

"Really?" I tilted my head to the left so he had access to the other side. He slid his thumb along the nape of my neck and I bit down on my bottom lip to keep from groaning.

"Really," he said, his voice just a low murmur in my ear.

I actually shivered a little. "Good to know. You have the most amazing hands."

"You've no idea."

My eyes blinked open and I met his gaze over my shoulder. Chemistry.

He placed his hands on the small of my back and gave me a little shove toward the bedroom. "Rest for a little while. Everything will still be here when you get up."

A little smile crept onto my face, and I couldn't resist teasing just a little bit. I swept my eyes up and down his frame. "Every single thing?"

"Keep looking at me like that, *chérie,* and you will find out sooner than you think. I'm a gentleman, but I'm a man first."

He didn't give me one of his famed grins when he said it, so I knew he was deadly serious. Without looking back, I fled into the bedroom and shut the door behind me.

14

What's Going On?

Beau—3:41 PM that same day

I was having the best damned dream. I was floating on a cloud, but I wasn't alone. Pressed against me, actually almost completely on top of me, was a fine female form. She smelled amazing, and she kept squirming her tight body against mine in a way that signaled a really good time was about to happen. Naked good times—my favorite pastime. So I rolled over in the cloud and caught her beneath me. Her arms came around my neck, and I shifted to take her hips in my hands. Lord, that felt right. We fit. She arched up; I pressed down while trailing kisses along her jaw. Her hips started moving in an insistent rhythm, and she moaned my name.

"Beau." She reached around and grabbed my ass with one hand to pull me closer. I obliged, nestling into her notch.

"*Tout va bien, ma petite?*" I pressed my hard length against her and rolled my hips.

"Yes, it's all good. It's so good. I want more."

I traced the long line of her neck with my lips. She smelled of rose petals.

The dream just got better and better. I knew what she wanted, I knew what she needed. And I was more than ready to give it to her. I reached for the zipper of her jeans when suddenly Marvin Gaye started singing . . . loudly.

What's going on? Hey, what's going on? What's going on? I gotta know what's going on. Hey, hey, hey, hey! Whoo!

Marvin usually sang "Sexual Healing" in my dreams. And he didn't keep getting louder as the song continued. My eyes flicked open. Ah hell. I was on top of Belle, harder than a slab of granite. She blinked up at me in sleepy confusion. Her breathing was ragged, and her nipples had that same granite thing going on. Marvin began another chorus.

"Oh dammit!" She pulled her hands off my ass, and I crawled off of her and ran for the phone. I didn't know if she was damning the fact that we were interrupted or that we almost had semi-conscious sex.

"Belle's phone," I barked into the cell.

"I take it I'm interrupting something?" Dalton's voice had way too much humor in it for my liking.

"What is it?"

"He's out of recovery and in and out of consciousness."

"We're on the way." I ended the call and looked back at Belle. She was sitting on the edge of the bed looking at me. "Your dad's waking up. We should go."

She nodded. "Where are your clothes?"

I looked down at myself. I was in dark grey cotton boxers. "After my shower, I just wanted to lie down for a second."

"Next to me."

"It was just for a second," I reiterated.

"I thought I was dreaming."

"As did I."

She sighed. "You're going to be the death of me."

"Don't be overdramatic. Let me pull some jeans on, and we'll head out."

She pointed at my boxers, where things were still at attention. "How are you putting jeans on with that?"

"If you stop looking at it like you want a taste and give me a minute, we'll be out of here in no time." The way she was eating me up with her eyes had me gritting my teeth.

"I do want a taste," she breathed with that fire burning in her eyes.

"Jesus, Belle, that's not helping!"

"You're talking to a woman who hasn't had a taste in a long, long time," she admitted.

My voice was hoarse when I asked, "How long?"

"A little under a year."

"What?!" How was that even possible?

"Yes. For someone who is just twelve hours past his last taste—I'm sure that's amazing."

I scowled. "Are you going to throw that up in my face forever? I said I was wrong; I apologized. I'm a man who likes sex—is that a crime?"

"Depends."

I suppressed a sigh. She was turning peevish again. I put my hands on my hips and stared at her. "Why?"

"Why what?"

"Why has it been a year since you—"

"Oh, no time and lack of interest. I'm past the scratching-an-itch phase."

I winced. That hit close to home.

"Sorry, I didn't mean it like that. I really am going to let it go."

"When?" Because I, for one, was thoroughly sick of the topic.

"Right now. Everything you've ever done with any other woman is buried. As of this minute, you have a clean slate."

I blinked, waiting for the catch. "A clean slate?"

"Yep."

"What's the catch?"

"No catch. But I get one, too."

"You haven't told me anything about your past relationships."

"True."

From the sound of her voice, she wasn't planning on it either. I didn't like it but . . . I wanted that clean slate. "Deal." I put out my hand to shake on it.

She walked over and took my hand and placed it on her waist, then she leaned up and kissed me with pure fire and want. Holy Mother of God. She devoured me with lips and teeth and tongue, and for the first time in a long time, I just went along for the ride. I tightened my hand on her waist and pulled her closer.

She stepped back. "You do make one forget one's circumstance. We have to go."

I growled in frustration. "You started it."

"You started it with the mattress bump 'n' grind act. But don't worry, pretty boy—I'll let you finish it . . . at some point. Now tame that thing so we can go see my daddy."

Muttering under my breath about women who tease and what they had coming to them, I yanked open a drawer in the bedroom.

"Why don't you take a look at the changes I approved on those three designs we discussed earlier while I get dressed?"

She reached for her iPad and scrolled through to her e-mail. "Yessir. You sure you don't need any help getting that gun back in its holster?"

"Nice. Dick-as-gun jokes. Is this where I say it's locked and loaded? Unless you're prepared to come handle the weapon, Ms. Richards—*calmez-vous*!" I shushed her.

Jeans weren't going to work out. I stepped into some loose-fitting navy drawstring linen pants and shrugged into a light-green summer-weight shirt, which I prudently left untucked. I stuck my feet into some old-school Top-Siders before shoving my wallet in my back pocket, cell phone in front. I walked back into the living room and picked up the hotel phone.

"Yes, we'd like to have the car brought around

please. Montgomery. Thank you, we'll be down shortly."

Belle stood up with her purse on her arm, peering at her iPad. "Is that a plum stripe in this shirt?"

I nodded and opened the door. "After you."

"I like it. I wouldn't have picked it, but I like it. Did you put a contrast thread in?" she continued as we walked toward the elevator.

"Kelly green spun silk." I pressed the DOWN button.

"Pricey." She sent me a look and slipped her iPad into her purse.

"But worth it aesthetically, don't you think?"

She threw back her head and laughed. "You know you're the only heterosexual man I know who can talk spun-silk aesthetics with me."

I grinned down at her as we stepped onto the elevator. "Am I, now?"

"Indeed. What were you going to pair it with?"

"The cream-colored, flat-front trouser from the resort collection."

She glided in front of me and leaned back against me, making sure to brush her ass right up against me in a way that made me hiss through my teeth. "I love it when you talk clothing to me."

The rose scent that clung to her wafted up to me. It was safer to concentrate on that than the gyrations she was currently performing with her hips. "Gets you going, does it?"

"Yes, sir, and you know what else?" she teased in a soft voice.

So she wanted to tease. I looked at my watch. It was still Monday. I promised not to make any moves on her until it had been twenty-four hours since Renee. That made me feel very man-whorish just thinking it. That damn Renee, always more trouble than she was worth. I sighed and took a step back. She eased back as well, not breaking contact.

"What else?" I tried to concentrate on the conversation at hand.

"It's very sexy. The fact that you can talk fabric and fit and cut with me and still be so . . ."

". . . So?"

"Male." She reached behind her and caressed me through the thin pants.

"Delaney Mirabella Richards," I scolded, loving the feel of her but hating the timing.

"Yes, sugar?" She looked up at me through her lashes and tried to look innocent. Damn difficult when she was stroking me to within an inch of sanity.

I reached down and clasped her hand in mine as the elevator reached the lobby level and the doors opened. "Payback is going to be such sweet revenge."

"You're mixing your clichés, *monsieur*."

"You knew what I meant," I said quietly as we strode through the lobby.

"I'm all over the place. Am I making you crazy?"

"A little bit, but I get it."

She raised a brow and climbed in the car.

I tipped the valet and slid behind the wheel. I slipped on the sunglasses I'd left on the dash and started the car. Glancing in the rearview window, I eased the car out into the lane and headed for the highway.

"So tell me—what do you get?"

I smiled; she really couldn't help herself. She wasn't the kind to just let something rest. "*Bébé*, you've been scared, pissed, disappointed, horny, and elated all in the span of a day. If you weren't on an emotional rollercoaster, I'd be worried about you."

"You're a good man, Beau. When you're not so determined to be bad."

"*Merci*, Belle. That's the best backhanded compliment you've given me."

"*De rien.*"

"Look at you, with the French phrases; we'll make a Cajun out of you yet."

"Slow down, Bayou Beau; one thing at a time."

We were definitely making progress.

15

Hey, Daddy

Belle—5:23 PM that same day

I was clasping Beau's hand so hard, I was surprised he wasn't protesting. But that was one thing about Beau: he was strong and didn't break. He constantly surprised me with additional facets to his character. Long gone was the *laissez le bon temps rouler* playboy. I realized now that was a façade that Beau used to keep people from getting too close.

From the moment I decided to hire Beau, the playboy persona had virtually disappeared. Oh, he still had the charm and the looks, but there was a less predatory air about him. He seemed more purposeful in his actions, as if he had a plan and a destination. Whatever it was, it was a potent combination.

If you had told me when I first met Beau that I would be clinging to him as I approached my father, I would have called you fourteen kinds of crazy. Yet here I was, holding on like he was a lifeline. The comfort I found just in holding his hand should have alarmed me. But I decided to just go with it.

"*Tout va bien, chérie?*" he whispered in my ear.

"Yes, I'm okay. Thank you."

We walked the long hallway of the CCU floor and finally stood outside my father's door. Peering in through the glass window, I took a deep breath. There were many things I could say about my father, but I had never seen him like this. Normally a tall, imposing man robust and full of life, he now looked helpless, fragile, and very mortal. It was a disturbing sight.

I pushed open the door and pulled Beau inside with me. We approached the bed and stood looking down at my father. The breathing tube had been removed; he had dressings covering his chest and he was propped up slightly. His eyes were closed and he was breathing deeply. We sat down on the small sofa across from the bed and waited for him to stir.

"You don't have to wait with me," I told Beau while not letting go of his hand at all.

"Right." He squeezed my hand and didn't move an inch.

"It's just . . . you know. My dad and I—we have a complicated vibe." That was putting it lightly.

"He loves you."

"He does, but he's not so approving of my life choices."

"You're beautiful, successful, smart—what more does he want?"

"Me married, barefoot, and pregnant. Preferably with a passel of kids, cooking grits and bacon every morning and chicken and dumplings every night. Some man's lil woman knittin' booties or some such thang."

"You know your Southern belle sneaks out in your voice when you're agitated?"

"Does it now?" He was a fine one to talk with the Cajun colloquialisms springing forth constantly.

"I'm curious though, Belle—do you even want any of that?"

"I wouldn't mind whipping up some chicken and dumplings soon."

He gave me a look that clearly said he knew that was a non-answer.

"Why Beauregard Montgomery, are you seriously asking *me* about marriage and kids?"

He looked a little uncomfortable and shifted with a waggle of his shoulders. "Sure, why not?"

"Notorious playboy letting the M-word fall out of his mouth?"

"I haven't been notorious with it in quite some time. You don't have to answer if it makes you uneasy."

"Like you, I'm rarely uneasy."

"Maybe it's just around me then."

"Maybe it is." He did have a way of getting under my skin and ruffling my feathers. I was a girl who liked to stay calm. Something to think about at another time.

"Well, *chérie*, you give me an unsteady breath from time to time yourself."

I was glad to hear it, so I answered his question. "I would like to get married one day. Two kids. House with a lawn and a pool. One day. I have time."

"You have all the time in the world."

"Just gotta find the right guy." I waited for his reaction to that one.

He blinked slowly. "Indeed. So, a man like your father, or no?"

My first instinct was to say *no*, and then I thought about it. "Yes and no. A family man, a man who believes in God, a man who adores every breath his wife takes. Yes please. But I want a man who respects my profession, isn't locked into traditional gender roles, and is more of a partner."

Beau nodded, and we fell into a companionable silence.

My relationship with my father had always been complex. I knew he loved me but I also resented the hell out of him for driving my mother to an early grave. He had made no secret of the fact that he thought my career was frivolous, but he didn't refuse the money I funneled toward the family for years. I'd never heard a *thank you* or a *good job* out of him. Now, with my sisters and brothers ready to make their own way, I just wasn't sure what the family dynamics would be. So while I definitely wanted him healthy and whole, I was conflicted about the nature of our relationship now.

We waited for close to an hour until my father started trying to sit up. I rushed to the side of the bed and raised the angle slightly. I placed my free hand on his shoulder to keep him from trying to get up and kissed his forehead.

"Hey, Daddy." Beau came and stood beside me, taking my hand in his again.

My father's eyes blinked open and his mouth lifted up in a smile. His voice was a little slurred and raspy. "Baby Girl. Who's this young man?"

"Beauregard Montgomery, meet Percival Elias Richards."

"Mr. Richards." Beau clasped his hand.

"Percy."

"Percy. Wish we'd met under nicer circumstances."

"Is what it is."

I could see the effort that staying awake and talking to us was taking. "Daddy, don't wear yourself out. We'll be back in the morning." I patted his shoulder and took a step back.

"Dallas?" My father rasped out the single word.

"We're not going back to Dallas until we know how you are . . . for sure." The doctors had given him a good prognosis, but I wanted to see him up and moving before I headed back.

"I'm fine."

"I know but . . ."

"You made enough sacrifices for us."

"It's not a sacrifice."

"I'm gonna be fine."

"Daddy . . ."

"But stay . . . please."

My eyes welled up with tears. My father was a man who did not say *please* ever. He was a man of few words, actually. You never knew what he was thinking. If he was asking me to stay and adding a *please*, this was serious. "Of course I'll stay as long as you want. We'll be back first thing in the morning. You just concentrate on getting well."

He nodded and closed his eyes.

The floor nurse came in, checked his dressings, and gave him some meds while quietly telling us that he was doing well.

After the nurse left the room, I stood watching my father rest for another moment before squeezing Beau's hand and turning away. We were a step from the door when my father's voice rang out stronger than before.

"Beau?" We turned back around to see him sending a surprisingly lucid and assessing eye in Beau's direction.

Beau stepped forward. "Yes, sir?"

"Watch your step."

Beau nodded. "Yes, sir."

"Delaney's very special."

"Daddy!" Where had this come from? I felt like a teenager bringing her prom date by for approval. This was crazy. I was *very special*? That was new also.

Beau nodded again. "Don't back talk your father. Sir, I completely agree."

My mouth fell open and I closed it quickly.

Percy's eyes lit up. "All right then."

Beau patted my father's hand. "Rest well, Percy."

I looked from my father to Beau and shook my head. Men.

"Go ahead on with the man, Baby Girl."

Beau grinned. "C'mon, Baby Girl."

All I could do was roll my eyes and follow Beau out the door. Before I could chat with him about whatever that macho nonsense was, we ran into Dalton and Tina in the hallway.

"How is he?" Dalton asked.

I had to smile. "Nurse said he's recovering quickly, no complications. He's well enough to have a word or two with Beauregard here."

"Oh yeah?"

Beau grinned. "*Mais oui.* Baby Girl here is very special."

Tina snorted. "In more ways than one."

"Are you going to make that 'Baby Girl' thing a thing now?"

"Maybe. I kinda like it."

"And if I started calling you Pontchartrain Poonhound?"

"Doesn't have the same zip to it."

Dalton sighed. "Not to interrupt y'all's banter but . . . so Dad's sleeping?"

"Knocked out," I supplied.

My sister Loren came striding down the hallway with a blanket, pillow, and duffel bag. "Family, hot dude Delaney brought with her—what's good?"

"Loren is coming up to stay the night. We thought we'd do shifts," Tina said.

"I drew the short straw; I'm on the night shift," Loren said.

"Aw, look at y'all all grown up. I like this new independence but keep me in the loop, okay?" I actually was growing okay with the fact that they didn't need me for every little decision. Letting go was easier than I thought it would be.

Dalton rolled his eyes. "Yes, Sis."

Beau asked, "Who's hungry?"

All of us Richards raised our hands.

"Least I can do is take Baby Girl and her fam out to dinner."

He was really getting into the whole "Baby Girl" thing. I was going to have to squash that . . . soon. "You don't have to buy us dinner."

Beau rolled his eyes. "I know, Belle. I offered— are you turning me down?"

I dropped his hand and put my hands on my hips. "Why are you so sensitive this afternoon, sugar? I didn't say all that."

"So enlighten me, Belle, what *are* you saying?"

"I was just giving you an out in case you didn't want to buy us dinner!" We stood toe-to-toe, and I pointed my finger in his chest to enunciate every word.

He took the back of his hand and moved my finger out of the way. "I wouldn't have made the offer if I didn't mean it."

"Well, fine!"

"You know what, *ma fifille?*"

"What?" I huffed.

He lowered his voice. "You are driving me absolutely crazy today."

"It's been a long day."

"It's getting longer by the minute," he agreed.

Loren's, Tina's, and Dalton's heads swiveled back and forth between the two of us as if they were watching a tennis match.

"Y'all need a moment?" Loren drawled.

Beau gave me a whatcha-wanna-do-now look, and I shifted forward to lean my forehead against his chest and wrap my arm around his waist. "I know. I'm sorry. I told you I require patience."

He stroked the back of my neck with his hand. It felt amazing. I leaned into the caress for a moment. His voice was a low rumble in his chest when he responded. "You did. I'll try not to run out."

Dalton cleared his throat. "Seriously, do y'all need a moment?"

I took a step back. "Sorry, let's go eat. Pretty Boy is paying."

16

You Sure about This?

Beau—Wednesday, May 4, 4:50 PM

I finished sending the last e-mail and shut down my laptop. Moving it to the desk in the hotel suite, I also double-checked my phone for messages before setting it next to the laptop. I plugged both of them into their chargers.

There was no way you could have convinced me that selecting models was hard work . . . but it was. Belle liked to create glossy one-page handouts that she called style sheets. She used those in addition to an order catalog, which we would work on next. We selected two male and two female models, sent Katrina out with the photographers to scout locations, and scheduled the shoot. We were halfway to the launch of the spring line.

Some of the sample garments had arrived this afternoon. We had been ripping open the boxes and examining each one. I have to admit to being proud of my contribution to making these designs come to life.

"We just got the FedEx. We've been running around with my family and taking laps to the hospital. He's doing great. Beau's been great." Belle was on the phone to Yazlyn. "I think the resort collection for the men is my favorite line so far."

I opened up the last box and pulled out a shrink-wrapped garment. As I shook it out, my mouth went dry. It was a sheer bustier in pink with an embroidered rose pattern across the straps and down the bodice; there was a matching pair of bikini panties. It instantly occurred to me that Belle would look *trés magnifique* in these. In fact, she would look better with me taking them off of her. Maybe with my teeth.

"Belle." I spoke in a quiet, serious tone.

She glanced over at me and held up a finger before turning away. "No, hold on to the rest of the samples. They are releasing my dad Saturday morning, and we should be in the office by Monday."

"Belle, hang up the phone and put these on." I walked toward her, unbuttoning my shirt as I went. I'd had it with waiting. For an instant-gratification kind of guy, my patience was sorely tested. I wanted what I wanted when I wanted it. And right now, I wanted Belle . . . with a crucial urgency. Gliding up behind her, I placed my lips on the back of her neck and unzipped her dress. She stopped talking abruptly. I smirked as her dress fell to the ground. I unsnapped her bra and started sliding the straps down her arms. She was beautiful. I looked down and watched as her nipples pebbled into points. I cupped her breasts in my hands; they fit perfectly. Greedily, I feathered my thumbs across the tips. I wanted all of her attention focused on me.

She looked over her shoulder at me. I lifted my eyes and met her look as I continued to stroke her. The heat between us went from warm to blazing just like that. Her breath stuttered and her eyelids lowered to half-mast. "Yaz, I gotta go." She ended the call and tossed the phone toward the sofa as she arched into my hands. "Jesus, that feels good." She pulled the bra the rest of the way off and kicked the dress out of the way. I sent my shirt to join the dress.

"I can make it feel better," I promised.

When she turned toward me, I had to catch my breath. She was a goddess clad in a whisper-thin thong and silver high-heeled sandals. Her skin looked like poured chocolate and I wanted a taste . . . badly. I craved it more than my next breath. Before I could reach for her, she kicked off her heels and jumped at me. She literally climbed up my body before wrapping her arms and legs around me. "You still want me to put the lingerie on?"

"Later," I growled and gripped her hips to mold her to mine. I shifted her in tiny increments against me just to drive both of us a little crazy. She was soft and blazing hot where our bodies were smashed against each other.

"About time; let's do this." She attached her lips to the side of my neck and bit down.

I barked out a laugh as I carried her toward the bedroom. "About time? I was waiting on you, *chérie!*"

She licked the small wound the bite left. "I appreciate that. The wait is over."

"*Certainement.*" It certainly was. I tipped her back onto the bed and settled on top of her. My lips met hers in a fiery kiss. We were eager to learn each other's taste and rhythm. Instead of dueling, our tongues danced. Each foray more heated than the last. Stroking my palm across her face, I had to ask, "You sure about this?"

"*Absolument,*" she said with a grin.

I put her arms up over her head with her wrists together. "Leave them there," I commanded as I started tasting her. Light licks and kisses across her jaw, down her neck, across her collarbone, nearing her breasts. I wanted to leave a trail of fire everywhere my lips touched. I explored her reverently, learning the beat of the pulse along her throat, the softness at the curve of her shoulder, the slope at the plump swell of her breast where a slight flower scent lingered.

She squirmed and brought her hands down to my face. "Beau . . ."

I stopped. "Where are your hands?"

With a low moan, she took her hands and placed them back over her head. I knew she would. Belle was the kind of woman who liked to be in control everywhere but in bed. She wanted someone to challenge her comfort zone a little, take her on a journey outside of herself. I was definitely up to the job.

"Keep them there, or I stop." I traced her left nipple with my teeth while circling the right with my fingers as incentive for her to comply.

"Okay, but hurry."

I stopped again. "What was that?" I smiled as she groaned deep in her throat.

"Who knew you'd be a control freak in bed?"

I kissed my way down her stomach and pressed a kiss in the center of her damp panties. "If you don't like it, I can stop."

She arched her hips up. "Don't you dare!"

I moved the panties to the side and dipped down for a taste. The taste of her arousal exploded on my tongue, and I was instantly addicted. With a hum, I settled in to enjoy the feast. I allowed my tongue to scrape and dart and plunge and tease until her breath hitched in her throat and she began to pant. Her legs fell open and then tightened around my ears as I nipped right there and then there and with extra pressure there.

I reached up and flicked a nipple at the same time that I sucked her nubbin into my mouth and thrust a finger inside her tight passage. She screamed and convulsed around me. I continued the pressure so she could ride the wave as long as possible. After a few moments, she settled and her legs fell limp.

"Beau?" Her voice was raspy and low. It was the sexiest thing I had ever heard.

"*Oui, ma belle?*"

"Get inside me, darlin'. Now."

I raised a brow at her tone.

She shimmied on the comforter. "Please. I need you. Please!"

I snapped, all thoughts of control and challenge gone. I needed this woman far more than I wanted her surrender. Impatient now, I ripped her panties and flung them across the room. Then I shucked off my pants and boxers. Pulling a condom out of the nightstand and rolling it on, I couldn't remember being quite this hard before. Settling back over her, I widened her thighs and placed a kiss on her lips. "You ready, *ma douce?*"

She opened her eyes and tilted her hips up in blatant invitation.

"I hear you, baby. Here we go." Without further ado, I slid in to the hilt. Jesus, she was tight as a fist around me. Belle screamed and I went still as a statue, worried that I'd hurt her in some way. "Are you okay?" I managed to ask as her impossibly wet canal pulsed around me. It was insane for a woman to feel like this.

"Better than okay; may I have more please?" she begged.

"*Je sais tout faire.*" Anything she wanted, I would do. Shifting up, I placed each of her legs over the crooks of my arms and opened her wide. We both groaned at the sensations caused by the deeper angle. I tensed my jaw and slid forward again and then again.

"Yes!" she hissed between her teeth and lifted her hips to meet each slow stroke.

"Belle, is this how you like it?" I asked for the first time ever. I wanted to make it perfect for her.

"I like it however you want to give it to me."

Great answer. I grew harder inside her and slowed the tempo more. "All right then." I inched out of her in a silky withdrawal before sinking just as slowly back into her warmth. I ground against her to plumb her depths. I looked down to where we were intimately joined, amazed that such a simple action could spark this kind of feeling.

When I looked up, Belle's eyes were trained on me. Her expression revealed the same awe that I felt, and a warmth that had nothing to do with sex seeped into my veins. *Not now Beau*, I lectured myself. This was no time to get all emotional. I had work to do. My job here was to dissolve Belle into a limp pool of happy. I altered the stroke to hit her G-spot and her eyes fluttered closed.

"Keep that up and I'm going to come again," she warned with a whimper, her hands still above her head and gripping the pillows tightly.

"Go ahead, Mirabella; there's more where that came from." A light sheen of sweat coated my skin as I held back my release to ensure Belle had her fill. She began to throb around me so I leaned down to nip at the sensitized tip of a heaving breast with my teeth. I sucked the nipple into my mouth and rolled it between my teeth and tongue. She gave a keening cry and roared up beneath me; I had to literally brace myself to keep from joining her in orgasm.

I watched in fascination as she fractured around me. "You like that? *Trés bien*, maybe just a lil more?"

Her head flailed from side to side on the pillow. "I can't, I can't."

I lowered her legs to the bed and slid my hands up to join hers. Linking her fingers with mine on either side of her head, I whispered, "You can. Just a lil more, *chérie*, for me?" I rocked against her.

Her knees came up on either side of my hips. "*Umm.* Maybe for you."

"*Merci, merci beaucoup.*" I continued my slow rock.

"Beau?"

How far gone was I that I was starting to love the way she said my name? "Belle?"

"Let go, baby."

"Beg pardon?"

"I know you're holding back to make it perfect for me."

She saw through me. "Maybe a lil bit."

"Don't. It's already perfect. It's everything I wanted and more. Now I want you to lose control."

I wasn't a man to lose control in bed. I enjoyed myself, yes, at all times, but I wasn't one to forget where I was and what I was doing. At that moment, she squeezed me with her internal muscles and stroked a hand down my back to sneak in between us. As I withdrew, she ran her finger along my base and across my sac, lightly scraping the skin with her fingernail. I lost control.

I made a sound that was part animal, part human as I reared back and slammed into her with all that I had. "*Sainte Mère de Dieu!*" I called on Mary and any other divine being that could explain the wonder of this moment. I thrust with pure passion and very little finesse, driving toward completion.

"Just like that. Just. Like. That!" Belle screamed and clutched me tighter.

The fact that she was with me stroke for stroke took it to a whole other level. "Stay with me, *bébé.*" It wasn't going to be pretty but it was epic in its goodness.

"I'm with you, baby. I'm right here." She began the shivers that preceded her race to ecstasy.

Ah hell. That got me. I caught her lips in another searing kiss, and our tongues tangoed to the same rhythm of our hips. Faster and more frantic until I felt flammable. Finally, I ripped my lips from hers and seated myself as deeply as I could inside her addictive heat. "Belle!" Her name flew from my lips as I let the explosion hit me. And at that crucial moment, I had one crystal clear and terrifying thought: I was home.

Without a single clue what to do with that thought, I rolled off of Belle and pressed a kiss to her forehead. I wrapped the condom in a Kleenex and discarded it in the trash can next to the bed.

"Can we go again in a minute?" she murmured. "I've been deprived, you know."

My lips curved up. This was familiar and comfortable territory. "You seemed to be making up for lost time."

"What can I say? You're like a potato chip."

I squinted at her. That did not sound flattering. "Ah . . . in what way, exactly?"

"You're instantly addictive. Once you have a taste, you want the whole bag. You know the catch phrase—bet you can't have just one."

"At last count, you had three, *chérie.*"

"Impolite, sugar," she tsked.

"Apologies."

"So that's a no?" she said, sliding her hand down my torso.

By the time her hand brushed against me, I was stirring back to life. "Have I ever refused you anything?"

"Well, you did make me play by your rules." She looked up at me through her lashes.

I pulled her on top of me and slid a finger across her buttocks. "You loved it. You like a little kink in your potato chip." I smacked her ass lightly and she shivered.

"You see too much," she muttered as she started to squirm against me again.

"Ditto. First cotton candy, now potato chips. Let's see what other tasty treat I can bring to mind." I slid my hand around to cup her. "Hmm, I'm thinking something with honey."

17

We All Make Our Own Choices

Belle—Sunday, May 8, 3:12 PM

I glanced at my watch and tried not to make the c'mon-with-it-already motion to my father. He was staying in a small house in Alpharetta we'd rented for him. All of his belongings from Valdosta had been shipped, unpacked, and set to his exact specifications around the three-bedroom, two-bath ranch house. My mother's picture hung over the fireplace in the living room. Percy Richards sat in navy blue lounging pajamas Beau had bought for him, with his feet propped up on a faded tan ottoman I remembered from my childhood.

The doctors were ecstatic about his progress, but I'd hired a home healthcare worker who was not only a registered nurse but a chef as well. Nina was a sturdy, no-nonsense woman in her early fifties who won all of us over immediately with her straightforward attitude. The full breakfast of grits, eggs, and ham hadn't hurt either. When she slapped a bowl of thin Cream of Wheat in front of my father with a look that said not to try her, I knew she was the perfect person for the job.

Beau and I had a plane to catch in less than an hour. My father had asked to speak to me alone and sent everyone else out of the room. That was three minutes ago. Since then he sat, staring at the picture of my mother.

With a deep breath, he finally started to speak, and his first words shocked the hell out of me. "Delaney Mirabella, I know you think I put your mother in her premature grave."

Whoa! I had no answer to that one. I did think it, but one didn't say such a thing out loud. So I sat silently.

"But I want you to know that your mother knew she had a heart condition. She lived her life exactly how she wanted. I never asked that woman to bear five children, work two jobs, and fetch for me like she did. That's what made her happy, Baby Girl."

"How do you know that?"

"She told me. And she left a letter. I want you to read it. I want you to understand." His voice shook as he spoke.

"Daddy, you're not supposed to get upset. It's fine. It's okay. I understand."

He slapped his hand down on the side of his lounge chair. "No, you don't! And you need to before it's too late."

"Don't say things like that!" Was he not feeling well? Was there a chance he wouldn't recover?

"Not too late for me, too late for you!" He was adamant.

"What do you mean?" I was thoroughly confused.

"When your mama died, a part of me shut down. It was like a lot of the color just seeped out of my life. I didn't feel the joy. I did the basics to raise your sisters and brothers, and I let them lean on you for the rest."

I let out a breath. "It all turned out all right." Now that he acknowledged it, I was willing to let the whole thing go.

"No, let me finish. From the day you were born, your mother and I knew you were special. At the age of four, you had me drive you to the city limits of Valdosta and you pointed and asked, 'What else is out there, Daddy?' I knew then that you were destined for more than I could offer. At the heart of it all, I'm just a good old country boy. I'm ashamed to say it hurt me some to see you so happy away from home. And then after you started making more money in a month than I made all year, I didn't know what to do with you."

"Oh." I never thought of it from his side before.

"Then, after I lost your mother, I had no idea how to be a father to you. I didn't think I could guide you or teach you nothing. You were always speeding so fast in the other direction. But I was always proud of you, Baby Girl. You done real good by all of us."

Tears welled up in my eyes. "Thank you, Daddy."

"Mirabella, you have your mother's heart and my stubborn pride."

"Well now—" I wasn't sure I agreed with that assessment.

"It's true girl, just own it. But don't let that pride block your blessings."

He lost me again. "Which blessings are those?"

"That pretty Cajun boy who can't take his eyes off of you."

"Now Daddy, we're just . . ." I cast around for the right word to use with my father. "Fooling around a little bit. It's nothing serious."

"No?"

"No. Beau doesn't do serious, and I don't want serious right now."

"Well, I don't know who's lying to who but somebody sho'nuff lying," he cackled.

"Beau is kind of a player, Daddy. He's not in love with me."

"Baby, every man's a player until he meets his other half. And that boy looks at you like you're his other half. Don't count him out and don't sell yourself short."

"Yes, Daddy." At this point, whatever it took to cut the conversation short.

"That's the tone you use when you just want your old man to shut up and change the subject. Listen good now. We all make our own choices, Dela-Bella. Your mother chose to live the time she had as she saw fit. She lived full out, no regrets. Will you be able to say the same?"

That was food for thought. I'd been so busy hustling, I hadn't stopped to reflect on the journey. "I don't know," I answered honestly.

"Well think about that. You've been a success in every area of your life except your personal one. I don't know if our stuff has held you back or you miss a mama to talk to about it. But either way, we've both learned that life is short and tomorrow ain't promised. You take what that boy offers with both hands, hear?"

Damn he was on a roll today. "I hear you, Daddy."

"Think on it, Baby Girl."

"I guess I have to." He hadn't left me much choice.

He reached beside his chair and pulled out a flat, square box. "Tuck this away and look at it in a few weeks."

I got up and walked over to retrieve it. "A few weeks?"

"Weeks, months, whenever you feel you are ready. Wait until after all of this has settled down and marinated a little bit."

"Okay." I tucked the box into my tote bag.

"Now, call everybody back in so we can let you and your young man get on up outta here. And Delaney?"

"Yes?" I paused on my way to get the others.

"I love you, Baby Girl. Don't ever doubt it."

I knelt down to hug him tight, and he kissed my cheek.

"Wipe those tears; you're too pretty to cry."

I wiped my eyes with a laugh. He'd been telling me that for as long as I could remember.

"Though I liked your hair longer, Baby Girl."

I rolled my eyes.

"But once you start having those bayou babies, you won't have time to keep yourself looking so perfect all the time."

"Now there's the Percy Richards I know."

"Yeah, I said it." He grinned mischievously.

I kissed his cheek and brushed his hair back. "I love you too, Daddy."

"Of course you do. C'mon now, you don't want to miss your plane."

I called everyone back into the room and the round robin of good-byes started.

Thirty minutes later, Beau and I were striding across the tarmac toward the jet.

"You do realize this is ridiculously extravagant, right?" I looked over at Beau through my dark sunglasses. It was a bright, sunny, and hot day in Atlanta, Georgia.

He shrugged in typical Beau fashion. "I figured we'd leave the way we came. Besides, I had to pay for the round-trip when I booked it. It would have been a waste to pay to fly commercial at this point."

"Well, when you put it that way." I flashed him a grin and trotted up the stairs. Now that I wasn't scared and tired and stressed and pissed off at Beau, I could appreciate the luxury of the jet. It sat ten people comfortably, more if you weren't concerned about the safety of those on the sofa.

There was a small galley with seating for the staff near the cockpit in the front. There was a sleeping cabin at the back along with the bathroom. I slipped into one of the chairs that folded down into a sleeping pod in the middle of the plane. The crew closed the plane door and the air conditioning came on. I got comfortable and watched Beau talking with the pilot.

He was wearing black cargo pants and a plum-colored fitted tee. The pants hung low on his slim hips, the tee stretched across his broad chest. Beau was the kind of fine that was undeniable. Match that with his features, tight cropped hair, and lethal who-me? smile—I don't know how anyone could resist him. On top of that, damned if he wasn't a far more decent guy than I'd given him credit for being.

Trailing my eyes along his tall frame, I all but licked my lips. Now that I knew what it was like to have him inside me, his eyes turning from gold to antique bronze as he stroked every inch of my body inside and out . . . I wasn't sure I could pull back from him . . . even if I wanted to.

I had hardly been a nun before I met Beau, but I could say in all honesty that no man had ever taken me to the heights of passion I scaled with him. It was almost embarrassing the way he could bend me to his will and make me want him again and again. I could completely let go with him. Thankfully, he seemed to be equally drawn to me. I didn't know if this would burn itself out or turn ugly, and God knew with the close way we worked together, the whole thing had the potential to get messy.

Even without my father's words ringing in my ears, I wasn't prepared to settle for a professional-only relationship with Beau. I wondered if everyone in the office would know just from looking at us that we were together. The energy around us was palpable. My siblings had teased me about it all week long. If the snap, crackle, and pop between us didn't give the relationship away, the way I couldn't stop eating him up with my eyes probably did.

My eyes returned to him as if pulled by magnets. I felt myself heating up just looking at him and knowing what he was capable of. He nodded at something Samantha, the smiling flight attendant, said before sensing my eyes on him. He shifted and caught the expression on my face. I watched as a tension came across him. His stance widened slightly, his jaw firmed, his nostrils flared, and his eyes went laser hot. He murmured something to the pilot and the flight attendant, and they turned and disappeared into the front of the craft, pulling the partition closed behind them.

He advanced toward me, a decidedly predatory aura about him. "You're gonna get what you're asking for, Baby Girl. You're gonna get it good."

Coming from anyone else, that would have sounded ridiculous. But hearing it from Beau when I already knew he could back it up? Well, that just made me hot.

He slid into the seat next to mine and examined me from head to toe. I was in a teal blue short-sleeve wrap dress with a ruffle around the neck and hem with peach wedge slingbacks and a peep-toe on my feet. I crossed one thigh over the other as his eyes ran down the length of my legs.

He crooked a finger at me, and I leaned in. He put his lips next to my ear. "You're wet already, aren't you?"

I shook my head to deny the truth. Who admitted that kind of thing?

"Tell me, or I'll reach down there with two fingers and find out for myself."

I shivered. Part of me wanted him to and part of me was scandalized at the mere thought of it. That gray curtain wasn't exactly a privacy screen.

"Belle?" His hand was on my thigh and sliding upward.

I put my hand over his to stop him. "Beau, there are other people on this plane."

"They're paid well for their discretion. Besides . . ." His hand slid higher and higher, hovering over the juncture of my thighs.

I bit my lip between my teeth and debated whether to part my thighs or not. I was entirely too easy when it came to one Beauregard Montgomery. "Besides?"

"The thought that they might catch a peek or hear you cry out has got you boiling."

With a deep breath, I uncrossed my thighs. Two long fingers he promised slipped under my panties to stroke the swollen and ready flesh there. We both groaned at the contact.

"You're dripping with it." He rimmed the opening before pressing once against the bud that was already hard and throbbing underneath his touch.

"I know, I can't help it," I murmured, keeping an eye on the curtain.

"I don't want you to. I love how hot you get for me. This is for me, right?" He scissored my button between his fingers in a fast staccato that took me to the edge in no time flat.

"It's for you."

"Only me."

I'd deal with this new possessive streak later. For now, I wanted what he could give me. "Only you."

"Are you ready to come all over my fingers?"

I really was. I nodded.

"I can't hear you, Belle."

"Yesss . . ."

He fluttered his fingers along my slit before thrusting both fingers inside me. The shock of it sent me over the edge. His mouth clamped over mine to muffle my scream. I shamelessly rode his hand as the delicious rapture sent me soaring.

My head fell back against the seat. "You make me forget myself."

He removed his fingers from me and began to lick them clean. Damn if the sight of that didn't get me worked up all over again. He sent me a look that said he knew what he was doing to me. "We'll finish this after take-off."

As if on cue, Samantha came out and asked us to buckle up. She promised to return after take-off with beverages. To her credit, she acted as though she didn't notice Beau was hard as a rock, I was squirming in my seat, and the air was scented with sex.

I straightened up and buckled the seat belt. "I can't decide if you're heaven-sent or the devil incarnate."

He sniffed his fingers and smiled at me. "Probably somewhere in between, *chérie*."

Only time would tell.

18

What Are We Arguing About?

Beau—Monday, May 9, 6:47 AM

"Y ou're almost there, aren't you?" I groaned into her ear. She was bent at the waist grasping at the vanity while I stood behind her, pistoning into her silky depths. I had stepped out of her shower to find her standing nude bent over the sink washing her face. That's all it took to get us from there to here.

"Yes. Don't stop. Don't stop!"

"Look at us." I pointed.

She raised her head and stared into the mirror. We were surrounded by the fog from the shower, making our reflection look surreal as we moved together. I placed the heel of my hand against her and ground down in a circle once and then twice.

On a long, low moan, she came around me, triggering my own climax. Our eyes stayed locked on each other as we rode out the sensation. There was that strange intimacy again. Beyond the physical and into a place that gave me pause. I didn't have time to pause this morning. Discarding the condom, I reached for a washcloth.

She cleaned up, splashed water on her face, and started applying makeup. "So being naked in front of you is just an invitation for kick-starting the good 'n plenty."

"Apparently, that's all it takes. Keep some drawers on about yourself," I teased.

"I'll remember that."

"And don't give me the 'do me baby' look when we have other places to be."

"So noted."

"Or wear those sandals that wrap around the ankle."

She shimmied into underwear and looked at me over her shoulder. "Doesn't take much to rev your engine, huh?"

"You're a fine one to talk, *chérie*. Who was all 'Beau, stay with me' last night?"

"Might have been me." She padded over to her closet.

"Who woke me up at one in the morning talkin' bout 'just a lil taste?' " I reached around her and pulled out a sheath dress in an ocean color. I handed it to her.

She sent me a look and stepped into it. "Might have been me as well."

I rifled through my garment bag. "*Mmm-hmm.* By the way, I'm out of clothes. Someone wouldn't let me go by Katrina's to pick something up. Unless you want me coming to work in a towel, I have to go."

"We have sample clothes, sugar. Now is as good a time as ever to see how they look on. And speaking of work . . ."

Something in her tone alerted me and I paused midstep. "Yes?"

"I don't want to advertise our . . . thing." She made an I-don't-know-what-to-call-it gesture with her hands.

"Thing?" I repeated the gesture.

She pulled on some eelskin sandals and looked at me. "You know what I'm talking about . . . the more intimate aspect of our relationship."

"Oh, are we calling this a relationship?" I kept my tone even and selected slate-gray dress pants with a mint-green pinstripe. I would have to go commando. I added the checked white and kelly green shirt. It shouldn't have looked good together but it did.

"As opposed to calling it what?" She put a hand on her hip.

No way was I going to start throwing descriptive terms around. "I'm Backseat Beau, remember? This is your show."

"I'm going to have to call bullshiggity on that. I'm running the show at work but uh . . . that's about it. The rest of the time, you set the music we dance to, sir."

"Is that a complaint?"

"It's not a complaint, Beauregard. Don't get all hot grits in a sizzling skillet on me."

"I'm pretty sure I don't do 'hot grits on a platter,' or whatever you just said. What does that even mean? *Mon Dieu*, I'm just asking if you want to have that 'what is this?' conversation right now. Do you have the answers to the questions?"

"Do you, darlin'?" She had the attitude of one spoiling for a fight. I wasn't in the mood to oblige.

"I'm in this. Whatever it is. You're the one trying to keep secrets," I shot back.

"I'm not keeping you a secret; I just don't want to be undermined at work."

"I think I can be counted on not to grab your ass from eight to five. I do have some sense of professional decorum about myself." I was starting to get pissed off. I was only good enough to bounce around with in the dark? Really?

"You're being deliberately snarky."

"You're being deliberately rude. If you don't want to claim me, just say so."

"Claim you?"

"Sure, if I'm just a cut buddy say it straight out. I'm a grown-ass man; I can take it."

"Would I have introduced a cut buddy to my family? My father?"

I shrugged. Who knew what she was thinking? I sure as hell didn't.

"This is one of those pretty boy problems, huh?"

"Beg pardon?"

"You're never sure if someone wants you for you or all your pretty."

I rolled my eyes. "Yes, cuz you're such a hag yourself."

She laughed. "What are we arguing about?"

"Were we arguing? I was just looking for clarity."

"Smart-ass. Can we not act like we just jumped each other when we get to the office?"

"*Pas de probléme.*"

"Can you not look at me like I'm the last slice of peach pie at the county fair?"

"I'm the soul of restraint, *mon ami.*"

"Like just now?" she said, looking toward the bathroom.

Okay, I had kinda run up on her. I'd own that. "I got it; no bending you over the conference room table and having my way with you."

"Yeah, *um,* none of that."

"No grabbing your hips and pulling them to mine while we share one of those long, slow kisses you're so good at."

She put her hand up. "See, this is how you start."

I gave her my most innocent look, "Me? *Mais non,* I'm going to be good."

"That's what I'm worried about."

19

All My Eggs in the Beauregard Basket

Belle—Saturday, May 14, 8:21 PM (later that week)

I checked my Facebook page on my phone as we waited to be seated. "Sweet Jesus, my father has posted another article about black single women over the age of thirty and their chances of achieving happily ever after. He's added a cheery 'Don't let this be you!' with the link. Whoever put that man on Facebook has a lot to answer for." Dad had been on a not-so-subtle matrimony theme since meeting Beau.

"My mother used to send me those. Now she's sending me reminders about babies and fertility treatments," Jewellen said. I hadn't spent a lot of time with Beau's sister-in-law, but what I knew I liked.

"Good Lord, that's wrong on so many levels," I sympathized.

"Wait until he forgets that Facebook is public and posts something really personal for all your friends to see. My mother is no longer allowed to post on my wall." Jewel shook her head. The hostess led us to a booth near the back windows.

"But let's flip the topic back, Belle. Speaking of happily ever afters, spill it," Katrina said the minute we put down our purses and slid into the booth at the P. F. Chang's in Northpark Center. We were all casually dressed in jeans and summer tops since it was still over one hundred degrees outside.

I smiled as the server handed us menus and walked away. "What are you talking about? I think I'm in the mood for seafood; how about you?"

"I never turn down seafood," Jewellen cosigned.

"Ms. Richards? Ma'am? Just who do you think you're talking to here?" Katrina said, running her eyes up and down the menu before setting it down.

I sighed. She was giving me the Montgomery pretty-eye stare. I'd seen it from Beau enough times to recognize it for what it was. It meant they wanted answers and they wanted them now. "Okay, what do you want to know?"

"What's up with you and Brother Beau, besides the obvious?"

I played dumb. "The obvious?"

"You two are clearly gettin' it in at every available opportunity."

I winced. "Kat."

Jewel blinked at both of us. "When did this happen? I'm so out of the loop."

Katrina said, "A few weeks now. They're still in that 'give it to me, baby' phase, where everyone knows what they've been doing all night."

I had no defense. "You're killing me, Katrina."

"Oh, I'm not supposed to mention the 'just got laid and laid well' vibe dripping off the two of you twenty-four seven, making the rest of us sick?"

I rolled my eyes. "No, you're not."

"Fine. We'll just bury our head in the sand on that one. But my brother hasn't slept at my house since you two jetted off for Hotlanta. I wanna know what's really happening. Is it a love thing or what?"

Excellent question and one that I did not have the answer to . . . at all. "We *uh*—we haven't put a label on it as yet." The waiter appeared beside the table and asked for our drink order.

"Ginger-peach iced tea, please," Katrina said to the waiter.

"Sprite," Jewel requested.

"I'll have the blackberry iced tea. And some lettuce wraps?" I added.

The waiter moved away after setting three glasses of water on the table. Katrina started back in again. "Let me see if I understand. He works with you all day and stays with you all night and you haven't defined it yet?"

"He moved in with you?" Jewel asked, eyes wide.

"Not exactly," I dodged.

"He might as well have," Katrina volunteered. "You all haven't had the *what are we doing* talk?"

"Not in so many words, not really." Now I was

tempted to squirm. I wanted off the hot seat, please.

Katrina clucked her teeth. "Belle, you are the most dot-the-i-and-cross-the-t person I know, and you're just winging it?"

Sounded bad when she put it like that, but . . . "Yes."

"That's okay as long as you're both comfortable with it." Jewel shrugged.

"Well, how do you feel?" Katrina asked.

"About what?"

"About *him*!" Katrina slammed her hand down on the table in impatience.

"Oh. Well, I like him." I did. I liked Beau a lot.

"Clearly," Jewel added.

"And I respect him."

"Another good thing," Katrina added.

My voice and expression went dreamy. "And since you brought it up . . . the things that man can do to me! Gets me every time. That Cajun has the most magical—"

Katrina squealed in protest. "Hold up, that's my brother you're sexually objectifying."

"I was going to say hands." No, I wasn't.

She shook her head violently. "No you weren't! *Eww!*"

Jewel grinned. "Those Montgomery men are . . . blessed with natural talent."

"Well, yes, they're given so much to work with." She and I exchanged a high five and a giggle.

Jewel leaned in. "Nothing like a big, strong, take charge man who knows what he's doing!"

"Amen!" I agreed.

Katrina's horrified gaze cut from me to Jewellen

and back. "You two can see me, right? I haven't turned invisible."

"Our bad," Jewel teased. "But you have to know your brothers are fine."

"Nuff said. Fine I can live with." Katrina put her hand up. "But beyond that, please ladies. Now, Belle, what else?"

"Oh I'm just not sure . . ." I wasn't ready to make any sort of declarations.

Katrina frowned at me. "What?"

"Katrina, you know your brother."

"I am familiar with him, yes."

"I can't put all my eggs in the Beauregard basket, know what I'm saying?"

"*Hmmm.*" Jewel crossed her arms and sat back.

"Clarify." Katrina tilted her head to the side.

"What I mean is—how do I know I'm not just Beau's current flavor? Your brother has cut quite the swath through the female population. I've never seen any indication that he was a settle-down-forever kind of guy."

"Six months ago, I would have agreed with you. But Beau has come into his own lately. He's on some grown-man flow. He's focused, he's driven, he's dedicated, and I'm not just talking about at work. Believe me, if you were just one of Beau's rotating cuties, he would be hanging out at night and coming into work late, taking long lunches and basically disappearing at random times. If Beau doesn't give a damn, he doesn't give a damn. He doesn't keep up appearances or sugarcoat. He's authentic one way or the other."

I laughed. "You're saying if your brother was just playing—"

"He would be acting like a playboy. He's into you, Belle," Katrina assured me.

Jewel nodded. "I have to agree. I have seen Beau in playboy mode. This isn't that. I knew something was different when he brought you to Sunday dinner. He's never brought a woman to the family dinner."

"Oh, it was really more of a casual thing."

Katrina shook her head. "No, it wasn't. Beau acts casual, but he's not."

That made me happy and nervous all at the same time. "I hear you."

"Please do. If you're not all in, cut him loose. He acts like he's made of Teflon and as if nothing hurts him, but underneath all that pretty is a sensitive soul."

"Another Montgomery trait?" Jewel asked with a smile.

"Maybe, but it's definitely more pronounced in Beau. Roman holds it in and then blows up, sharing every thought and feeling until he's positive you've heard and understood him. Beau is the smiling, silent one. He's all swirling emotion and heart under the surface, behind that easy smile."

My heart hitched a little. "I know. Every now and again, there's this vulnerability that shows through. Just grabs you right there, you know? You wouldn't believe how great he was with my family. My father all but called him 'son.' "

"Well, then . . . you know I'm down for another sister-in-law."

"Amen again," Jewellen said, clinking her drink glass with Katrina's.

I hastened to set them straight. "Hold up ladies, we're still at early stages yet; you all have us marching down the aisle. Everybody just take a step back and give us some time."

"*Hmpfh.* You're not getting any younger," Katrina muttered.

"And those eggs don't stay fresh forever," Jewel said, trying to keep a straight face.

I sent both of them a side-eye and motioned for the waiter. "Can you bring a round of pear mojitos for the table, please? A few of us need to mellow out."

20

You Turnin' In Your Playa Card?

Beau—9:09 PM the same night

"Did your brother share with you that he is completely and totally whipped?" Carter asked Roman. My father walked back to the table at that moment with a pitcher of beer.

"My eldest? Whipped? *C'est inconcevable!*" Avery Senior set the pitcher in the center of the table and sat down in between me and Carter. We were relaxing at a table in a sports bar watching the NBA playoffs.

"It's not only possible, it's entirely true." Carter laughed and poured himself a mug.

I sighed. "I'm already regretting inviting you out to Montgomery Man Night."

"I like to think of myself as a Montgomery man

just through length of acquaintance and the fact that your mama loves me."

"She does love the boy." Pops nodded.

"God only knows why," I muttered.

Roman rolled his eyes. "So back to the whipped part? By who? How? And since when?"

"Gotta be that Belle; she was something special." Pops gave a sly grin.

I almost spit my beer across the table. "*M'excusez?*"

"*Hmpfh.* You're excused. I'm married, not dead, boy. I have eyes in my head; I'm gonna use 'em. That's a good-looking woman with a nice shape and some sense in her head. You might wanna lock that one down."

I exchanged a look with Roman. Pops was in rare form today. Roman smiled. "So, you and a former supermodel. I'm stunned."

"Don't start. It's not even like that."

"No?" He quirked a brow.

Carter said, "He chartered a jet to take her home when her father was in the hospital. And he went with her. And he stayed."

Pops whistled. "You met the family?"

"*Mais oui.*"

Roman's eyebrows went up. "That's different. Beau actually opening up his wallet?"

"I pay for things," I snapped, irritated at the inference.

"No one is calling you cheap," Carter explained, "but you are not one to make extravagant gestures."

"It wasn't an extravagant gesture," I countered.

"Son, you chartered a private plane to fly yourself and a woman you had known for less than a month eight hundred miles. I ain't one to put labels on things, but that spells sprung to me," Pops pointed out.

Roman and Carter roared with laughter. I had to smile. "Maybe it was a little over the top, but it got her attention." After that slip-up with Renee, I needed a grand gesture. That flight back had been worth every single damn penny.

"I see by that smile it must have been worth it," Carter said.

"You know a gentleman never kisses and tells. But I'd do it all over again."

"So what does this mean?" Roman asked. "We're a little past the point of using terms like *girlfriend.*"

"You boys are past the point of having girlfriends," Avery Senior said. "Well past time for the house to be running over with grandchildren. At least this one gotta wife and a son. You need to get on it, Beauregard."

"We're not there yet. Well, she's not there yet." I knew if I got the slightest sign from her that she was looking for a serious commitment from me, I was ready. Even if it gave me a little unease.

Carter slammed his glass down on the table. "Wait a damn minute! Are you talking about turnin' in your playa card?"

I considered it for a second. "Maybe so. Maybe so."

Roman smiled. "So this is the one, huh? She's it?"

"I think so, bro."

An attractive young woman walked up and tapped me on the shoulder. "Excuse me?"

I flashed a grin. "Yes?"

"My friends and I are wondering if you and your friends would like to join us for a drink?"

I didn't even turn to look at the table of friends she was referring to. "I'm sorry *petite fille*, not tonight. But tell your friends we appreciate the offer."

She nodded and walked away. I turned back to the table and found three sets of eyes staring at me with varying shades of disbelief. "What?" I asked defensively.

Roman exclaimed, "I've never seen you turn a good-looking woman down."

"Why did you speak for all of us? I'm not shackled up like you three," Carter complained.

Pops said, "I'm proud of you, Beauregard."

I shook my head. "You guys are killing me. I haven't been *that* bad, have I?"

"Man, don't get us started."

"Pontchartrain Poonhound sound familiar?"

"You've made some changes. Some of them just because it was time and others are directly from having this woman in your life. I like what I'm seeing." My father nodded as he spoke.

"Do we have to hug it out or can we just watch the game now?" I asked, feeling more than a little bit self-conscious.

Carter teased, "So we're in agreement on that whipped thing?"

"You wish you were whipped," Roman said. Pops and I toasted him for that one.

21

We Have a Problem

Belle—Thursday, May 26, 3:33 PM

Three weeks away from Dallas Fashion Week and we were ahead of the curve. The samples were gorgeous. Beau worked with a set designer and came up with the most awesome stage concept for the live runway show. The models were ready. The style-sheet shoot went off without a hitch. We managed to make a rooftop in Downtown Dallas look like a tropical resort and an urban club all in the same day.

I looked at the latest updates to the marketing plan, and I was pleased. Yazlyn's plans for the women's line were looking sound. Across the room, Beau stood towering a full foot taller than my finance director, Suzanne, who was in town from New York. She said she couldn't believe his grasp of forecasting and cost projections. Neither could I. Had you asked me what Beau knew about finance, I would have said, "His AMEX black card balance." Showed how much I really knew about the man. Seemed as though I kept underestimating him, and I had no idea what to think about that.

We had fooled absolutely no one with our "platonic in the workforce" attempt. The very day we walked in trying to act like nothing was different, my male receptionist called out, "Dude, you finally hit that? Thank God, maybe now we can get a coffee break around this place."

The whole office broke into applause and laughter. I just shrugged it off in the end. No one's attitude toward me changed because I was lying next to Beau at night. And yes, perhaps I was wound a little less tight now that I was "relaxing" after hours.

Overall, though—no complaints.

Before I could even bask in this contentment, my cell phone beeped insistently. I flipped it over to read the screen.

We have a problem, call ASAP!

The text was from Yazlyn. I punched in her number and put her on speakerphone.

"What's up?"

"Pull up your e-mail and check out the link I sent."

I opened the e-mail app on iPad and clicked through. The glossy Web site heralding Arizona Wind Designs opened up. The header read: Sneak Peek at New Spring Line. That page led to four designs that looked like very poor and cheap imitations of the BellaRich Man line.

"Irritating," I said and caught Beau's eye across the room. I waved him over. "But more importantly, troublesome. These aren't well done, but they are close enough to let me know she's seen either a sketch or a technical spec. Less than ten people, excluding the three of us and Katrina, have access to those. So where is she getting them from?"

Beau looked over my shoulder and raised a brow. "Not just copied but watered down. She's not using the same quality materials or paying attention to the details. It's the detail that sets ours apart."

I grinned. He was right. And I loved how proprietary he was over the work.

He glowered. "This does mean that you have a leak somewhere. We need to find it and plug it before she copies the entire campaign."

"We?" I teased him.

He shrugged. "Somebody."

"No you're right; we need to get ahead of this sooner rather than later."

Yazlyn piped up from the phone, "How do you want to handle it?"

"We could hire somebody to look into it. Maybe a corporate security specialist?" I suggested.

"Or . . ." Beau said with a sly expression.

"Or?" I could tell he had something already up his French-cuffed sleeve.

"We could set a trap," he announced dramatically.

Yazlyn squealed, "I like it! What do you have in mind?"

Beau had a twinkle in his eye. "Very cloak and

dagger. Let's walk into the conference room to talk about it."

We strolled toward the wall of windows at the rear of the floor where the conference room was located. Shutting the door behind us, we dialed Yazlyn back.

"Here's what I'm thinking," Beau said. "We generate eight new designs that we have no intention of producing and give one each to different people in the company, saying that these will replace a piece for the spring line. We tell each of them it's confidential and we're keeping it as a surprise."

I nodded. "And then we see which one ends up in Arizona's hands."

Yazlyn concurred. "That's perfect. And a little bit diabolical."

"Well, that's Beau for you."

He grinned. "You think I'm perfect, *chérie?*"

"Leave it to him to concentrate on the part he likes." Classic Beau.

Yazlyn laughed. "Oh there you two go with the banter bickering. Before you go full-scale flirty chatter, can we talk about banking?"

"What about banking?" I asked.

"Suzanne is going to bring it up with you later. We're not happy with the way our accounts and lines of credit are being handled right now. It's time for a more sophisticated banking scheme. If we continue to grow at this rate, we need a bank that backs us and gives us incentives to stay. Do you know anyone?"

I couldn't think of anyone.

Beau spoke up. "I know a guy. His name is Gregory Samson. He's a wealth investment manager that both my brother and sister-in-law have worked with. He also handles a few of my personal accounts—Katrina's too."

The name was familiar. "Why do I know that name?"

Beau slid a slow look my way. "Not sure; it may have come up before."

"Where did you meet him?"

"He's engaged to a friend of Jewellen's."

Suddenly it clicked. "Wait a minute, Renee's ex-fiancé? Dude you cuckolded at the dance? He manages some of your money?"

He shot me a look. "Do you want to discuss this right now?"

Yazlyn piped in. "Um—I'll let you two get into that. I'll get back to work while y'all decide whether you are going to draw daggers or make googly eyes at one another. Let me know what you want me to do to assist with the master plan. I fully expect you will have come up with a code name and a spreadsheet breaking down the plan by day's end."

"Hey, we're not that bad!" I protested.

"Yes. You both are. Two more perfectly suited personalities, I've never met. Later." With that, she hung up.

We stood there looking at each other.

"Perfectly suited?" Beau asked with a cock of his left brow.

"I don't know about that. We spend a lot of time bickering."

"I prefer to think of them as exploratory conversations."

The man had a way of putting a positive spin on things. "Nicely put."

"You know me."

"I'm not sure I do, but I'm working on it," I answered honestly.

Both of his brows rose. "Whoa! *Extrêmement intéressant.*"

"Extremely interesting?"

"*Mais oui.* You don't think you know me?"

"I know you, but I don't *know* you," I clarified.

"How sad is that I actually understand what you mean by that. So what do you need? The life story? The ex-fiancée? The childhood years? The world traveler days?"

I blinked. Did I know that he'd been engaged? "Wow. Now that you dangled those carrots out there, I kinda want to at least hear the high-level summary on a little bit of everything."

"And you'll reciprocate?"

"I've told you a lot."

"But I haven't heard about your ex-fiancé. Any of your exes, really."

"I wasn't sure you wanted to."

"*Vraiment?* Why?"

"You don't seem the sort of man to hear about the ones who have come before."

"Actually, I don't mind. I always assume I'm setting a new standard. What came before has nothing to do with me. I'm here now."

It was so quintessentially Beau that I flung my head back and laughed. "Of course you do. My bad."

"I don't like to sit around making lists and comparing numbers, but if there was someone who mattered to you, who changed the way you look at relationships now? Yes, I'd like to hear about that."

"Fair enough. We should do that sometime."
Not a conversation I was looking forward to.

"Let's make it a date."

I looked beyond him to see a woman walking into the offices. "Speaking of dates, here comes someone you're familiar with."

He looked over his shoulder. "*Merde!* What is she doing here?"

"I suspect she's meeting with Andrew about putting BellaRich together with Royal Mahogany for some sort of advertising campaign." I crossed my arms and leaned against the table.

"You're not meeting with her?" Beau shot me a look. We watched as she strolled on five-inch heels in a skintight safari dress to the reception desk.

"I opted to delegate. Something about her rubs me the wrong way. Unless you'd like me to spend time with her?" I didn't think that would go so well.

Beau answered prudently. "Whatever works for you, *ma douce.*"

Renee turned, spotted both of us across the room, and gave us a completely insincere five-finger wave. We gave her twin smiles that broadcast absolutely nothing. I paid close attention as her eyes scanned Beau from top to bottom, and I knew she was remembering the last time she saw him. I didn't like it at all. I worked extra hard to suppress the urge to step closer to him and somehow broadcast the fact that he was currently warming my bed.

Possessive much, Belle? I scolded myself quietly. Even if Beau and I hadn't defined our relationship, he had all but moved in with me. We were exclusive and I didn't want anyone thinking they could poach. I found myself wanting to stamp MINE on his forehead, just so she'd quit thinking she had a chance at a repeat performance any time soon.

And then, unbidden, came the curiosity. What was it like between her and him? Was it as explosive and intense as it was with us? Beau was a man who knew how to make love. It was a gift that he'd perfected over countless practice sessions. But he also had the ability to figure out exactly what a woman wanted or needed from him and give it to her.

My eyes narrowed in something akin to jealousy as I wondered exactly what he had given to her and how. Irrationally, I wanted to erase that experience with one of our own. And I wanted that right now. This minute. Mine.

"Mirabella?" Beau had stepped closer and spoke low into my ear.

"Hmm?" I flicked my eyes upward.

"Please recall that you specifically told me not to bend you over this table and have my way with you."

"I recall." My breathing quickened.

"*Mais oui*, the way you're looking at me right now and the way that pulse is fluttering at the base of your lovely neck is saying something altogether different."

"You're Mr. Restraint, remember?" I murmured.

His voice was a little hoarse. "I have my limits."

"These walls are glass," I said inanely.

"Too bad. I know you like it like that," he teased.

I closed my eyes and pulled it together. You simply could not bait Beau with things like this. He was sexually fearless. He would, given the slightest provocation, follow through on that conference table fantasy and not give one single damn who was watching. I might have a little kink in me but my freak flag didn't wave so high that I was willing to be taken in front of my staff and his ex-what-ever-she-was. I took a deep breath and a step back.

"So. Renee's ex-fiancé is your banker?"

"He's a good guy." He shot me a knowing look at my abrupt change of subject.

"Clearly. He forgave you but not her."

Beau gave an easy shrug. "I wasn't wearing his ring."

It made a twisted kind of sense. "True. Is it mean of me to want to schedule a meeting with him for the next time Renee comes in?"

"*Un peu.* Just a little bit." But he smiled as he said it.

At that moment, the conference door swung open and Renee stuck her head in. "Hey, you two, am I interrupting anything?"

"Just a meeting about finances. What's up, Renee?" I asked with stilted politeness.

"I just wanted a private word with Beau, if you have a second?" she asked with a gleam in her eye that I didn't care for at all.

I made to leave the room and Beau pulled me back before clasping my hand. "Belle stays. What can I do for you, Renee?"

"That's what I wanted to talk about," she said in a seductive tone.

"Apologies, *'tite fille*, I'm only available for professional and platonic liaisons, if you'd like to discuss one of those?" he said politely. He was so smooth with it you had to take a second to realize he had just turned her down.

Her brows arched high and her glance skittered between the two of us. "Oh it's like that now, huh?"

Neither of us answered for a moment. Beau reiterated, "It is indeed like that. What do you need?"

"Oh, I was hoping for something that it doesn't look like I'm going to get. Not any time soon anyway. I'll check back." She smiled slowly. "Belle, you are a lucky woman."

"*Hmm*," I answered noncommittally.

"Isn't he just wonderful in bed?" Renee cooed and took a step forward.

So tacky. The woman had zero couth. I contemplated tripping her just for the pleasure of watching her fall and decided I was being childish. "He's wonderful everywhere, sugar. Beauregard is extremely talented in so many areas."

Renee blinked twice as if it had never occurred to her that Beau was useful when clothed. I wanted to smack her for that alone. I met his gaze and noticed that he was part irritated, part embarrassed, part amused, and part resigned. Suddenly, I had some insight into what it was like to be Beau. And it wasn't the cakewalk I had previously assumed. I squeezed his hand. "Did you need something else, Renee?"

She studied us for a moment or two more before reaching some sort of conclusion. "I guess not. See you around, Beau."

"*Au revoir*, Renee."

She turned and tipped out of the room with one last backward assessing glance.

"Beau?" I probed in a thoughtful voice.

He brought our joined hands up to his mouth and kissed my knuckles. "Belle?"

"How often does that happen to you?"

"What, *ma douce*?"

"Women assuming you're an empty-headed easy lay."

I saw something shift in his eyes before he shrugged. "I've never played hard to get well."

"But you've never been stupid. Why do you let people think you're . . ."

"Cotton candy?" he asked and met my gaze.

Ouch. I had called him that. "I'm sorry, darlin'. Right after I said it, I felt bad. But you're not, you know. You're so much more than that. Why won't you let people see it?"

"Sometimes it's easier to just let people think what they want, *chérie*. And for many years it was easier to live down to others' expectations than to live up to my own."

"But not now."

"No, not now. The job, this work, you—you've reinvigorated me. I've found a passion for more than passion."

"And you're happy?" I wondered.

"*Oui ma petite*, I'm happy. Are you?"

I had to admit it. "You know, before Yazlyn called and Renee sashayed in, I was just thinking that I'm pretty pleased at the moment."

"Let's see what we can do to keep it that way."

"Yes, let's."

22

I Don't Run to Drama

Beau—Sunday, May 29, 1:11 PM

"Word on the yard is that I'm whipped," I told Belle as we strolled through the Nasher Sculpture Garden. We had gone to church earlier and then inside the Dallas Museum of Art checking out an exhibit of African masks. The day was sunny and pleasantly warm with a light breeze that kept it from being too humid outside. We stepped onto the back decks to look at the outdoor exhibits.

"Who said that?" She laughed lightly as we stopped to watch water cascading down a wall.

"Carter, Roman, my father of all people." My own father.

"Pops?" She snorted in surprise.

"He was quite amused with himself. He says I'm

different with you, that you bring out my better qualities."

"Have I really? I haven't been able to break you of your unnatural obsession with Lil Wayne's music."

"You have no room to talk with T.I. in constant rotation on your playlist, beautiful."

She rolled her eyes. "Whatever, Poonhound. You still rip my panties off at inopportune moments."

"You love it. I've heard zero complaints."

"Moving on . . . So do I?"

"Do you what?" Once we started talking about panties I forgot the rest of the conversation.

"Do I bring out the best in you?"

I turned to face her. "Truthfully?"

"Of course," she said earnestly.

"I was at a serious crossroads the night I met you. I had a shoe thrown at me by a woman whose name I still can't remember; I had been fired from my job and kicked out of my brother's house. I was, for all intents and purposes, homeless and jobless with nary a plan forward in sight. I'd like to think that I would've straightened out my act on my own. But meeting you and getting the opportunity to work with you and generally not wanting to let you down has helped me tighten up my game."

"You don't want to let me down?" She gave me an incredulous look.

I took her hand in mine and started walking again. "No *chérie*, I don't. I don't want to let you down."

"Is that what happened with your ex-fiancée?"

"Alexa?" I knew we'd have to get around to this walk down memory lane at some point. Apparently, that point was right now.

"Was that her name?" Curiosity sparked in Belle's eyes.

Heaving a sigh, I told the tale. "Her name was and is Alexa Little. We met on a shoot in Rome. She's British, beautiful, and a bit of a diva. I don't know if I let her down as much as I didn't care as much as I should have."

"Why did you ask her to marry you?"

"I thought it was time. We'd been seeing each other for a while, we got along well, and that's what I thought I was supposed to do," I honestly admitted.

Belle looked horrified at my answer.

"I know, Mirabella, I could've sugarcoated it for you, *chérie*, but I thought you deserved the unvarnished truth."

"I'll take a little varnish next time, if you don't mind."

I thought of the best way to say it. "I was very fond of her."

"Oh damn." She winced.

"I get now that there should have been far more intense emotions on my side. She wanted more, can't say I blame her, and she moved on. We've remained friends."

"So that's it. That's the big love-of-your-life story?"

Her response irritated me. "*Une seconde s'il vous plait*, I never said there was some great, sweeping, epic, love lost story. You wanted to know about Alexa. Now you know."

"I guess I was expecting more drama."

"*Chérie*, contrary to what you may think—I don't run to drama. Drama does at times, most unfortunately, run to me. But I have, in fact, spent quite a lot of my life avoiding it at all costs."

"Renee?" She slanted a glance my way.

I sat down at a small table and folded my arms across my chest. "Are you going to throw her up in my face every time you want to score a point?" Frankly, I was sick to death of the subject. I counted Renee as a mistake I made more than once out of sheer restlessness. But that was then and this is now. I couldn't undo it, and I sure as hell wasn't going to keep apologizing for it.

She sat down next to me. "Sorry. You're right, darlin', that's not fair. It just seems like you haven't shown the best judgment when it comes to women. Like maybe sometimes you were thinking with the little head and not the big one."

"What man hasn't? But really it depends on how you look at it. I never pursued a woman that didn't show interest in me first."

"Um . . ." She frowned.

I shot her a chiding glance. "C'mon now. You showed interest, Mirabella. We can pretend that you were a lamb led to slaughter but we both knew where this was headed from jump. I've never lied to a woman and told her the situation was any more than what it really was. Did I allow them to believe there were possibilities beyond what was real? Perhaps. Now, was I prolific in my enjoyment of the fairer sex? Yes. Was I sometimes too eager to move on after the initial physical hunger was slaked? Yes. But I'm always honest about it."

She absorbed my words for a minute and then tilted her head in consideration. "What you're saying is that it's different with me."

"I'm still here, *n'est-ce pas?*" To me it was simple. If I was with her, I was with her. If I wasn't, I'd be gone.

"You are here," she acknowledged with a smile. "But what about when the initial physical hunger is slaked?"

"Are you seriously worried about it?" I asked incredulously.

She shrugged. "Maybe I'm just another pretty face."

I laughed shortly. "Good thing I'm just as attracted to your mind then."

"Isn't that a slick answer?"

When she said things like that, I realized she wasn't 100 percent sure of my intentions toward her. There was still a part of her who wondered if it was all just a game. I wasn't 100 percent sure myself. The only way to find out was to stick around and show her. "Slick but true. One doesn't negate the other, *ma belle.*"

"You have a point," she conceded.

"I generally try to."

I loved our conversations, even when she was being deliberately challenging, which she tended to do from time to time. To me, our talks were just as stimulating and satisfying as our physical interactions. One fed the body, one nurtured the mind. Heavenly Father, I'd begun waxing poetic over this woman. Maybe I *was* whipped. But turnabout was fair play.

"What about you, Delaney Mirabella? Who's the man who made you decide that men are more trouble than they are worth?"

She looked startled and then she frowned. "Did I say that? I don't think I ever said that."

"Your actions said that. They all but screamed 'I don't have time for one of you trifling men to be making any moves.' "

She put her hand on my arm and howled with laughter. "Why, Beauregard, I should be upset that you can read me so well, but I'm tickled pink."

"*Fais attention*, Belle, your deep South is showing."

"Aw sugar, if you French it up every other sentence I can let a lil Georgia drip from my lips from time to time."

"Fair enough. So you want to get to sharing here or on the way to Sunday dinner?"

"On the way to Sunday dinner; let's go."

23

Well, and So That's That

I had to admit, I hated talking about past relationships. It was an uncomfortably reflective process, irksome, a reminder of failure, and often had very little impact on what you had going on currently. But Beau hated the "so what happened to you" conversation twenty times more than I did, and he had been unflinchingly candid.

"Katrina says we're making everybody sick with our sex vibe," I shared as I slid into Beau's car and buckled up.

"I'm not sure how I feel about *ma petite sœur* talking about our sex vibe."

"Worse, your sweet baby sister said we had a 'just got laid and laid well' vibe."

He sent a teasing look my way before sliding on his sunglasses and starting the car. "Maybe we should look less satisfied?"

"Ha! Let 'em hate."

He grinned and put the car into drive. We eased out into traffic and headed south.

Nothing left for me to do but tell the tale. "So I'll make it short and sweet. I met a guy. He was a model. His name was Lucas. We got together. I thought it would last forever. I wanted a picket fence, suburbia, the whole picture. My career went ballistic in a good way; his imploded in a bad way. He took to lounging around looking pretty and feeling sorry for himself. Which wouldn't have been too bad except for the fact that he was lounging around my apartment with other women, spending my money."

"How *déclassé*." Beau scowled.

I nodded curtly. "Quite tacky. Even worse, he tried to flip it around and make it seem like it was my fault he couldn't keep his pants zipped."

"And the money?"

"He would 'borrow' a credit card and run it up to its limit and forget to mention it until the bill came in."

Beau winced. "Go on."

"Apparently I forced him into this kind of behavior because I was too focused on my career and didn't give him the time and attention he needed."

"Did he mention that before or after he started doing random females in your bed?"

"Exactly. Nonetheless, I felt guilty for outshining him, I guess. I was young, and I felt bad that I was succeeding when he was failing."

"*Bébé*, you know there was nothing you could do about that. You shouldn't have to hide your light under some bushel for a man."

And that right there was what I adored about Beau. He was secure enough in himself to not only let me shine but also use an old-school phrase about lights and bushels. "I know, but I thought I loved him. And, like you, I thought it was time to get married."

He nodded in understanding.

"Anyway, when I broke it off, he turned a little nasty. I had to fight to get my keys back from him. Then he tried to blackmail me with some fake nude photos . . . it just soured me for a minute."

"Understandable. What was his name?" Beau's tone was deadly calm and even. Too calm.

I glanced over at him; his jaw was tight and behind the dark glasses his eyes had turned dark and stormy. "I'll tell you, if you promise not to hunt him down and beat him up."

"I'm a lover, not a fighter, *chérie*." He fashioned a grin that didn't match his eyes.

I snorted. "You forget I've seen you work out. You're a fighter too, sugar."

"I promise not to hunt him down and beat him up," he recited grimly.

"Lucas Turner."

His mouth turned down. "That dude?"

"Yes, that dude. I take it you know him?"

"*Un peu*, he's a selfish prick."

"Okay, you know him more than a little bit."

"We ran in similar circles for a short period of time. I didn't like the way he treated women; I told him, he took offense."

My eyes were wide. The world could be a surprisingly small place sometimes. "Reading between the lines, you're telling me that you've already kicked his ass."

"*Vraiment.* That I did." He looked more upset than the situation warranted.

"What's that look on your face about?"

"You don't think I'm him, right?" Clearly, the thought of that comparison had him agitated.

I have to admit when I first met Beau, I did think they were similar. Tall, pretty men who oozed sexuality and charisma, enjoyed women indiscriminately, and didn't take life seriously. But beyond the oozing sex and charm, Beau was nothing like Lucas. "I did in the beginning, before I really knew you—but now I don't. You're nothing like him and he's nothing like you and that's a good thing. Lucas cared about Lucas. You care about me."

"I do care, you know."

"I do know."

"Well, and so that's that."

"Pretty much."

"So I've restored your faith in men." He gave a smug grin.

A laugh bubbled up from my lips. "Well, I've definitely decided that you are worth the trouble."

"Whew! That's something at least." He wiped his hand across his brow.

"Very funny. So are we good. Enough trips down memory lane?"

"Please and thank you."

I leaned back in the seat. That wasn't as hard as I thought it was going to be. Then again, nothing with Beau ever was.

24

Delayed Gratification

Beau—Saturday, June 19, 7:18 PM

Belle walked out of her bathroom in a dress that stopped my heart, sent my blood rushing south, and emptied my head of coherent thought. It was a long, clingy, spaghetti-strap dress in the exact same tone as her skin but shot through with metallic strands, so it appeared that she was almost naked but for the gold streaks. Her makeup was gold and copper with smoky chocolate on her eyes and lips. She looked absolutely freaking amazing. Don't get me wrong—Delaney Mirabella was a beautiful woman. She looked good every single day without trying. But when she looked like this? You could see supermodel from every angle. She took my breath away.

"Woman, you must not want to leave this house tonight, looking like you look." I took a step toward her.

She put a hand up. "Hold onto that thought, playboy. I just got all this makeup on; don't bring all the sexy over here. Don't. Bring. It. Here."

"*Merde*! I already know I'm going to have to check some fool for eyeing you up."

She beamed at me. "Yes, cuz you're such a hag yourself." It had become a standing joke between us.

I was wearing one of her new BellaRich for Men suits in a slim-fitting linen and silk blend. It was a well-tailored suit in a dark tan color with a slight sheen to it. A honey-colored shirt went under it. "They say the clothes make the man."

"You know you're wearing the hell out of that. We'll take preorders tonight just based on all of this caramel sexy you've got going on." She waved her hands around. We were headed to the launch party for BellaRich for Men. It was being held on the penthouse floor of the Stoneleigh Hotel. Even though we weren't officially taking orders until after the show, we wanted to get the buzz going with pre-publicity. Preorders were always welcome.

"Back atcha. So let's go get this money, *chérie*."

She laughed and picked a tiny gold purse. "You crack me up. Urbane and suave one minute, rough and rowdy the next. You go from cultured to Cajun before I can blink my eyes. You're never boring, Mr. Montgomery."

"Guess you'll have to keep me around until you figure me out."

"Looks that way." Our eyes met for a suspended moment.

The tone was casual but there was an obvious undercurrent there. A discussion needed to happen but now wasn't the time or place to have it. I held out my hand and she stepped forward to clasp it tightly. We rode downstairs in companionable silence. When she went to walk across the parking garage, I tugged her hand to guide her in the opposite direction.

"We're riding this evening, *chérie*," I announced with a smile.

She looked at me questioningly. "What have you done?"

"The star of the show doesn't drive herself, *ma douce*." I escorted her toward a black Town Car limousine parked near the loading dock.

The driver swung the back door open. "Good evening, Mr. Montgomery, Ms. Richards. My name is Gary; it's my honor to drive you tonight."

"Thank you, Gary," she murmured and slid into the car. That's when I noticed the slit in the side of the dress.

I followed her into the car and, when Gary shut the door, I slid my hand along her silky thigh. "You are borrowing so much trouble right now, you know that?"

Her mouth curved upwards in a purely feminine way. "I thought you might like this dress. I also thought we'd try something different *ce soir*."

My pulse tripped in anticipation. I was always down for whatever. Something different tonight? I was all in. "Now you're speaking my language; what did you have in mind?"

"A lil something called delayed gratification, sugar." She let out a peal of laughter as my face fell. "Wait, listen. You know how we are: I say something, you give me a look, and next thing you know we're in the supply closet getting Post-it notes stuck in uncomfortable places."

"The Post-it notes weren't as bad as the paper clips." Those damned paper clips were sharper than they looked.

"We at least salvaged most of the paper clips."

"If you hadn't shifted like that near the end, we wouldn't have had to throw out that whole box. But to be fair, Mirabella, you issued a direct challenge, and you weren't wearing any panties." What was a man to do?

"I admit my culpability. I seem to have zero resistance to your many charms."

"It's a mutual obsession at this point," I conceded.

"So all I'm saying is . . . for one night— tonight, let's get through the evening with our drawers on."

"And without your lip prints on mine?" I teased in a quiet voice.

She closed her eyes for a second. "You had to bring that up? I bought you another three pair, darlin'. Who knew that peach color was so hard to rinse out?"

"They call it all-day lip stain for a reason, beautiful. If you had given me a minute to get them all the way off . . ."

She cut me off. "Like you do? We are quickly approaching the point of needing a lingerie expense account."

I shrugged. "I told you to order extra samples of those rose joints."

"What is it about those? You've ripped two pair already!" she scolded.

"Have you seen yourself in that getup?" She looked like walking sin.

"*Um*, no, sugar, you rend them in two and have them hanging from the ceiling fan before I get the chance to catch a glimpse."

"I did warn you." From the moment I'd seen that pink with the rose pattern, I'd lost my damned mind. I don't know why it affected me the way it did, but I'd given her fair warning. Come out wearing the fancy rose drawers and it was going to be on.

"So you did," she agreed.

"Sir, madam? We're pulling up to the venue," Gary called out from the front seat, his face and neck bright red.

"See now, *chérie*, you've embarrassed Gary."

She leaned forward with an apologetic smile. "I apologize, Gary. Hope we weren't too out of pocket with our indiscreet chatter."

"Not a problem, ma'am." Like what else was Gary going to say?

She turned back to me. "So do we have a deal?"

"Delayed gratification?" I ground out.

"Yes."

Whatever the lady wanted. "Deal."

She flashed a brilliant smile and squeezed my hand. "Thank you."

"Anything for you, Belle. *Je t'aime*." We both went still. I seriously had not meant to blurt out that I loved her as we were climbing out of the limo for one of the biggest nights of our professional life. I actually hadn't really even owned the feeling yet. But there it was. Couldn't take it back now . . . dammit, Beau.

"What . . . what does that mean?" she stuttered in a shaky voice.

I gave her one of my patented "no worries" smiles. "It's just a term of endearment. You ready to go? Your public awaits."

She looked into my eyes for a second and then looked outside to see light bulbs already flashing. "Okay." She nodded, the brilliant smile back in place. "Let's do this."

25

This Could Get Messy

Belle—7:32 PM that same night

I smiled and nodded and said all the appropriate things walking up the red carpeted entrance to the Stoneleigh. I fielded a few intrusive questions about the nature of Beau and my "collaboration"—yes, the reporter actually used air quotes.

I watched Beau charm the hell out of male and female reporters alike; why was I surprised? We climbed into the elevator to the penthouse with the buyer from Neiman Marcus and a photographer who was doing a spread for Italian *Vogue*.

When we entered the penthouse, the party was in full swing. We had screens up playing the flash presentations of the new designs. Drinks were being poured and the models were working the

rooms. Beau and I separated and I did a full cir-
cuit of hellos and chitchat before grabbing Katrina's arm and pulling her into the penthouse
bathroom.

She was wearing a Trés Belle tank dress in white
that only the very tall and very thin could pull off.
"Girl, what is it? I was chatting up the jewelry
buyer from Nordstrom."

"What does *Je t'aime* mean?"

Her eyes narrowed. "Why? Who said it and in
what context?"

"Katrina, just tell me!"

"Oh my God, did *Beau* say it? To you? In a non-
joking way?"

"Katrina!" I snapped impatiently.

"It means *I love you.*"

I exhaled slowly, doing nothing to calm the flut-
ters in my stomach. "I thought so. But then I
thought, maybe it's more casual like *I really like you*
or *I enjoy being naked with you.*"

Katrina shook her head vehemently. "Nope. It's
love." She shrieked. "Woo! What did you say
back?"

"Well, since he told me it was just a simple term
of endearment, I just said, 'Okay, let's go.' "

Katrina slammed her hands onto her hips and
glared at me. "You left my brother hanging with
the love thing in the air?"

"He didn't admit that it was the love thing," I
justified.

"Now that you know, what are you going to do?"

I pulled out my phone and opened the app for
French-to-English translation. I looked up a phrase
and smiled. "I'm good, sugar. I got this."

"What are you going to do?" she persisted.

I patted her on the shoulder. "Stay outta grown folks' business, Katrina. Get on out there and dazzle some buyers, will ya?"

She pursed her lips. "That's how it's going to be?"

"That's how it is." I freshened my lipstick, smirked, and zipped out of the bathroom. Walking down the stairs, I walked out onto the terrace. Beau was out there talking to our new banker.

"Hey, Greg, glad you could come out," I greeted him and leaned in to kiss his cheek. Gregory Samson was the buppiest brother I'd ever met, but he knew money. He knew how to keep it and make it multiply. He was cute in a preppy way, hovered around six feet tall, with the complexion of a Hershey's Kiss. I didn't need him to be cutting edge on fashion as long as he could help us grow the business. He was in a gray jacket and navy pants with a white shirt underneath. Basic, but he wore it well. On his arm was a tall, gorgeous, curvy woman with shoulder-length natural hair, olive-toned skin, and a beautiful, wide-mouthed smile. I extended a hand to her. "I'm Belle."

She ignored my hand and gave me a hug. "I know, honey. I've been a fan forever and ever. Now if you would just come out with some women's sizes, I'd be even more grateful. I'm Veronica." We stepped away from the men for a second.

"Well start sending gratitude my way, because all of the new line goes up to a size 24. What are you, a 16 or 18?"

She nodded. "Depends on the cut."

"I might have a thing or two for you to preview; swing by next week. Just be sure you mention me on your show." Veronica hosted a sexy nighttime radio show that was syndicated nationally. It was a blend of music and talk. She went by the name of Veronique.

She beamed. "I wasn't sure if you knew who I was."

"With your distinctive voice? I don't miss much, sugar; just like I am not missing that rock on your hand! Congratulations—when's the big day?" Veronica was sporting a canary yellow diamond that was no joke. That ring was so flawless that I had to look at Greg in a whole different light.

Her whole expression turned tender thinking about it. "September. We're just going to run off to the beach, lift a glass of champagne, and call it a wedding."

"Ni-ice. Do you have a dress yet?" I could already picture the perfect one in my mind.

Her eyes grew wide. "I don't . . . could you possibly . . ."

"I'm thinking jeweled straps, surplice bodice, very blinged out, and then it floats away in sheer layers to the ankle. In a champagne color."

"Ooooh, I want it!" she breathed.

I smiled. "You shall have it, and you'll look incredible."

"She always does," Greg said, stepping over to put his arm around her.

I couldn't resist teasing him. "I must say Greg, having this lovely lady on your arm has upped your cool factor significantly."

"That's why I keep her around," he joked.

Veronica jabbed him in the ribs. "Boy, I'm the best thing that ever happened to you."

Beau laughed. "She definitely has your number, Samson."

"Who picked out the ring?" I wondered.

Greg inclined his head. "You can say that my taste is impeccable, go ahead."

We all laughed.

A voice from behind us interrupted. "Well, isn't this an interesting group. Nothing like running into my exes."

As one we turned to see Renee standing at the entrance to the deck with a snarky pinched expression around her face. I squelched a sigh. I hated drama, but I had the feeling that Renee dined on it.

Did I mention that I really didn't like this woman? Beau slid beside me and we linked fingers.

"*Bonsoir*, Renee," Beau murmured.

"Ray," Greg said, acknowledging her presence while keeping his arm around Veronica.

"Greggy, you look well. Roni Mae, I guess picking up my sloppy seconds is working out for you." Renee was instigating in a sing-songy voice. Slapworthy.

"No one really calls me Roni Mae anymore, but it always took you a second to catch up with reality. Yes, I would say life is rather sweet for me right now, Nay Nay." Veronica lifted her hand to push her hair behind her ear and that ring caught the light. Renee's eyes went straight to it. Renee's face turned hard and her eyes narrowed. She was not pleased by the ring or the nickname.

Oh. Ouch. This could get messy. I didn't need the publicity that a scene would generate. I decided to try and defuse the situation before it turned ugly. Uglier, rather.

"Not that it's not great to see you, Renee, but

what brings you to the party?" It was invitation-only, and I knew damned well she wasn't on the guest list.

"I came with a friend. He has a fashion blog. Here he is now." A slim Hispanic male wearing a pink plaid jacket over a white polo shirt and white skinny jeans approached us. She laced her arm through his. "This is Ricardo. Ricardo, this is the designer, Belle Richards."

Ricardo was making a name for himself as a popular blogger who went behind the scenes to get in-depth interviews with the hottest designers. He had actually been invited. I was more than a little stunned to see Renee as his plus one. For a number of reasons.

I shook his hand. "So pleased you could attend. This is—"

"Beau Montgomery," Ricardo reverently announced. "I remember you from that cologne ad when you wore the blue Speedo on the rocks in Greece."

Beau grinned and gave Ricardo what I called the full Cajun twinkle. "*C'est très aimable à vous.* I always enjoy meeting a fan. That was a flattering photo, for sure."

Ricardo looked as though he would pass out. "Are you still modeling—is that how you met Belle?"

"Actually, we met through my sister. I'm the creative director for BellaRich Men," Beau explained.

"How marvelous! Is this one of the designs you're wearing?" Ricardo ran his hand down Beau's arm.

Beau leaned in closer. "It is *très magnifique,* no?"

"I love it!" Ricardo gushed.

"*Merci,* maybe you can give us a shout-out on your wonderful blog?" Beau produced a business card seemingly out of thin air and handed it to Ricardo. I knew for a fact that Beau had never heard of this kid or his blog, but he made that sound smooth as silk.

"I'd be honored; can we take some photos?" He pulled a small digital camera out of his pocket and handed it to Renee. Then he slid in between me and Beau.

"Why not?" Beau exchanged an amused glance with me as we posed beside Ricardo.

"This is such a thrill for me, you don't even know. You look great, too, Ms. Richards." Renee took several pictures before handing the camera back to Ricardo.

"Thanks, darlin'," I said, struggling to keep my model smile in place and not dissolve into giggles. Upstaged by my man at my own launch party. Typical Beauregard.

"We don't want to take up any more of your time. Thanks for the invite. Beau, I'll be calling!" He grabbed Renee and practically bounced away.

We stood in silence for a moment after they left.

"Do you think she knows he's gay?" Veronica queried.

"Yes," Greg and Beau answered simultaneously. Then they exchanged glances.

This caused me and Veronica to exchange glances. She didn't like their shared history any more than I did.

I had no idea what Renee was up to. "Good for him and all that, but do you think she thought she could pass him off as not gay for some reason?"

"Who knows why Renee does what she does," Beau sighed.

"I doubt she even knows," Greg agreed.

There was something that had been bugging me for a while about the entire Renee story. Finally, I had to ask. "May I ask you two something?"

"*Mais oui, chérie,*" Beau responded as Greg nodded.

I clarified. "Well, two somethings. First, what did you ever see in her? Besides the obvious."

Greg shifted uncomfortably. Beau raised and lowered a shoulder. "I'll admit to getting stuck on the obvious."

Veronica said, "She wasn't always this bad. She actually was one of my best friends. But where before she was a little self-centered and snarky, now she's completely self-absorbed and bitchy. It's not pretty. But when she first met Greg, she was a softer person and her flaws were more . . . redeemable."

I understood. "My second question, how is it that the two of you are friends after . . . you know?"

"You mean after I caught Beau in a compromising position with the woman I thought I was going to marry?" Greg asked.

"Well . . . yeah."

Greg explained. "It occurred to me that if it wasn't Beau it would have been someone else. Renee is a woman never satisfied with what she has. She always thinks there is something better just around the corner. So, in retrospect, he did me a huge favor."

I had never thought of it like that. That whole

things happen for a reason ideology was probably the best way to look at it.

Beau added, "Plus, I apologized by bringing in a few large accounts for Greg to manage."

"I accepted his apology." They chuckled.

"So all's well that ends well," I concluded.

"Always been my philosophy," Beau stated.

"That doesn't surprise me." I sent him a look.

He tugged at my hand. "C'mon woman, we have a party to work. Clothes to sell. People to dazzle."

I waved to Greg and Veronica as we walked away. "Veronica, call me!"

"Don't think I won't!" she called off with a rolling laugh.

We walked back inside the main room. Renee was nowhere to be found. I had to admit, that was okay by me. We mingled for another two hours or so before the party started winding down. Yazlyn came over in all her glory in a tight red mini-dress and heels that put her well over six feet tall, not counting the towering curly Afro.

"We rock," she announced as she handed me and Beau glasses of champagne.

"Yes, we do. What specifically for this time?" I asked with a smile.

"The preorder app that Beau dreamed up— huge hit." Beau had suggested that beside each of the large displays we mount a touch screen where buyers could click a button to inquire about ordering the item they saw. "The hottest items are the clothes you two are wearing right now. I'm thinking the two of you will need to revisit the cat-walk at the Dallas show."

I looked at Beau. "What do you think?"

"I like life off the runway just fine."

"Me too." I did not miss my catwalk days at all.

"But I'm game if you are. Whatever it takes." He smiled down at me.

When Beau said things like that, wholeheartedly supporting me without a thought, I knew exactly how I felt about him. He needed to know, too. I pulled out my phone and sent a quick text message. He gave me a curious *what is this* look as his phone vibrated in his jacket pocket. I held my breath as Beau retrieved his phone and read the message: *Je t'aime aussi.* French for *I love you, too.* He looked at me with a strange expression on his face. It was a cross between bewilderment and joy. Then his eyes heated to that laser intensity as he tucked the phone back in his pocket.

He turned to Yazlyn. "See you later, Yaz." The next thing I knew, he took my hand in his and hustled me toward the exit. He literally growled at me as we trotted along. "Here or your house?"

"Beau . . ." So much for that delayed gratification.

"Here. Or. Your. House?" He was not playing. The look on his face told me I had a very narrow window to answer him or he was taking matters into his own hands. Just thinking of those hands had me liquid and heated.

"My house."

"*Bien.*"

Maybe I should have been embarrassed as we hurried past the last of the party attendees, including his brother and sister, with barely a wave . . . but I wasn't. I wanted to get behind closed doors with the man I'd fallen in love with and celebrate the night.

We were in the back of the limousine in the blink of an eye. Deliberately, we sat apart and did not touch. I crossed one leg over the other and Beau sent me a look. "Fifteen minutes. Wait."

I nodded, trying to gather my emotions and composure and failing miserably.

"So did you mean it?" His voice was soft, his eyes intent.

"The text?"

"Yes."

"I meant it. Did you?"

"I did. I do," he answered sincerely.

"Then, why did you try and take it back?"

"I wasn't sure you wanted to hear it or even if I was ready to say it. I've never said it to anyone who wasn't related to me and biologically required to reciprocate." He gave a wry grin.

"No one?" That surprised me.

"Not a soul," he adamantly confirmed.

"Not even your ex-fiancée?"

"Not even her."

"Wow." Our eyes met. "I need to thank you for those words then. With repeated enthusiasm." I uncrossed my legs and recrossed them in his direction.

He wrapped his hand around my ankle and lifted my leg onto his thigh. He stroked a hand along my calf. "Wasn't delayed gratification your idea?"

I shifted on the leather seat. "It seems like a silly one right about now."

"So impatient," he teased.

"I know what I want."

"I plan to give it to you."

"Promise?" I shot a sultry look his way.

"Have I failed you yet?" His hand crept up past my knee to draw lazy circles along my thigh.

I shuddered. "Not once, no."

"I don't ever intend to," he answered gravely.

That was quite a promise. "Not ever?"

"Not if I can help it."

It was the sexiest thing anyone had ever said to me. "See now, that makes me hot."

"You make *me* hot. I'm trying not to rip your clothes off right now," he muttered, casting a look at the stoic limo driver.

I wished he would move that hand just a little higher. "There we go embarrassing Gary again."

"It could be worse for him," Beau said.

"Right—he could be Samantha, the smiling flight attendant."

With a laugh, he recalled the flight. "Her face when we walked out of that tiny bedroom."

"Maybe if you'd put your shirt on first. I don't know if the sight of your bare chest or the knowledge of what we'd been up to flustered her more."

"Ah well, these things sometimes happen."

"Around you? Yes, they do. Frequently."

He squeezed my thigh and put my foot back on the floor. "Five minutes and we'll be home."

I smiled. It was the first time he'd called my place home.

26

Are You Done Playing?

"**A**re you ready for this, sugar?" Belle's sultry Southern drawl teased as she slithered into position over me.

"Woman, quit playing," I ground out between gritted teeth.

In the months that Belle and I had been together, I'd taken control in the bedroom. But on this night, she demanded to have her way with me. I acquiesced, and have her way she did. She teased and touched and tantalized until I was hanging on with the barest thread of restraint.

I held back when she performed a striptease that almost sent me to my knees in supplication. When she dropped to her knees instead and took me in her mouth, I called on all the saints to preserve me. She pushed me onto my back and made it her mission to explore every nook and cranny on my body, paying special attention when I drew in a quick breath, broke out in a sweat, or swallowed a groan.

At long last, she slid a condom on me and then settled her moist warmth on top me and rocked back and forth without letting me inside. "Belle."

"*Hmm?*" She licked the side of my neck.

"Are you done?" I arched my hips up and let my hardness slide through her moistness, making sure to hit that tiny pleasure nubbin with my tip before settling back near her entrance.

Her eyes drifted shut and her head fell back. "Am I done doing what?"

I repeated the action once and then twice. "Are you done playing?" I twisted my hips away when she tried to take me inside.

"Beau," she groaned.

"Yes, beautiful?"

"Help me."

"*Mais oui, cherie.*" I grasped her hips in my hands and guided her onto my shaft. With an upward thrust, I fit myself inside her as deeply as I could.

"Dear God, that just gets better." Her walls gripped me. We fit. I was home.

"It really does. Now go, baby, take us there."

She sat up and pulled her thighs in close and then began to ride. Slowly at first with a slight swivel on each downstroke. I drove up to meet each stroke. Her head came down and our eyes met. I watched as a myriad of emotions rolled across her expressive face, I caught my breath as the passion turned into so much more. "Beau . . ."

"I know, *mon coeur*. I know." It was almost too intense. I was literally shaking as I rolled her underneath me. It had never felt quite like this before. Not with anyone. Her legs automatically came up to circle my waist, and I slid back in to the hilt.

It was a dance, a slow, steamy dance where hard met soft, tongues met skin, and eyes stayed locked on each other. I sunk into her with a gradual roll of my hips, loving the heat and grip of her before easing out to repeat the motion again. As I watched, tears welled up in her eyes and spilled over. My breath caught in my throat and I leaned in to kiss each tear away.

"I didn't know. I didn't know it could be like this with you," she whispered.

I was so humbled to have her. Humbled to have her love me and share her life with me. Before I knew it, tears were in my eyes as well. "You know I love you, right?"

She nodded and wiped my cheeks as we rolled onto our sides. We wiggled and rolled against each other exploring different angles. We sped up the pace and then slowed it down in an attempt to draw out the transcendent experience.

"Now. Please," Belle whispered in my ear, and I knew exactly what she wanted.

Rolling again until I was on top, I rearranged her so her ankles were over my shoulders. She started moaning just at the shift in position. I smiled; my baby liked it like that. "It's gonna be quick and hard."

She shuddered. "Do it."

I grabbed her ass in my hands and went in hard and fast with a flurry of thrusts. She went orgasmic immediately. I loved that about her. She squirmed against me.

"Just a lil bit more," she pleaded.

"*Avec plaisir.*" It was my pleasure, within moments I felt the most monstrous climax of my life building up. "*Mon Dieu*," I prayed as I lost all semblance of control. My hips began moving in a rhythm foreign to me. My hands clenched and unclenched on Belle. She literally keened with pleasure as I swelled within her. Finally with a roar, I erupted inside of her. The feeling went on and on, her feminine flesh spasming and milking everything I had to give.

I shuddered against her, trying to take in breath and not crush her with my weight. Finally, I stood and stumbled to the bathroom to dispose of the condom before sinking bonelessly beside her on the bed. I brushed a kiss across her shoulder. "Woman, what the hell was that?"

She smiled dreamily and snuggled close while her breathing returned to normal. "That, Mr. Montgomery, was making love. The real deal."

"It almost killed me."

"I've no doubt of your ability to recover, darlin'."

So that was making love? I liked it. I wanted more of it. And I wanted it forever.

27

You Hold On To That

Belle—Sunday, June 20, 12:54 PM

It was Father's Day, and I couldn't reach my father on the telephone. The only reason I wasn't worried was that one of my brothers or sisters would have called me if something was wrong. I would try to catch him before going over to Beau's parents' house for dinner.

Pulling up to the address in Preston Hollow that Beau had texted me, I stared in confusion and a little wonder at a gorgeous Italian-villa style home. He had hopped out of bed this morning as if the devil was chasing him and then sent this cryptic text:

Meet me here at 1:00 pm.

Truthfully, I assumed that the crying/emotional/ orgasmic sexfest from the night before freaked him out. Hell, it freaked me out. We had always had an amazing chemistry that manifested itself into explosive passion, but what happened last night was beyond biology and into spirituality. It seemed like just declaring our love took us to a whole other level overnight.

To be perfectly honest, I kept waiting for the Beauregard freak-out. A guy like that who hadn't had to commit to anybody or anything in thirty-eight years? I still wondered if it was just a matter of time before he decided this was all a lark and took off to Monte Carlo with a Brazilian lingerie model.

Yes, I believed he loved me, but I wasn't sure he was built for that long-term happily ever after. That damn charming Cajun had snuck in under my defenses and made me fall for him. So I was in it, come what may. With a sigh, I climbed out of my car and flung my purse over my shoulder.

I walked up a charming slate walkway and admired the landscaping. Whoever owned this home lived in a lovely setting. As I approached the front door, I was startled to see my father standing in the doorway. I ran forward to greet him.

"Dad! Happy Father's Day, what are you doing here? I thought you said you were staying in Atlanta?"

"Well, Baby Girl, your man invited me on out here, so I decided I better come on out."

"But what are you doing here?" Now I was seriously confused but happy to see him.

"Come in and find out." Percy grinned at me like a child with a secret they are dying to tell.

I walked into a grand foyer with marble tile and stucco walls. It was two stories high with a cupola in the center. To the far left was a wide, curving staircase; the rest of the foyer opened into a huge great room. At the end of the great room was a tall wall of windows looking out onto a shaded patio and a pool beyond.

Stepping down into the great room, I saw Beau lounging against a long granite bar. The look on his face said he had something up his sleeve. "Beauregard."

"Mirabella. Welcome."

We met in the middle of the room and exchanged a light kiss. "Did you wake up early to steal a house?"

"Actually, I bought this house about three months ago. Right around the time someone called me 'cotton candy.' I've been working on it a little at a time. There's still a lot of furniture and finishes to add but there's all the time in the world for that."

I was stunned speechless and pivoted in a circle to take in the majesty of the house once again. My father was cheesing from ear-to-ear. "I'm . . . I'm confused. You're moving out of the loft?"

He nodded. "I am moving out of the loft and into here. Care to join me?"

I looked from my father to him and back again. "*Ummm . . .*" I know he didn't just invite me to shack up with him in front of my Southern old-school father.

Beau got down on one knee. What in the entire hell was he doing? My heart stopped when he pulled a ring box out from behind his back. "Delaney Mirabella Richards, I love you and respect you. You are the best person I know. Will you do me the grandest honor of becoming my wife?"

"What? Are you serious?" He opened the box to reveal a cushion-cut chocolate diamond surrounded by clear round baguettes. It was breathtaking.

My father sucked his teeth. "This girl slower than molasses all of a sudden. Of course, he's serious. Do you think he would have flown me in here on Father's Day and asked for my blessing for a laugh?"

I had no idea what to say. But even I knew when the word *yes!* didn't immediately spring to my lips that there was a problem. "I just . . . wow. I did not see this coming."

Beau's face changed from warm and open to guarded and curious. "*Chérie*, you're kinda leaving me hanging here."

I blurted the first thing that came into my mind. "But you're not the marrying kind!"

Instantly I knew it was the worst thing I could've said. He got up and closed the box. "Apparently, I am. Apparently I'm not the kind that *you* want to marry. *Pas de problème*, we won't speak of it again. Apologies for overstepping."

I could feel him retreating into himself with every word. I reached out and grabbed his hand. The one with the ring box in it. "Wait a minute, wait a minute. Just give me a second here. You sprung this"—I gestured toward the house, my father, and the ring—"on me all at once. I just need a minute to take it all in. Do you think this is kind of fast?"

"I'm thirty-eight years old, Mirabella. I know what I want when I see it. And it's all right here in front of me. I thought you felt the same way about me."

"I do, but I just need some time. I'm not saying no, I'm just saying not right now. I want you to be sure."

My father spoke up from the corner. "I'm going to step outside and enjoy this fine weather we're having for a moment." He cut his eyes at me as he walked past, clearly broadcasting his disapproval of my answer.

The minute the door closed behind him, Beau started talking rapidly. "If you're not sure of me, say that but don't presume to know what I want and what I'm ready for. The long and short of it is that you think I'm still that guy. That guy who is looking for the next adventure and the next pretty face. *Je préfère plutôt mourir que* hurt you like that. That means I would rather die than let you down. Do you understand me? Do you hear what I'm saying to you?"

"I think you're moving too fast." I knew he was moving too fast. We hadn't even known each other for six months. We hadn't had a major fight, we hadn't slept apart, and we hadn't been battle tested. Marriage was something I only planned to do once. Right and forever.

His eyes were piercing in their intensity as he spoke passionately. "I think you're underestimating me. Again. I'm not a boy. I'm a man with experience and life lessons under my belt. If I say you're what I want, you're what I want. Did you hear me when I told you I'd never said the words *I love you* to another woman?"

"I heard you, Beau. I hear you."

"*Bon*, then this is about you. Don't try to say you're giving me more time. I don't need it. This is about you being unsure about me."

He looked so hurt in that moment that I wondered if I should just put aside my misgivings and say yes. But the damage was already done. "Beau, I do love you, and I believe you love me. But I think we both owe it to ourselves to take our time and make absolutely sure this is our next step. How do you know your feelings won't change tomorrow?"

He nodded once in a jerky, stilted manner. "And there it is." He handed me the ring and pulled his keys out of his pocket. "You hold on to that. Can you take Percy over to Pops' house? They wanted to meet."

His quiet tone scared me. "Where are you going?"

"I'm just going to drive around a while. Clear my head. I'll be by in a lil while."

I reached out to grab his hand and pull him toward me. "We're okay, right?" Now that was a stupid question. Clearly, we were not okay.

He fashioned a smile that didn't reach his eyes and was tinged with sadness. "*Mais oui*, we're fine."

I wrapped my arms around him and hugged him tight. I didn't want to lose him; I just wanted to be sure. After a short pause, he hugged me back.

"Please understand," I whispered.

"Please believe in me," he implored.

"I do," I assured him and squeezed him tighter.

He pulled away, and from the shuttered look in his eyes, I could tell it was more than a physical withdrawal. His voice was wistful. "Your words tell me that, your actions? Not so much."

"Beau." I wanted to talk some more, make sure he understood. I wanted to say something, anything, to make it right. But I wasn't sure I could.

He stepped out of my embrace. "I'll see you later."

"Promise?"

He smiled that sad little smile again, turned, and walked out the back door.

28

You're a Good Man, Beau Montgomery

Beau—8:12 PM that same night

I sat alone and in the dark on the one piece of furniture in the living room of my new home. Well, not exactly alone. I had a crystal tumbler, an ice bucket, and an opened bottle of Patrón Reposado to keep me company. Nothing like premium tequila to cure what ails you. Or at least make you forget what ails you for a little while. I needed a few glasses full of forget. My cell phone was turned off and flipped screen side down next to the ice.

This day had not gone like I had planned at all. In fact, I'd have to put it up near the top of Beau's Suckiest Days Ever list.

I'd done everything right this time, hadn't I? I picked a woman I actually loved who said she loved me back. I had a plan for the future. I bought a house. I worked my ass off. I got the ring, asked her father's blessing, even flew him in from Georgia, for Christ's sake. And what did it net me?

I looked around the house with no little bit of irritation. I topped off my glass and sat back with a sigh. I imagined that Father's Day dinner at Pops' house was a doozy. They had been expecting a newly engaged couple and instead got the woman who turned me down and her father. I just couldn't go. I couldn't do it. I didn't want to have to make explanations or play like it was all okay.

Because it really wasn't. As a matter of fact, it totally wasn't. It was so far away from okay that Belle hadn't slid that ring on her finger and said, "Yes, of course I'll marry you!" while jumping into my arms, raining kisses on my face, grateful and happy for the chance to become Mrs. Beau Montgomery.

But she hadn't. And here I was working up a good mad and trying hard to get my drunk on. The patio door opened and in walked Percy Richards with Katrina. I looked down at the drink and blinked. Maybe I'd had enough.

I stood up. "Kit-Kat? Sir?"

He walked over to the sofa, put his hand on my shoulder, and sat me back down. He sat next to me. "Boy, that was a damn fool thing my daughter did today."

"Well, uh . . ." I was in the difficult position of not being able to agree without insulting his daughter but not wanting to disagree either.

"The statement was rhetorical, son. It required no answer."

"Yes, sir." Katrina took the tequila out of my hand and replaced it with bottled water.

"But if she says she needs time, you have to give it to her and forgive her this bit of foolishness," Percy continued.

"Yes, sir."

"I like you, Beauregard. I like you for my daughter. It shows me something that you bought this grand house and that fancy ring and sent for me."

Too bad his daughter didn't seem as wowed. Again, I kept my thoughts to myself.

"And you have a mighty fine family. I enjoyed breaking bread with them this evening."

"Thank you, sir. I'm sorry I missed dinner." I did feel a little bad about not going.

"Well, I figured you looked to get a little of your own back by leaving Belle to make those explanations on her own." Percy slid a sly grin my way.

I actually hadn't even thought about it. I just didn't want to go. So I didn't go.

Percy continued. "Your lovely sister offered to bring me back around to say my piece. You're not going to give up on my girl, are you?"

"No sir." Honestly, I'd been thinking of doing exactly that.

"I raised that girl, son. I know she can stretch the patience of Job."

"I'm not Job."

"Few of us are, Beau. Few of us are. But don't get discouraged. You two smart, pretty people found each other, and you fit somehow. Don't let that go."

I didn't know what I was going to do so I answered in a neutral tone. "Okay, sir. I appreciate that."

"All right, then. The offer to stay here still stands?"

"Of course, sir." Who was I to question why he wasn't staying with his daughter? I certainly wasn't going to put the man in the street because his daughter trampled all over my feelings.

"Well, then, I'll just head on into that nice room you showed me earlier and let the TV watch me for a spell." He stood up and patted my shoulder again. "You're a good man, Beau Montgomery."

"Thank you, sir."

Katrina handed him a bottle of water and walked him toward the downstairs master bedroom. "You know now, Percy, if you decide you're in the market for a younger woman . . ."

He gave a deep belly chuckle. "Little girl, you are a mess. What would you want with an old man like me?"

"They say age brings wisdom, and I reckon you still have some wind in your sails."

He laughed so hard, he had to stop walking for a moment. "You just made my month. If you weren't my daughter's age, and I wasn't afraid Avery would get the shotgun out, I'd have to teach you a thing or two, young lady."

"I bet you could. Good night, Percy."

"Have a good night, sir," I called out from the couch.

"Good night, Montgomerys. You are an entertaining lot, that's for sure." He closed the door behind him, still chuckling and shaking his head. I set down the water bottle and picked back up the tequila.

Katrina walked back and sat down in the space Percy had vacated. "You all right, *mon frère?*"

"Never been better." I saluted her with the glass.

"Now Beau . . ."

"Now what? Katrina, she said no. To me. Beau Montgomery. She actually said no." I was tempted to pout. I settled for a scowl.

"She said not now."

"If it's not a *yes*, it's a *no*," I snapped.

"That's kind of black and white, don't you think?"

I shrugged. "How bad was dinner?"

"Actually, it wasn't so bad. When Belle and her father walked in without you, we all knew something hadn't gone as planned. So we just dropped it. Scraped *congratulations* off the top of the cake and kept it moving. You won't be surprised to know that Avery and Percy got on like a house of fire."

I smiled imagining the two of them together. "That doesn't surprise me at all."

"Belle spent the whole time watching the door, checking her watch, and calling your cell phone."

"*Hmm.*" Did I mention that the woman said no . . . to me?

Katrina nudged me. "Don't shut her out, Beau.

She loves you. She just needs *une momente* to turn the corner."

"*Apparement.* I'm not going to shut her out, but I'd be lying if I said I wasn't a little angry."

"Only a little?"

"Maybe a lot," I acknowledged.

"Any chance that's your ego talking?"

"Maybe *un peu*, but I keep coming back around to the fact that if she loved me enough or trusted me enough, she would've said yes." That was the crux of it. No getting around it.

Katrina took the tequila glass away and set it on the coffee table. Then she pulled me over and cradled me in her arms. "You were always a good man, Beau. Perhaps just a little too pretty and spoiled for your own good. Things came easy to you. Maybe it's best that you work a little harder for forever, you know?"

I blinked up at her with a disgusted snarl. "Seriously, Kit-Kat? This is my karmic boomerang, then? For all the ladies I loved and left?"

She rolled her eyes. "So overdramatic! She hasn't left you and if you play your cards right, you'll win in the end. You're a better man now than you were three months ago, and you'll be a better one still in six. Just don't do anything stupid, Beau. *Tu m'entends?*"

"I hear you. Stupid like what?"

"I don't know . . . like fall naked on some skank just to feel better about yourself?"

"Oh, stupid like that. That's the old Beau."

"It better be. Don't blow this over some bruised feelings." She kissed my forehead. "I don't want to disappoint that charming older man in there. And for some crazy reason he has his heart set on you as his son-in-law."

"Speaking of which, what were you doing flirting with him? He's over sixty years old, Katrina!"

"Just because you and Roman are all about your love thing, don't ruin my fun. I'm not ready to settle down and be Mrs. Anybody yet."

"Please tell me you're joking." I looked at her with dismay.

"About making a move on Percy, yes. That was just harmless teasing. About Katrina funtime? No sir. As soon as we wrap Dallas Fashion Week, I'm outta here. Kit-Kat needs a spa vacation where I can find a buff masseur with magic hands, narrow hips, and loose morals."

"*Ugh!* TMI, lil sister." I had to smile at her audacity.

"But I made you smile, didn't I?"

She had. Something I would not have thought possible mere moments ago.

29

Is It Me, or Is It Gettin' Hot in Here?

Belle—Monday, June 21, 11:48 AM

I used to make my living standing in front of the camera emoting whatever feeling was necessary on my face and through my eyes. But it took every ounce of acting skill I possessed to remain cool and calm in front of the cameras today.

I had a fashion show starting in close to ten minutes. We had rented the empty warehouse space across the street from my office to put on the show. It had been completely transformed with lights, fabrics, furniture, and props to resemble an upscale theater where the middle aisle was a runway. I was both elated and terrified to see that the place was packed. Standing room only at this point.

The Style Channel was filming a "Behind the Scenes" segment, reporters and journalists wanted to squeeze in one last question, and my father was standing in between Beau and Katrina taking in the chaos.

Speaking of Beau . . . well, I wish I could. Beyond the brief "Hey, let's go get 'em" that he'd murmured as he strode past, he hadn't said two words to me since yesterday. And yes, I was more than a little tart that my father had chosen to stay with him rather than me. I mean, c'mon now, really? Percy was too much. He announced on his Facebook page that I was a "damned fool child" and posted pictures of his room in Beau's house. I guess I knew where his allegiance stood.

Someone thrust a microphone in my face as a camera swung toward me. "Ms. Richards, can you give us a hint about the theme for the show?"

I turned my smile up to full wattage and leaned into the microphone. "You'll just have to wait and see. But I promise it will be worth the wait."

"Five minutes, everyone to their places. Final model check! Regina, are you ready?" Sergio, our show producer, snapped at the announcer and circled briskly backstage barking into his headset and physically moving people into place.

My father went to sit out front next to Mr. and Mrs. Montgomery. Katrina was in a business suit from the Trés Belle collection waiting for her cue. Beau stood with his arms crossed staring at the monitor that panned the crowd and showed the stage. Something on the screen caught his attention, and he turned to look for me. Catching me watching him, he motioned me over with a crook of his finger.

"*Regarde ça!*" He pointed.

"Look at what?" I walked over and watched the audience again. There two rows back in the center sat Arizona Marks. Second-rate designer, third-rate design stealer, and all around trifling personality. "That's bold. I would have her kicked out but she'd just lap up the attention."

"Well, what can she do at this point? Our show is today, hers is in two days. We'll look and see which decoy design she chooses and handle it then," Beau suggested.

"That's true. I can't wait to confront her about this."

"As a matter of fact," he nodded toward the camera filming the "Behind the Scenes" show, "why don't we let the camera come along and capture the moment?"

I clapped. "I love the way your devious mind works, Montgomery."

"Do you?" He quirked a brow. The set of his jaw was the only indication of deeper subtext going on between the two of us.

I lowered my voice. "You know I do."

He placed his mouth next to my ear and his hand at the small of my back. To observers, it looked like we were sharing a secret just before showtime. In a silky tone he murmured, "Prove it and marry me." Before I could respond, the lights went dark and applause broke out as my logo was flashed onto the screens and fabric in the theater area. He stepped away and applauded with a loaded look back at me.

I'd asked Veronica to act as announcer for the show. She'd agreed. Her rich voice boomed out over the speakers. "Welcome to Dallas Fashion Week and welcome to the House of BellaRich. You've fallen in love with the Trés Belle line of clothes, swimwear, and intimates for women, but today you'll see so much more. It's a season in the life of a BellaRich Man."

The show was designed so that the set and scenery changed with each ensemble. We started with the business suits, showing male and female models in the boardroom, at a lunch meeting, and at the airport. I watched as Katrina strutted down the "tarmac," dragging a male model behind her as if they were rushing to catch a plane. The audience roared with laughter as he struggled to keep up. I let out a sigh of relief. It was going well and not coming across as too campy.

"Belle, you ready to change?" Sergio pulled me away from the monitor as we highlighted the resort wear. Seasonal raingear was next followed by weekend wear, club clothes, and lastly, sleepwear and lingerie.

"*Ugh*, I almost forgot I agreed to do this." I looked around for Beau and couldn't locate him. I ran behind a partition and changed into a short hot-pink silk negligee embroidered with my signature rose pattern. The makeup artist dusted me down from head to toe with a glittery powder and touched up my makeup. There was a matching floor-length sheer robe in a lighter pink color. I stepped into four and a half inch baby-pink sandals with crystal straps that wrapped around the ankle.

Stepping out from behind the curtain, I still didn't see Beau anywhere. Two of my staff whistled at me. "Looking good, boss lady." I rolled my eyes and waited for my cue. The plan was for the male model to be waiting for me at the end of the runway. I would stride down, circle around him, and then drop the robe. I would turn and walk slowly back to where a bed was going to be wheeled out on stage, all the while trailing the robe behind me. He would follow me; we would climb under the covers and the bed would be wheeled off as the lights faded to black. End of show.

I took a deep breath as Sergio waved me forward after they cued the male model. There in the wings, I couldn't see the monitor or the stage. I heard a collective "Oh!" and then wild applause broke out. I raised a brow; one of the male models knew how to work a crowd.

"The only thing our BellaRich man needs now is his Trés Belle woman." That was my cue. I put my head up, shoulders back, made sure my stomach was sucked in, haughty smile on and hands on my hips. I started my signature sexy strut down the lacquered runway. Toe, heel, hip roll, and repeat. The lights were blinding and kept changing colors. All I could see was the back of the male model as I approached him.

I blocked out Veronica's voice as I hit the end of the runway and struck a pose, jutting one hip out. I turned to send a sultry look to the male model and met a smiling pair of hot gold eyes staring back at me. Beauregard, in all of his splendor, stood in a pair of navy pajamas, drawstring bottoms resting low, and one button undone on the shirt.

He cocked a brow in silent challenge as if to ask, *What are you going to do with me now?* My smile turned mischievous. I sent a *Don't you wish you were me?* look at the audience as I sashayed over to him. Instead of circling, I stood in front of him and unbuttoned the rest of the pajama top. The crowd went wild as I yanked the shirt off of him and tossed it toward the front row. Then I ran a hand across his chest and down his abs, pausing right above that drawstring.

"Is it me, or is it gettin' hot in here?" the announcer asked and our sound man dutifully cued up Nelly's *Hot in Herre.*

Picking up on the beat, I kind of danced a few steps away before Beau reached out, caught my hand, and spun me back to him. I was on tiptoe, with his arm around my waist, and we looked into each other's eyes for a hot second. Then he spun me around to face forward and without a bit of warning ripped the sheer robe off me.

A collective gasp went through the audience as the two halves fell to the ground and I stepped out of the shredded remains. I stood in the nightgown and heels knowing as the flashbulbs popped furiously that this would look amazing on film. He turned me so that we both faced sideways to the audience. As if we planned it, we started dancing together to the beat of the music while making our way back up the runway. Halfway up, he pulled me to him and kissed me briefly but long enough to make a statement.

"*Ooo-wee*!" Veronica squealed. "If that night-gown can guarantee this response, sign me up for a dozen!"

He stepped back and a slow smile spread across his face. Wicked enough for me to wonder what he was up to now. His smile widened into a grin as he lifted me off my feet and into his arms and carried me toward the bed. If not for all the hoots, hollers, and clapping, I would've thought we were at home about to do a lil sumthin' sumthin'.

Remembering the audience, I threw a big smile and a wave over his shoulder. He set me down on the bed and lay down next to me. The smiles on both our faces disappeared as he leaned over me. That look in his eye had me reaching up to slide a hand behind his head and stroke his nape. His eyes flickered closed. His lips were a hairsbreadth away from mine when the stage went dark.

"Who else knows how *that* story is going to end?" Veronica announced, breaking the spell as the audience broke into laughter.

"Jesus, Belle," he breathed as they rolled the bed offstage. He got up and strode backstage without a backward glance.

More shaken than I'd realized by the encounter, I took a deep breath and stepped into the less sheer matching robe that someone held out to me. The models were lining up to go out on stage for the final walk as Katrina sidled up to me with a Cheshire grin on her face.

"Well, Ms. Delaney, that was hot—was that planned?"

"Not exactly," I muttered.

"You two kill me." She chortled and pranced out on stage.

"The design director, Katrina Montgomery, ladies and gentlemen."

Beau had slipped on a long navy robe, which he left open, the ties dangling on each side. It was patently unfair that pools of drool formed in my mouth as I watched him swagger out onto the stage.

"This gent is no stranger to the fashion world either. This piece of eye candy is the total package—brains, brawn, and beauty. The creative director of BellaRich Men, Beau Montgomery." He bowed and stepped to the side.

I stepped out from the wing and walked down the runway with a huge smile. I never got tired of this feeling after a successful show. A job well done.

"Proving that she can still set the runway on fire: our founder, creator, and the chief executive officer of Bella-Rich—Ms. Belle Richards!"

I smiled and waved and took the microphone. "I'd like to thank everyone for coming out. I hope we put on a good show for you." I waited until the applause died down to continue. "This new line, BellaRich Men, would not have come to fruition without two of the smartest and prettiest damn people I know. Katrina and Beau Montgomery." I motioned for them to step forward. Beau smiled and inclined his head while Katrina gave a curtsy.

"And because I don't often get the opportunity, and yesterday was Father's Day, I'd like to give a special shout-out to the man who once said, 'You can get out there and strut like a peacock as long as you don't shed all your feathers'—my father, Mr. Percy Richards. Stand up, Dad."

My father stood up and waved once before sitting back down. This was the first of my shows he'd ever been to, and I wanted to show off a little for him.

"Again, thank you so much. We've got food and drink in the back for you. God Bless."

I handed the microphone back to Veronica and marched back off the stage followed by the other models. Once backstage, I thanked all of the models, staff, and crew for their hard work.

Yazlyn raced over and enveloped me in a huge hug. "OMG! That rocked so hard! Did you and Beau plan that?"

I stepped behind a curtain to change back into my dress, a short, belted safari-style number in a coral color. I searched for the matching shoes while I answered her. "Um—not so much. I didn't even know he was going to model."

"Well, wow and bravo! The media is all abuzz. Honey, you two almost set off a fire alarm up in here."

I slipped my feet into the sky-high slides and beamed. "Whatever gets them going, I guess. That is one thing about doing shows outside of New York and Paris; you can be a little more creative with them. It's not just straight-faced stomp, stomp, music, clothes, stomp." We crossed the floor to head over to the cocktail area.

"Dallas has lit you up from the inside. If I were you, I would just keep the small showroom in New York there and move everything else down to Dallas. You've come into your own here, Mirabella, professionally and personally. You could really have it all."

I stopped and abruptly switched course. I zipped into a small office near the back of the warehouse and pulled Yazlyn in with me. I sat down in a chair and put my head in my hands. "Oh shit, Yaz. I think I really screwed up."

She sank down on the desk and crossed one long limb over the over. "What did you do now?" Her voice indicated that she'd been waiting for this.

"Beau asked me to marry him yesterday," I announced baldly.

She squealed, and I hopped up to clap a hand over her mouth. "*Sssh!* I don't want anyone running in here right now."

She grabbed my hand. "Where's the ring? I know he got you a fantabulous ring."

"The ring *is* fantabulous. It's at home, in a drawer. I didn't say yes," I mumbled.

"What?!" she shrieked, and I threatened to put a hand back over her mouth. She leaned back. "Delaney Mirabella Richards, *what* did you just say?"

"I didn't say yes. I didn't say no, but I didn't say yes, either."

"What the hell *did* you say?" She looked at me as if I'd grown two heads.

"I said I needed more time."

"More . . . what? I knew from the moment you said his name that he was the one for you. Are you crazy?" She was approaching shriek level again.

"We haven't known each other for very long."

"When it's right, it's right, though. This isn't either of your first time at the dance. Are you crazy?"

"What if I'm just a whim for him?" My voice wavered.

Her mouth fell open, and she eyed me in disbelief. "For that man? The one who just got half naked and claimed you in front of God, man, and your daddy? Again I ask, are you crazy?"

"I have to be sure of him." At this point, I didn't know if I was trying to convince her or myself.

As usual, Yaz did not hold back. "Mirabella, you're an idiot. That man makes you orgasm with half a sideways glance, he puts up with all your artsy-assed mood swings, he is brilliant in your industry of choice, and he gets you. What more are you looking for?"

I sighed. "I want him to be sure. Beau isn't Lucas."

"Damn right he isn't. Thank God for that."

I clarified. "What I mean is, I actually want this to be right from start to finish. He matters, he really matters. Lucas, well—he wasn't so hard to get over when it all went to hell. But with Beau? If it all goes south? I don't know."

Yaz stood up and shook her head. "Just so you know, you're certifiably crazy. Completely Looney Tunes." She started gesturing wildly with her hands. "For someone so smart, honey, you're acting like a damn fool. And to cosign your original statement—yes, you screwed things up."

"Thanks. Thanks a lot for the pep talk." I pursed my lips.

"Whatever. What did the ring look like?"

"Cushion-cut chocolate diamond, at least four carats with—"

Yaz put her hand up. "I can't talk to you right now. I'm going to drink and schmooze and forget that my best friend is a super-talented lunatic." She stormed toward the door.

I grabbed her arm to stop her. "Yaz, wait! How do I fix it?"

"Well now you done hurt that man's feelings. The only way I know to smooth ruffled feathers is to stroke the hell out of them."

30

Now That's Just Hitting Low

Beau—Thursday, June 24, 7:23 PM

"I hope to be back for the engagement party before the year is out," Percy Richards declared as he climbed out of Roman's truck at the airport. As much as I loved the Porsche, Percy struggled climbing in and out of it so I had baby bro give us a lift.

I laughed shortly, stepping down from the back to grab Percy's suitcase and walk it over to curbside check-in. "You are a far more optimistic man than me, sir."

"This is just how Delaney is, son. She's over there plotting and formulating a plan before she makes her move."

"Is that what she's doing?" I hadn't spoken to her outside of the context of business all week.

"Have patience, Beauregard. She's worth it," he reassured me.

"Yes, sir. *Merci beaucoup.* I appreciate you coming in. Please tell Dalton, Davis, Loren, and Tina hello for me. I know it wasn't easy for them to turn you loose on Father's Day."

"I was glad to get away from that crew for a second. Always crowding around, double-checking that I haven't dropped dead—it can wear on a man."

I held back my chuckle. "No doubt."

"Plus, I wanted to see my baby girl in action. That was some show you two put on the other day." His eyes sparkled.

I grinned. "We gotta give the media something to talk about."

He gave me an astute look. "You keep telling yourself that was all for the cameras." He turned and waved at Roman. "You send my regards to your wife and son, ya hear?"

"Yes, sir," Roman called out through the window.

Percy clapped a hand on my shoulder and brought me in close for a quick hug. "It'll all work out. I have faith in both of you." He stepped back and pulled out his ticket to hand to the attendant. "Don't be a stranger and tell that sister of yours to slow down. She doesn't have to race through life; it comes at you no matter what. Ha-ha!"

"I'll let her know. You called Belle to tell her you were leaving?" I watched as the skycap checked him in and took his bags.

"We had us a good chat; don't fret none. Oh, I sent you a friend request on the Facebook. Don't leave me hanging, son. Percy out!" Mr. Richards headed into the terminal.

With a final wave, I climbed into the passenger seat of Roman's car. "You know, the thought of him and Pops hanging out on a regular basis is more than a little scary."

"Imagine the trouble those two could get into chattin' it up on 'the Facebook' together?" Roman drawled.

"*Terrifiant.*" Terrifying.

"So where to, AB?"

"Home, James," I teased and leaned back in the seat.

"Look at you, Mr. Maturity. In a real house, with your name on the deed. All the stuff you've accumulated over the years finally out of storage and on display."

"Shut it, Montgomery."

"I can't even get a jab in that you bought a house less than ten minutes away from mine? It kind of warms my heart from the inside out."

"You done?" I rolled my eyes.

"I'm done." He snickered.

"Okay then." I leaned back against the headrest and closed my eyes. It had been a hell of a week. The show and then the endless interviews, all with the camera crew following us around. In the midst of all that, I found I couldn't be around Belle without wanting to either throw an epic tantrum or strip her naked while I worked that tight body into submission. Neither one seemed like a good idea, so I kept my distance.

"One more thing, though," Roman added.

"You're worse than a nagging wife!" I complained.

"How would you know?" he shot back.

"Now that's just hitting low."

"Apologies. If you don't mind my asking . . ."

I heaved a sigh. "You're going to ask anyway, so go ahead."

"Don't you have another show to go to tonight?"

"I could've gone to the Arizona Wind show." I looked at my watch. "It's wrapping up right about now. She's the chick who has been stealing Belle's designs and trying to pass them off as her own. But I'm tired, and Belle can handle it without me."

"This is how you fight for your woman?" Roman threw a skeptical glance my way.

I had to express amusement. "This from the dude who sat on his back porch in a ripped shirt and sweatpants with Sade on repeat before you and Jewel worked it out?"

"I wasn't that bad!" Roman protested.

"Man, you were worse. Remember that one whole four-day stretch when you didn't bathe, didn't eat, didn't leave the house? Just sat around moaning, 'What if we can't work it out, what if she can't be what I need? I just love her so much' over and over again until I wanted to go get her for you. Good Lawd, you were whiny."

Roman let one side of his mouth tilt up. "I was so far gone over her; still am, I guess."

"Well, good for you. I'm still trying to get there. So quit sweatin' a brother, can you please?"

"Look, why don't you go to the show, give her that look you give."

"What look?" I had no idea what he was talking about.

"I don't know. That pretty boy thing that makes women throw their panties at you."

"Again, pot . . . kettle." I pointed from him back to myself.

"Hold on, homeboy. My ass is ruggedly handsome; you're just pretty."

I rolled my eyes. "*Ça suffit*! Please tell me you have a point."

"My point, O Pretty One, is that you want to see her and get the conversation going again? Go get her and seduce her. Women are always more amenable when they are getting done and getting done well."

"Thank you so much for that nugget of wisdom." I could've gone my whole life through without having this particular chat with my younger brother.

"Hey, there's nothing like multiple orgasms to facilitate a conversation."

"Does your wife know you still talk like that?"

"My wife likes what I do with my mouth just fine."

"That's nasty, bro; I'm so not trying to hear that out of you."

"Just sayin' if you need some tips . . ."

"*Mon Dieu*, this is what it's come to? Sex tips from the younger, lesser Montgomery? Thanks but no thanks. I'm good."

Roman pulled in behind my garage. "Seriously, though, I'm here for you, *mon frère*."

We exchanged a brotherly fist bump as I climbed

out. "Appreciated. Go home to your woman. I'll be all right."

I walked in the house, pulled some leftovers out of the fridge, and turned on the Fashion Television network while I waited for the food to heat in the microwave. I remember the days when I turned on ESPN first, I thought with a self-deprecating laugh.

"Scandal at the Arizona Wind show tonight in Dallas, and we have the scoop for you, right after this!" the commentator touted with a wide grin.

I grabbed the plate along with a fork and a bottle of green tea and headed for the sofa. Three commercials played and then the news show came back on.

"Arizona Marks, once touted as a brilliant mind in cutting-edge fashion was outed this evening for plagiarizing the designs and concept from her former classmate's, Belle Richards', fashion line. As many of you know, the fabulously innovative Bella-Rich show was earlier in the week and showcased not only Ms. Richards' new menswear line but her new man, Beau Montgomery. Can we say yummilicious?"

I choked on that last bite. "Oh come on, now. Yummi-what? *Quelle folie!*" How crazy was that?

A snippet of the footage of the two of us stalking each other on the catwalk ran before cutting back to the Arizona Wind show. "Tonight's show looked eerily familiar, as did some of the designs." They put pictures up side by side of our BellaRich model and the Arizona Wind model in a similar outfit. "When confronted backstage by Ms. Richards, Arizona attempted to claim that Belle had stolen

ideas from her for years. That theory fell apart
when Ms. Richards revealed her original designs
along with a decoy design she put together pre-
cisely for the purpose of catching Ms. Marks in the
act. When asked to produce her original designs,
Arizona quite frankly . . . ran out of wind.

"No word yet as to whether the BellaRich camp
will seek legal and financial damages but stay
tuned, big things are happening in Big D." The
show went to commercial.

"So what do you think? Should we sue her for
every penny she's got?" Belle said from inside the
foyer. She wore a silver mini-dress that clung to
every glorious inch of her curves. On her feet, she
wore hot pink stilettos with roses across the back of
the heel. Completely impractical and totally hot.

"So it was Irena, the assistant in garment construction, who was leaking the designs?" I asked.

"Yep, but she was scared to send the actual designs so she redrew them from memory."

"That explains the half-assed copy job and lack
of detailing."

"That explains it." She nodded.

"So, all's well that ends well?"

"Are we still talking about the designs?"

I set my half-empty plate on the coffee table
and leaned back with my hands fisted at my sides
to keep from grabbing her. On the one hand, I
was happy to see her. On the other hand, I didn't
know what it meant in the overall scheme of
things. I guessed there was only one way to find
out.

31

That Was Beau Laying It All on the Line

Belle—9:01 PM that same night

Beau's voice sounded slightly hoarse when he asked, "How did you get in?"

I twirled the key around my finger with a false bravado I didn't feel. "Daddy gave me the key when he said good-bye earlier."

"What are you doing here?" he continued in that same impersonal and measured tone.

"Why wouldn't I be here? You said we were okay. If we're okay and we love each other, then I want to see my man."

He crossed his arms across his chest and looked across the dark room at me. *"Vraiment?"*

"Yes, really." I stepped into the living room and prowled across the marble floor to him. "And another thing . . ." I paused to gauge his reaction.

"*Un autre chose?*" he repeated in French.

"I missed you," I said softly, kicking off my shoes, tossing my purse on the coffee table, and climbing into his lap. I straddled him so that my thighs were on the outside of his and then I shifted forward. He unfolded his arms and set them on my thighs.

"Did you?" He still looked wary and slightly bored.

"More than you know. I've grown accustomed to having my Beau twenty-four seven. I miss Breakfast Beau and Ride to Work Beau. I miss Laughing at Work Beau and Working Out at the Gym Beau. I miss Watching Television Beau and Fresh Out of the Shower Beau. I miss talking to you and bickering with you."

"*Hmm.*" He no longer looked bored.

"I'll admit it. You have me hooked. I miss these lips." I traced his lips with my tongue. "I miss these broad shoulders to lean on." I rested my head on his shoulder and bit his neck. "I miss this chest to cuddle up against." I brushed my chest against his. "I miss these powerful thighs." I shifted on top of those thighs. "I miss these hands. Holding me, touching me, stroking me." I took his hands and drew them across my aching nipples, down my torso, and up my thighs. His hands slid the rest of the way up my thighs to cup my ass. He gasped at what he found.

"*Mademoiselle* Richards! Have you been running around all night without any panties on?" He grasped the back of my thighs to part them wider and stroked through my moisture with his thumb. "Answer me."

I didn't know what it was about him that turned me into a needy, mewling sex kitten with just one touch, but I loved it. I loved him. "No. I had them on earlier. I took them off when I decided to come here. To you."

"You are soaking wet and so hot, it's ridiculous," he hissed, continuing to stroke me.

"You make me that way. The mere thought of seeing you tonight, hoping you wanted to see me, and I got all humid."

"Why wouldn't I want to see you?" he murmured in a confused tone.

I had to pull his hands away for a second. "Wait, I can't concentrate when you touch me like that."

He rested his hands on my knees. "I said, why wouldn't I want to see you?"

I gave a little shoulder wiggle. "You're mad at me."

He took my chin in his hand and tilted it so my eyes met his. "I'm not mad at you. I'm hurt you don't want to be what I want, what I need. I'm hurt you don't trust me. I'm hurt, Belle."

Whoa. That was Beau laying it all on the line. I couldn't help but reciprocate. "Just give me a little time to get there. You have to understand, sugar. I thought I was coming down to Dallas to launch this line, hand it over to somebody, and head back up to New York. I didn't plan or want to meet anyone. When I met you, I was sure that we'd have a short, hot fling and walk away from each other. Then you were so freakin' smart about my designs, and then with my dad and my family you were so damn wonderful and caring. You snuck up on me, Beau. So maybe I started thinking if I'm having trouble making the mental leap, maybe you are, too.

"But after talking to my dad and your mom—"

"Madere? When did you talk to her?"

"We talked on Sunday, when you sent me to family dinner to face the music by myself." I slanted a pointed look at him.

He sent me one right back. "Ah yes, Sunday. A hard day for all of us."

I inclined my head in acknowledgment. "Anyway, after talking to my dad, your mom, Katrina, and Yazlyn, I realized something."

"What's that?"

"You're serious. When you said you were all in . . . you meant it."

"*Mais oui*, I've never lied to you."

"Remember when I asked you to be patient with me?"

"I do."

"Well, I'm calling in that favor now." I leaned against him and wrapped my arms around his neck. "Please darlin', don't give up on me."

He tightened his arms around me and squeezed. "If you're asking me not to let you go, I won't let go."

"Don't let go."

"*Entendu!*"

"Which means . . ."

"Done!"

"So we're good for now?"

"For now, Mirabella."

"Understood." I reached for his hands and put

them back on my thighs. "Put your hands on me, Beauregard."

"*Avec plaisir.*" His hands slid to the juncture of my thighs to tease and play, and I knew I wasn't in the mood for foreplay.

I unzipped his jeans, reached in, and lifted his length out to pulse in my palm. "Hello, my lovely friend, I have missed you so."

He literally guffawed. "Woman, are you whispering to my dick?"

"Yes. I was afraid he was gone forever."

"You realize it hasn't even been a week, right?"

"What can I say? You've created a monster. I don't want to go without. I have needs." I reached behind me, opened my purse, and snatched a condom out. "Shift down a little."

"Yes, ma'am. I'll have to make sure I can accommodate these needs of yours." He looked amused and tolerant as I struggled with the logistics of moving his clothing out of the way and sheathing his length with as much speed and efficiency as I could muster. "*Chérie,* are we in a hurry?"

"Yes, yes we are." Without further ado, I crawled back into place and sunk down on him and arched to take him all in one hot liquid slide.

"*Oooooh,*" we both said at the same time.

"So then." His eyes turned copper and his voice turned gravelly. "No foreplay?"

"No, thank you," I hissed as I rose up and slid back down. I moaned low in my throat and threw my head back. "Beau?"

He ground his hips up in a tight circle. "Yeah, babe?"

"Quick and dirty, okay?"

"*Ce que tu veux.*" He put his hands on my hips and sped up the tempo.

"I can't think in French when you do that! God, you're hitting my spot."

"I said, whatever you want."

"I like that," I hissed out as his strokes went deeper.

He did some sort of crazy motion where he corkscrewed his hips and bounced me on top of him at the same time. "What about that? You like that?"

I had to take a second to whip the dress over my head. I tossed it away. I was on fire from the inside out. "You know I do."

"But do you love it?" He seemed to reach deeper with every thrust, sending already sizzling nerve endings into full blaze.

"I love it," I whimpered, racing toward an epic climax. "I love you."

"Damn right you do. *Je t'aime aussi mon cœur, je t'aime aussi.*"

I lost the rhythm as the wave hit me by surprise. Shrieking, I grabbed his head and held it to me as I ground against him taking what I needed. As the last tremors fluttered through me, he drew a nipple into his mouth and sucked hard. I went over again.

He joined me with a long moan, holding me open while we crested together.

I stayed on top of him as he rocked me gently in the aftermath. "Babe."

"*Hmm?*" he responded.

"We're getting rid of this white sofa." The sofa,

while gorgeous, was not practical. It would not maintain its pristine appearance for much longer at the rate we were going.

"Not one of my best ideas."

"We're way too freaky for white furniture."

"Excellent point. Does this mean you're moving in?"

"Or camping out if you don't want me to stay. I have some stuff in the car."

"As soon as my legs work again, I'll help you bring it in."

"Just like that?"

"Just like that. You're home."

I relaxed and nestled my head against his shoulder. I was home.

32

I Think There's Rain in the Forecast

Beau—Wednesday, October 6, 3:41 PM (four months later)

I glanced at my watch. We had one more hour until the buyers' showcase wrapped at our temporary showroom in Market Hall. This was an opportunity for buyers and store representatives who hadn't already placed preorders for the spring line to come in, see the clothing, and order. The place had been a madhouse all day.

Not that I was complaining. It could have been worse. I could have been back at the office ducking Renee, who was there for the final campaign sign-off for the BellaRich joint venture with Royal

Mahogany cosmetics. There wasn't a single time when she walked into the office that she didn't try and stir some flavor of bullshit up, just because she could. I was thoroughly sick of it, but Belle said not to make a thing of it until we closed this deal. So I left it alone.

"Mr. Montgomery, can I ask you a question about this suit?" an attractive female buyer from a small chain of stores in the Midwest asked in a flirty tone. It was her tenth question, and she kept coming up with reasons to touch me when I came within a foot of her. Time was I would have encouraged her and taken her up on her offer. But I was now one of those guys who was completely satisfied with what he had at home. I wasn't even the slightest bit tempted.

But as it was in my modeling days, sex sold clothing. I dialed up my smile and walked over to her. She brushed her breast against my arm as she held up the jacket.

"You had a question? *J'ai la réponse,*" I said silkily, taking a small step back while keeping my smile firmly in place.

"I bet you have all the answers," she said, peering up through her lashes to see if I was taking any of the bait.

"Ask away, ma'am," I prompted, resisting the urge to glance at my watch again.

"Oh, you can call me Helen. Does this material breathe and move? You know, with the wearer? Whatever he happens to be doing?"

Jesus, let me not roll my eyes at this woman. The fact that I used to find this banter entertaining was a bit shaming. Actually, you know what? I was never this lame. I blinked innocently at her and decided to play dumb. "Most silks do. Especially with the additional engineered threading we've added in. The wearer could go skydiving in this suit, land, and go straight to a business meeting."

"Not quite the movement I had in mind. But I'll place an order anyway," she said with a slide of her hand against mine.

"Honey, he knows what you had in mind," Renee's voice rang out from the doorway.

I stifled a groan. Would this day never end? My phone buzzed in my pocket and I pulled it out, turning my back on both irritating women. A text message came up on the screen.

Suspect Renee on her way there.

I typed back:

You suspect correct. She just walked in.

Deal is done. Feel free to get snarky.

I'm going in.

Need reinforcements?

Care to defend my honor?

I was heading that way anyway. CU soon.

Hurry.

"Helen, do you have any more questions?" I turned back with a pleasant smile fixed on my face.

She slid a look Renee's way before stepping in front of her. "Any chance you'll be visiting the stores once the merchandise comes in?"

I placed some regret in my tone. "Oh, I doubt I'll have time for that. We're starting work on the next season's line and planning some runway shows in Europe."

"Are you going to be doing any more modeling? I saw footage of your work; I'm a huge fan." She drew the word *huge* out in a long syllable.

"Well, thank you, but I think my runway days are behind me. I'll leave that to the youngsters. Can I take your order form?"

She handed me the form, and I keyed it into the system before handing it back to her. She put it back in my hands. "You hold onto it. It has my information in case you have any questions about anything. Anything at all."

"Well, thank you. I'll just tuck that away for future reference." I took her hand and airkissed the back of it. "*Enchanté.*"

She giggled and waggled her fingers on her way out of the store.

"So I see you're still slaying 'em in the eyes, killer," Renee smirked.

With the other customers being handled by staff, I was free to give my undivided attention to Renee. I had to give her credit, she kept herself looking good if not a little bit obvious. True to form, she was shrink-wrapped into a dress that showed off all of her boom-boom-pow and strapped into some heels that were just a little too sexy to be professional. She always stayed a few shades above skanky. But she wasn't getting any younger and the sophisticated "it girl" act wasn't going to work for her too much longer. Where before she'd been edgy, she was now coming across as hard and brittle.

I sighed and dipped into my patience reserve. "What can I do for you, Renee?"

Her eyes flicked around the store. "Can we go somewhere just a little more private for this discussion?"

Since I didn't want the other staff members to hear what I had to say, I agreed. I escorted her to the storage room in the back of the store and ignored the smug smile on her face.

Stepping in after her, I gestured for her to sit in the chair. I leaned against the wall. "So what is it, Renee? What is it that has you sniffing around now?" My tone was far less warm than before.

She started. "I like to think that you and I are different sides of the same coin."

I tried not to look as appalled and insulted as I felt. "Do you really?"

"I think we understand each other," she continued.

"I definitely understand you," I countered.

"I think there's a reason that we stay in each other's orbit."

"Besides the fact that we know the same people and live in the same city?"

"You know how it is. We said the rain check is never off the table between you and me." She got up and leaned against me. "I think there's rain in the forecast."

I had to give it to her: that was a good line. I might have used something similar back in my player days. Don't get me wrong, it wasn't working at all but it was a damn good line. I had to give credit where credit was due.

She pressed herself against me and placed her hand against my pants. "Can little Beau come out and play?" She pressed and stroked with more than a tinge of desperation.

Ignoring the fact that I hated penis nicknames, little Beau didn't even stir. Not even the tiniest twinge of interest. *Hmm.* That was noteworthy. I had a beautiful woman plastered against me rubbing me the right way and I felt . . . nothing. "Renee, I don't think little Beau wants to come out and play."

She paused. "What?"

"He said, he doesn't think little Beau wants to come out and play," Belle repeated as she stormed into the backroom.

Renee took a step back. "Hey, don't get mad at me because your man was putting the moves on me. You know how Beau is."

Belle nodded. "Yes, yes I do. This is why I'm positive he never touched you."

"Yes!" I pumped my fist in the air. "That's what I'm talking about! Validation at last."

Belle giggled. "You're so easy, sugar."

"*Seulement pour vous*, only for you, Mirabella."

She walked over to me, and I wrapped my arms around her from behind, pulling her tight against me. "I've been noticing that. Funny, I never have any problem getting little Beau to come out and play. As a matter of fact, our problem is getting him to stay inside."

"You know you love it," I murmured and nipped her ear lightly with my teeth.

We cackled until Renee cleared her throat behind us. I spun around.

"Oh, are you still here? My bad. I forgot you

were standing there. Listen, *chérie*, it's not gonna happen. You can assume that rain check has expired. Nothing personal, we've had some good times, you and me. But I'm not that guy any more. And God willing, never again."

"You're seriously trying to be a one-woman man?" Renee sneered with blatant skepticism.

"I already am," I answered unswervingly.

Belle's eyes snapped with fire. "And he's going to stay that way, thank you very much."

Renee added, "Girlfriend, come on. Do you have any idea what it takes to get and keep a man like Beauregard Montgomery?"

"What's 'a man like me'?" I was mystified at the direction this conversation had taken.

Belle snuggled in closer. "Oh sugar, I'm sure she means hardworking, considerate, and silver-tongued in all the right ways."

"*Chérie*, you make me blush." I grinned.

"Avery Beauregard, you haven't blushed a single day in your natural life."

Renee interrupted our repartee. "You really think you've got him?"

"If I don't, I'll figure out. But darlin', I will tell you one thing . . ."

"What?"

"I won't be taking man-keeping advice from the likes of you!" Baby Girl was taking no prisoners.

After a heated moment, Renee snarled, "It won't last." She whirled around and stomped away. The storage room door slammed shut behind her.

Belle let out a pent-up breath. "What is *wrong*

with that woman? It's like she's incapable of having a grown-up conversation. Not to mention, she's relationship poison."

I shrugged. "Boggles the mind."

Belle changed the subject. "I saw the orders for today. How many women did you flash the pearly whites at to reach these numbers?"

"*Ma douce*, you have no idea how hard it is being me."

She rolled her eyes. "There you go with those pretty boy problems again."

"*Mais oui.*"

33

We Can Go Again

Belle—Saturday, November 7, 11:29 AM *(one month later)*

Beau and I sat in the airport lounge in New York. We had been in Paris and Milan and were heading back home after closing up my SoHo apartment and downsizing the New York office. Nothing but the storefront and a small staff would remain. I'd finally made the decision to move the bulk of BellaRich operations to Dallas. Labor was cheaper, taxes were lower, and most importantly, I was happier there.

I didn't have to prove I could make it in the big city anymore. I was there. I had done it. Without patting myself on the back, I could honestly call myself a success. Professionally, everything was happening for me as I'd always dreamed. Now it was time to get my personal house in order.

A few weeks ago, I finally opened up the package that my father had given me. It was a scrapbook of all my accomplishments dating as far back as my first runway show at age sixteen. My mother had started keeping the book, and after she passed, my father had taken over. I had no idea he'd been paying attention for all those years.

The other item in the package was a letter my mother had written before she died. It was mostly addressed to my father, with advice on how to raise us after she was gone, but there was a small section in there that she had written just to me. She said she knew I planned to be a very different woman with a different life than the one she'd led. But she wanted me to know that she lived exactly the way she wanted and if she had it to do all over again, she wouldn't change a thing. Her only wish for me was to live a life filled with love and no regrets.

I already had a few regrets, but I was determined not to have too many more. Reading that letter had kind of unlocked the last door I had in my mind about what marriage was and could be. When we got back home, I planned to tell Beau that I was ready. Ready to be his wife, ready to get this happily ever after thing kicked into overdrive. I couldn't wait to see his face when I told him.

Bless his heart, he'd stopped even bringing it up, and I knew he wasn't expecting it. The man let me redecorate his dream house without a single conversation about whether I would be there long term. He traded in his Porsche and bought a

Benz. Granted, it was still a convertible, but it sat four and my father could climb in and out of it without the Jaws of Life to assist him. Now if that wasn't unconditional love, I didn't know what was.

Digging around in the side pockets of my purse, I found what I was looking for. I took the ring out of the zippered compartment in my purse and slid it on. I wondered how long it would take him to notice I was wearing it.

"Are we there yet?" he said moodily, shifting on the sofa. He was dressed in black jeans, a plum buttoned shirt, and a leather jacket. Even sulky, he was giving off the caramel sexy.

"You're so bougie," I teased him.

"I'm just saying, if we took the jet like I wanted to, not only would we be almost home by now, we could be naked in the back cabin."

"I wasn't going to spend that kind of money just so we could play bouncy-bouncy at 30,000 feet. We are flying first class; it's not as though we're in the peanut section."

"We can afford to splurge every now and then," he reminded me.

That prompted me to ask about something that had me curious. "Just how much money do you have stashed, anyway?"

"Enough that we don't have to sit in this airport lounge right now."

"Enough that you're spoiled, you mean."

Beau just rolled his eyes and picked up another magazine to flip through. That meant he was through talking about it.

"Belle?" a male voice said from over my left shoulder.

From the look on Beau's face, it wasn't anyone either of us wanted to see. I turned my head to see Lucas Turner smiling down at me. He was about six feet two, light-skinned, broad-shouldered with almost delicate features and close-cropped hair. His eyes were hazel. I looked at him and felt ashamed that I had ever thought he and Beau favored one another in any which way, shape, or form.

"Hello, Lucas, how have you been?" I responded dully.

"What kind of way is that to greet the man you almost married?" He reached out and tugged me out of my chair and into his arms. I felt nothing except impatience and a little irritation.

I watched Beau's face turn feral as he stood up to his full height. Oh hell. This could get messy. I pushed out of Lucas' embrace and turned into Beau, lodging myself under his arm.

"Turner," Beau said.

"Montgomery."

Lucas looked at me. "I thought you said you were through with hangers on and pretty boys?"

"Oh I am."

"Well, what is he?" He gestured toward Beau disdainfully.

"The best thing that ever happened to me, thanks for asking."

Lucas took a step forward and Beau did the same. Lucas frowned. "What? You're gonna kick my ass just for speaking?"

Beau let a slow, dangerous smile ease onto his face. "I'm sure you've done something to deserve it. It's not like I haven't done it before. We can go again. Just say when."

Lucas looked at me. "Seriously, how is he better than me?"

I broke it down. "Uh—in every way possible, but I assume you want specifics. How about the fact that he's hardworking, honest, conscientious, puts me first, and is more into me than he's into himself?"

Lucas looked at both of us with disgust. "Well, I guess all those rumors are true. He's got you wide open. He'll toss you aside when he's used you up. Hope you don't think he'll ever marry you. His kind never do."

I raised my hand and flashed the ring. "We'll just add this to the long list of things that you are wrong about. The wedding is next summer. Your invitation will unfortunately be lost in the mail."

Lucas curled his lip in a way that was so unattractive I wondered what I'd seen in him to begin with. Thank God, I hadn't tried to build a life with this foolish boy. He sniffed, "I don't know what I ever saw in you. You're not that hot."

Funny, I was just thinking the exact same thing about him. "So, did you want something?" I asked.

"I guess not."

"Aw *petit garçon*, don't be mad that you dropped a dime and I picked it up," Beau said in the snarkiest tone ever.

"You two deserve each other," Lucas tacked on.

"Yes. We do. Thank you so much for noticing," I retorted, leaning back against Beau as he walked away. Beau's arms came around me.

"Mirabella?" Beau murmured in my ear.

"Beauregard?"

"You gonna marry me, *chérie?*"

I turned in his arms. "Well, if you're fool enough to still want me, I'm smart enough to say yes."

He picked me off my feet as he kissed me and whirled me around. Setting me down, he threw his head back and laughed. "When did you put the ring on?"

"Right before you started bitchin' about the private plane, sugar."

He guffawed again. "Bet you wish we were on it now, don't you?"

"You know, I think this lounge has a sleeping room," I whispered mischievously.

"Woman, I like the way you think."

"You've corrupted me; what can I say?"

"You love it." He started easing toward the back of the lounge.

With a sigh, I grabbed my purse and let him lead me toward what would no doubt be shameless behavior. "I do, I really do."

"*Bon*, cuz you're stuck with me now."

Glossary of Terms

'Tite chat	Little cat
À ce qu'il paraît, mon ami	So it would seem, my friend
Absolument	Absolutely
Allons manger	Let's eat
Apparemment	Apparently
Au revoir	Good-bye
Avec plaisir	With pleasure/My pleasure
Bébé	Baby
Bon appétit	Happy eating
Bon nuit	Good night
Ça se comprend	It's understood
Ça suffit	That's enough
Calmez-vous	Chill out/Calm down
Ce que tu veux	Whatever you like
Ce soir	This evening/tonight
Certainement	Certainly
C'est formidable	It's incredible/amazing
C'est inconcevable	That's impossible/inconceivable
C'est rien	It's nothing
C'est tout	That's all
C'est très aimable à vous	How very kind of you
Cette fille est différente. Elle est spéciale.	This girl is different. She's special.
Vous l'aimez, n'est-ce pas?	You like her, right?
Chérie	Sweetie/Darling
De rien	You're welcome/Think nothing of it
Déclassé	Unrefined, tacky

Étouffée	Cajun rice dish
Enchanté	Enchanted/Pleased to have met you
Entendu!	Done!
Extrêmement intéressant	Very (extremely) interesting
Faire un petit sommeil	Take a nap
Fais attention	Watch out
Fille	Girl
J'adore	I love it!
Jamais, mon frère	Never, my brother
Je préfère plutôt mourir que	I would rather die than
Je sais tout faire	I can do anything you want
Je t'aime	I love you
Je t'aime aussi	I love you, too
Jolie fille	Pretty girl
La vérité de Dieu	God's truth
Lagniappe	A little something extra
Laissez le bon temps roulez	Let the good times roll
Les femmes gâtées	Pampered women/Spoiled women
M'excusez	Excuse me/Pardon me
Ma belle fleur	My beautiful flower
Ma douce	My sweet
Ma fifille	Sweetheart/My little girl
Ma petite chou/tite chou	My little cabbage, term of endearment
Ma petite sœur	My little sister
Mademoiselle	Miss/Young lady
Mais non	Of course not
Mais oui	Yes/Of course/But of course

Merci beaucoup	Thank you very much
Merci, ma famille	Thank you, my family
Merde	Damn
Mes douceurs	My sweets
Mignon chat	Cute little cat
Mon ami	My friend
Mon coeur	My heart
Mon Dieu	My God
Monsieur	Sir/Mister
N'est-ce pas?	Isn't it/Is that right/ Right?
Où est mon frère	Where is my brother
Oui, ma belle	Yes, my beauty
Pas de probléme	No problem
Passer le temps	To pass the time
Pourquoi pas	Why not
Que caliente (Spanish)	That's hot
Quelle folie!	How crazy!
Quelque chose	A certain something/ sumthin'-sumthin'
Regarde ça!	Look at this!
S'il vous plait	Please/If you please
Sainte Mère de Dieu	Sainted Mother of God
Salut, ma mère	Greetings, Mother
Seulement pour vous	Only for you
Terrifiant	Terrifying
Tout à fait	As you like/Of course/ Certainly
Tout va bien	It's okay/It's all right
Tout va bien, ma petite?	All good, little one?
Trés bien	Very good
Trés magnifique	So wonderful/Very magnificent/Excellent

Tu comprends?	Do you understand
Tu m'entends	Do you hear me/Do you understand
Un autre chose	Another thing
Un instant	An instant/A moment
Un peu	A little/A little bit
Une chose	A thing
Une seconde s'il vous plait	One second, please
Vraiment	Really/Truly

The Montgomery series continues with

Any Man I Want

Available August 2014 wherever books and
ebooks are sold

Prologue

I don't regret much

Katrina—Saturday, May 21—10:22 p.m.

"Y ou will rue the day you ever discarded me!"
Kevin Eriq Delancey declared dramatically as he
slammed his belongings into a designer suitcase
that cost more than my first car. Thankfully, we
were in a private villa of an exclusive resort in
Barbados and no one was close enough to hear his
ranting and banging around. "Rue the day! *Do you
hear me?*" he repeated, punctuating each word
with the hard toss of an object into his luggage.

I blinked twice and then deliberately looked
back at the thumbnail I was slowly filing. It didn't
seem prudent to laugh, but really—he sounded
like a poorly written soap opera character. I
coughed to cover up the giggle that threatened to

spill out. *Rue the day?* I thought—okay, sir. I refrained from sighing deeply or rolling my eyes.

"Yes, I hear you, Kevin." I stayed still while keeping my eye on the fuming man pacing around the spacious accommodations. This trip had been successful professionally and disastrous personally. My photo shoot went flawlessly; my relationship went up in flames.

With growing detachment, I watched as Kevin railed at me, so angry that spit was literally flying from his mouth as he spoke. I had deliberately waited until tonight. I thought I'd staged this perfectly. We had a lovely dinner; I made sure he drank the lion's share of the wine. Our week here in Barbados was nearing an end. I'd hoped he'd be mellow enough to avoid just this kind of scene. True, there's never a good time to break up with someone, but seeing as how we'd only been dating a few months and neither of us were fooled into thinking this was any sort of love connection, I thought it safe to cut the ties before we headed back to the States.

I had long since given up dating models or photographers or designers. I was sick of men who required more pampering, ego-stroking, or mirror time that I ever would. I was tired of men who just wanted a trophy for their arm, a playmate for their bed, or photo op to boost their careers. Some of the blame fell on me. I hadn't always chosen my companions wisely. I was a busy woman. I didn't want to put a lot of work in and I wanted it to be easy. But I'd found that easy men were like cheap shoes: You got what you paid for, they were usually uncomfortable, and you shouldn't expect them to last long. I decided it was time to put at least as much effort into picking my men as I put into picking my wardrobe. Priorities, you know.

At first glance, Kevin seemed to be a great choice. He seemed different in a good way. He was supposed to be my anti-drama boyfriend. The grown-up, sophisticated, 'bout-his-bidness man who made the rest of them look like preschoolers. Educated, sophisticated, wealthy, and articulate; Kevin Delancey was supposed to be a step up on my dating food chain. Someone I could try and build something with for the long haul.

Yet here we were . . . again. Kevin was the CEO of a hugely successful online purchasing Web site. Serengeti was similar to Amazon.com, but the products were primarily manufactured and sold by people of African descent and targeted the African-American community. He started the company in his dorm room at Morehouse fifteen years ago, took it public for a ton of cash, and then went private again. He was now listed somewhere between Michael Jordan and Warren Buffett on the Forbes Richest Americans list.

Unfortunately, those riches had not bought Kevin very much in the way of couth, class, or chill. As my nephew Chase liked to say of ill-behaved people, "Dude had zero chill." Kevin put the X in extreme everything. And I'd missed the initial warning signs. Totally my fault. Kevin rolled up on me at an event for BellaRich Designs, the fashion house I ran jointly with my future sister-in-law, Belle Richards, and my brother, Beau. Beau and Belle were also former models. Since I was phasing out modeling for anyone other than BellaRich, I'd been more focused on design and promotion. It was at a BellaRich party where Kevin came over to compliment us on the line of evening wear we'd debuted.

At first impression he came across suave, sophisticated, stylish, and supremely confident. Just a shade under six feet, he was olive-skinned, easy on the eyes, and had a smile that no doubt closed many a deal. I admit to being somewhat fooled at first. I had to dig down a few layers to find that he was all about the surface and not much else. At this moment, I narrowed my eyes at him as he continued to pace and pontificate. Perhaps he should've finished Morehouse—they generally turned out a better product.

The thing was, people met me and saw the packaging. Light skin, light eyes, long hair, proportioned body. They don't take the time to see the sum of my parts. They assumed that as a model, designer, and business owner I was all champagne, caviar, red carpets, and flashbulbs. Really, I was most at ease curled up in front of On Demand with chicken wings and cheap Chianti. Kevin didn't get to know that side of me. He had no interest in the sweatpants, T-shirt, hair-in-a-ponytail, chill-on-the-sofa side of me. We started off as arm trophies for each other and I took my time over the course of the next few months deciding if I wanted it to be more than that. Our dates were glossy: high-profile restaurants, club openings, movie premieres, charity events. I didn't like the way he treated people he didn't seem to think were his equal. Rarely did he find anyone to be his equal.

Our schedules were so crazy that I didn't spend

a lot of time with him so I thought perhaps I was judging him too harshly. After all, the man ran a gabillion-dollar business; he didn't necessarily have time for all the niceties.

I came into this week thinking that it was going to be our make-or-break week. Kevin and I had flown down to Barbados for a shoot showcasing the newest line of BellaRich resort wear. Belle and I decided to go with Caribbean-inspired colors and prints for the line. Kevin had placed a substantial order after seeing the initial drawings. Seemed like the perfect time to mix business and pleasure for both of us. If only Kevin had shown a tenth of the prowess and presence in the bedroom that he did in the boardroom—we wouldn't be in this situation. Okay, that's not fair. I wasn't breaking up with Kevin because he was terrible in bed. Being terrible in bed was the last of many nails in the Kevin Delancey coffin.

And believe me . . . it wasn't just tragic bedroom game. Wait, let me say that again: *Tragic. Bedroom. Game.* A man of his age should not only know how things work, but should at least know where to find them. I mean, this is Anatomy 101. It's just not that hard to locate a minimum of three erogenous zones. That level of ineptitude indicated both selfishness and laziness. I'm sad to say I had to fake my way through it . . . twice. Once to give him the benefit of the doubt. The second time hoping he improved his game. At my age, faking it? Ain't nobody got time for that.

Before you judge me, know this—I was not so shallow that I couldn't overlook or provide hands-on assistance to someone with subpar swerve

skills. The fatal flaw that put the dagger in whatever Kevin and I had? He treated people like crap
all the time. Not just when he was stressed or busy
or multitasking. He thought everyone was there to
cater to his every whim. He cussed out the waiter,
made a maid cry, shouted at his subordinates,
threw a tantrum when the gift shop was out of the
lotion he preferred, and snapped his fingers and
pointed when he required something. The third
day of the trip, when he pointed at the coffeepot
and then to his cup, I raised a brow.

"Did you . . . need something?" I asked silkily.

He snapped his fingers twice and said, "Katrina,
you know I'm better when I have my coffee."

"Is there a reason why you cannot pour it for
yourself?" It wasn't that I was opposed to pouring
his coffee; it was the way he expected me to respond to a double-snap of his fingers. What was I,
a dog? No, sir.

He sneered. "Oh, I forgot, Princess Katrina, you
are too bougie to serve your man. You've never
had to lift a finger a day in your pampered life.
You're too cute to pour a simple cup of coffee,
huh? Never mind." While I sat there, astounded,
he called the front desk and ordered a butler to be
assigned to our suite. This fool could've poured
four cups of damn coffee in the time it took for
him to insult me, call down for assistance, and wait
for someone to arrive to fetch his caffeine. After
that, I was done. I played the "oops, I have my period" card and moved to the other bedroom in the
suite. You would think after a week of me ducking
out before he woke up and dodging him all damn
day he would be a little less surprised at my decla-

ration. I even softened the breakup by saying (cue an epic eye roll here) that he was just too much man for me.

"Are you listening to me, Katrina?" He stood by the front door of the suite, hands on hips. The much-maligned butler holding his luggage stood warily beside him. His expression indicated that he wished he was anywhere but here. I could empathize.

"Of course, Kevin," I lied smoothly.

"Well, hear this. You remember this moment. This is the moment you made an enemy of Kevin Eriq Delancey. You will regret this moment for the rest of your days."

I flung my hair over my shoulder and met his gaze directly. "I don't regret much. Life is too short for regrets."

His nostrils flared as he fought visibly to control his anger. "You *will* regret this."

Clearly nothing I said was going to make this go smoothly. "I'm sorry you feel that way, Kevin."

He swung the door open and motioned for the butler to walk out ahead of him. He stepped through and turned back. "You bet your sweet ass you'll be sorry. Also, I'm taking the jet. You can fly commercial." With that, he slammed the door shut behind him.

"Whew." I sighed and flung myself backwards on the sofa. Reaching for my cell phone, I punched a number. Belle, my business partner, best friend, and future sister-in-law answered on the first ring.

"Did you ditch Kevin Clueless yet?" Belle said in her husky southern drawl.

"Yep. He just stormed out, slammed the door for extra effect and everything."

"I guess he had his mad on?"

"Livid. He had that vein that men get in their forehead when they're agitated on full throb."

"Well, good riddance, I say, sugar. He can try and cause trouble, but the contracts he signed were airtight. If he backs out of the orders, we'll raise a stink. We're not without influence."

I let out a breath. "He says I'll 'rue' this day. Regret it the rest of my life."

She snorted. "Really . . . rue? You know I love an old-school turn of phrase, but c'mon now. What is he, a Victorian villain?"

"He's something. Best of all, he's gone. But really . . . I think we're okay. Like you said, he can make some waves, but how much trouble could he really cause?" After a bit more chatter, I wished her and Beau a good night and hung up. *How much trouble could he really cause?* I mused as I headed to the bathroom for a long, relaxing soak.

1

Not the dumbest thing, but so damn close

Katrina—Monday, May 23—10:46 a.m.

Glancing at my watch, I had about four hours until my flight left for Miami en route home to Dallas. Since I had a little time, I calmly clicked through the photos of myself from this past week's photo shoot with detached interest. Even though I was two months from turning the big three-zero, I still looked pretty much the same as I had when I started modeling ten years ago. I cannot lie. I was genetically gifted. Thanks to Avery and Alanna Montgomery's DNA, I stood 5-10 1/2 in flats. I had wavy, tawny brown hair that fell to my waist. My eyes were often compared to those of a lion, golden in color, slightly tilted and generously lashed. Being named Katrina and originally born in a small town in Louisiana—people heard the name and thought of the disastrous hurricane. It wasn't that far of a jump for my nickname to be Cajun Kat. Not very original, but it worked.

As the last child and only daughter of this generation of Montgomerys, I could have been anything I wanted in life. I had the brains, the beauty, the unconditional love, and the ambition to be whatever made me happy. I had started modeling at age sixteen after graduating early at the top of my high school class. I really never wanted anything else. I loved the world of clothes and fashion. I loved creating and wearing beautiful things. I knew I wasn't going to model forever and had been slowly phasing out the modeling and spending more and more time involved in the design and business end of the fashion house. In my midtwenties I took time to get a degree in art and fashion media from Southern Methodist University in Dallas. I thoroughly enjoyed not only the clothes but the best way to display and market the clothes across different media platforms. This shoot was the last of the artwork we needed for our next catalog.

I was deciding whether the gold bikini or the pale peach one piece would look better on the spring resort-wear catalog cover when a few things happened simultaneously. My cell phone rang, the doorbell of the villa rang, and the sound indicating that I had incoming e-mail beeped repetitively from my laptop. That couldn't be good.

I rose to move toward the door and caught sight of a photographer leaning over my balcony and pointing a huge lens at me. I snapped the curtains shut and looked down at the display on my phone. It was my agent, Fredrika Young.

"What's going on?" I answered.

"You haven't been online today?" she asked cautiously.

"No . . . but I have photographers at my windows and door and my e-mail is blowing up. What happened?"

"Kevin happened," she deadpanned.

I sunk onto the chaise lounge with a feeling of dread. "What do you mean, Kevin happened? What did he do?"

"Before or after he released the sex tape?"

"*Sex tape?*" I screeched into the phone. "I did *not* participate in a sex tape."

"He has the two of you on film, naked and in bed. Granted, it's grainy and there's not a whole lot of action, but it's definitely you, Kat. He says you offered him sex in exchange for the Serengeti business and once he'd signed the contracts, you discarded him. Discarded. He actually used the word *discarded.*"

"Yeah, he's all dramatical like that. Earlier, he used *rued* in a sentence."

"Wow. Anyway, it's total bullshit, of course. Everyone knows you aren't a sex-tape kind of girl and you've never considered pay-for-play a business tactic. If nothing else, we go after him for filming you and distributing without your consent."

"I can*not* believe this. He did say I would regret breaking up with him," I muttered.

"Do you?"

"Hell, no. I regret ever dating him in the first place." I huffed a brief and insincere laugh.

"As you should. From the looks of this tape he was a lousy bed partner."

I snorted. "To say the least."

"In addition to sucking in bed, he's a scoundrel and a liar."

"*Scoundrel* is a sexy word for someone devilish and charming. Kevin is neither of those two things."

Fredrika chuckled. "Duly noted. *Liar.* Not charming."

"Well, he did say one true thing," I admitted.

"What might that be?"

"I did discard him. I most certainly the hell did. Apparently, not a moment too soon."

"He is alleging that this is how you've closed deals for BellaRich Designs and stayed on top in the modeling field."

"Oh no, he didn't!"

"Yeah, he did. Said he has lists of other fashion execs and photographers that you've slept with. It's a slow news day, Kat. This is everywhere. They are calling you the Cajun Coquette."

I closed my eyes. Over ten years in the industry maintaining a flawless reputation in the media, playing nice with people who didn't understand the meaning of the word, smiling while half naked in rain, beach, snow, and shine and now this. . . . I was considered flirty but fun, sexy but not skanky,

pretty but professional. People took me seriously. I
worked hard to be more than a pretty face. I
scrapped, clawed, and kicked my way into design.
My designs were smart, sultry, and sought after. I
carried my weight at BellaRich Designs and I'd be
damned if a pompous ass with hurt feelings and
no bed game was going to ruin all of that.
"Thanks, Fredrika. I need to call Beau." My older
brother Beau was a man who was often underesti-
mated because he was so easy on the eyes. But of
the three Montgomery offspring (me, middle
brother Roman, and Beau), Beau was the one who
not only knew how to play dirty, but relished the
opportunity. He was sharp as a tack and knew how
to think like both an angel and a devil.

Fredrika exhaled. "You're calling Beau? Good—
he'll fight fire with fire. Call me when you know
your next move."

"Drika?"

"Yes?"

"Thanks for believing in me."

"Katrina. You're no angel, but you don't play
around when it comes to business. No worries. If
you need me, I'm here."

"Thanks again." I hung up, ignored the knock-
ing on the villa door, and dialed another number.
It was answered on the first ring.

"Baby girl, how many times have I told you that
your extraordinarily bad taste in men would bite
you in the ass?" Beau's slightly accented voice
poured out. Though we all had some Creole influence, Beau tended to lean more heavily on his
than Roman and I did. "I swear, Kat, all the lovely

male influences in your life and you have to hook up with the slimiest *cochon* out there. Not smart, sis."

I rolled my eyes at my older brother's rant. "Dating Kevin is not the dumbest thing I've ever done . . . but close. How bad is it?"

"Well, *chère*, I won't be playing that video at the next family reunion."

Scowling into the phone, I answered, "How is that possible? We did it twice. Both times badly. In the dark for less than fifteen minutes."

"I really didn't need details."

"I'm just saying. It was over in an instant. How in the world did that make a juicy sex tape?"

"Are you sure?" Beau queried.

"Quite. Why?"

"This tape might be doctored. The one I glanced at—and believe me, *'tite chou*, I never want to see anything like that again—has you in sunlight outside, near a beach in a hammock."

That sounded familiar and wrong all at the same time. "The only time I've been in a hammock here was for the shoot. I was topless, modeling the swim shorts. There was a male model; we did some flirting for the cameras but nothing that could be a hot sex tape. Not even close."

"This jerk must have meshed different footage together or something. Okay, I know what we're dealing with now. You need to lay low while I figure out how to go nuclear on Mr. Delancey."

All of a sudden, I remembered my team. "What about the crew?"

"We got everyone out on the first flight this morning. I'm sending someone to get you."

"What? No. That's unnecessary. I can fly home on my own, Beau. My flight is in a few hours."

"We already cancelled it," he declared.

"Oh, come on. This will blow over in a day or so."

"I doubt it. He's out for blood. Says he has proof that you've slept with half of your photographers, most of our clients. Says a lot of the BellaRich contracts were sex for signature transactions. He's claiming your entire professional career has been based on you passing out the good-good on the regular."

"*What?* I never—"

"I know that. I'm the last one you have to convince. When you think about it, it's actually kind of funny."

"In what possible way is this humorous?" I screeched incredulously.

"Out of the three of us—you, me, or Roman—which of us was more likely to be accused of using sex to get ahead?" Beau said ruefully.

My brother Roman was a straight arrow. He was happily married for the second time to a great woman named Jewellen. Beau, however, had been a notorious hound dog in his day. Not even just in his day—in everybody else's day as well. The trail of broken hearts and discarded panties he left behind was legend. He was bow-wowing right up until he met my friend Belle. We had modeled together. When she and I decided to go into design, I loaned her my condo. Beau had been kicked out of Roman's house and was trying to figure out what to do with his life and decided to stay at my place. That's how they met. After a few stumbles, they appeared to be on the path to happily-ever-after. I guess you *can* teach an old dog new tricks.

"I would say this is more ironic than funny—but hey, it's just my life imploding, laugh it up," I snapped testily. I rubbed my temple. I could feel a headache coming on. I twisted the top off of a large bottle of water and drank deeply.

"Chill, sis. Look, we all know this is ego-driven crap, but Delancey is throwing enough dirt around that we need a solid game plan before the media gets hold of you. We're releasing a statement today denying everything. In the meantime, you need to spend a few more days away from prying eyes and then come back to Dallas and stay somewhere the media can't find you for a while."

I exhaled. "How bad can it really be? I can't just step outside and laugh this off and it will go away?"

"Katrina, you're beautiful, you're rich, you're single, and you're famous. As much as people love you, they love a messy scandal more. They smell blood in the water and they're going for broke. This is going to take a little time and clean-up. But no worries, I'm on it. And I'm sending help."

I frowned down at the phone. "What kind of help?"

"Big Sexy is on his way."

I exhaled shakily. Carter "Big Sexy" Parks, super-hot former football player, one of Beau's oldest and dearest friends, currently a real estate mogul, was heading in my direction. Did I mention that he's super-hot? A man doesn't get and keep the nickname of "Big Sexy" without earning it. And he really did. Even more telling, no one questioned the nickname. It fit. Everything about him oozed big and sexy. I'd thrown all sorts of "do me" hints over the years and though he never said no, he never said yes, either. Never even looked all that tempted, much to my chagrin. I was a girl who was used to men wanting me and chasing me. The fact that he didn't seem to care one way or the other? Quite frustrating in a "but I can respect it" super-hot way. "Carter thinks I'm a pain in the ass."

"We all think you're a pain the ass, but we love you anyway."

I sucked my teeth in exasperation. "Carter Parks does not love me."

"Probably not, but he loves this family and he knows how to play tough. He'll keep you safe."

"I don't need a babysitter, Avery Beauregard."

"No, you don't, Audelia Katrina. You're a big girl. I know you're grown or whatever. But you do need an exit strategy and a hiding place where no one can get to you. Carter can and will provide both of those."

"Fine," I snapped out, already over it.

"I'm sorry, Kit-Kat. I didn't hear you. Was that a 'thank you' that you muttered so graciously, sis?"

"*Merci, mon frère*," I thanked him through gritted teeth.

"That's what I thought I heard. *De rien.* Keep your head up, sis. We'll talk later."

"Later."

"And Katrina?"

"Yes?"

"Don't look at it. It will just piss you off."

"Okay," I agreed, knowing full well I planned to look as soon as I hung up.

Beau used his sternest big-brother voice. "Katrina, I mean it."

"Got it. Not looking." I used my most innocent, agreeable voice.

He sighed. "I'll talk to you after Carter gets there."

"When will that be?" I glanced at the clock.

"Knowing him? Less than two hours. He was on the jet the minute after I called him."

Carter Parks was on his way, a sex tape with me on it was floating around the Internet, and it wasn't even noon on a Monday yet. "Fine."

"You okay?"

"You know us Montgomerys—we're always okay." I hung up and reached for the laptop.